Jón Kalman Stefánsson

ABOUT THE SIZE OF THE UNIVERSE

A Family History

Translated from the Icelandic by
Philip Roughton

MACLEHOSE PRESS
QUERCUS · LONDON

First published in the Icelandic language as *Eitthvað á stærð við alheiminn*
by Bjartur, Reykjavik, in 2015
First published in Great Britain in 2018 by MacLehose Press
This paperback edition published in 2019 by

MacLehose Press
An imprint of Quercus Publishing Ltd
Carmelite House
50 Victoria Embankment
London EC4Y 0DZ

An Hachette UK company

Copyright © Jón Kalman Stefánsson, 2015
English translation copyright © 2018 by Philip Roughton
Edited by Andrea P.A. Belloli

Icelandic
LITERATURE
CENTER
MIÐSTÖÐ ÍSLENSKRA BÓKMENNT

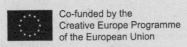

Co-funded by the
Creative Europe Programme
of the European Union

The moral right of Jón Kalman Stefánsson to be identified as the author of this work has been
asserted in accordance with the Copyright, Designs and Patents Act, 1988.

Philip Roughton asserts his moral right to be identified as the translator of the work.

The lyrics quoted on page 146 are from the song "Long are the Corpses" (*"Löng eru þau lík"*) by
Megas, from his 1986 album *In Good Faith* (*Í góðri trú*).

The poem quoted on page 356, "Diatribe Against the Dead" (*"Diatriba contra los muertos"*) is by
Ángel González Muñiz (1925–2008), originally published in *Prosemas o menos* (1984).

A CIP catalogue record for this book is available
from the British Library.

ISBN (MMP) 978 0 85705 602 3
ISBN (Ebook) 978 0 85705 601 6

10 9 8 7 6 5 4 3 2

Designed and typeset in Minion by Libanus Press, Marlborough
Printed and bound in Great Britain by Clays Ltd, Elcograf S.p.A.

Keflavík

— PRESENT —

About the Size of the Universe

— A FAMILY HISTORY —

ð, like the voiced *th* in *mother*

þ, like the unvoiced *th* in *thin*

æ, like the *i* in *time*

á, like the *ow* in *town*

é, like the *ye* in *yes*

í, like the *ee* in *green*

ó, like the *o* in *tote*

ö, like the *u* in *but*

ú, like the *oo* in *loon*

ý, like the *ee* in *green*

ei and ey, like the *ay* in *fray*

au, no English equivalent; but a little like the *oay*
sound in *sway*. Closer is the *œ* sound in the
French *œil*

Also by Jón Kalman Stefánsson in English translation

Heaven and Hell (2010)
The Sorrow of Angels (2013)
The Heart of Man (2015)
Fish Have No Feet (2016)

———

JÓN KALMAN STEFÁNSSON's novels have been nominated three times for the Nordic Council Prize for Literature and his novel *Summer Light, and then Comes the Night* received the Icelandic Prize for Literature in 2005. In 2011 he was awarded the prestigious P. O. Enquist Award. He is perhaps best known for his trilogy – *Heaven and Hell*, *The Sorrow of Angels* (longlisted for the *Independent* Foreign Fiction Prize) and *The Heart of Man* (winner of the Oxford–Weidenfeld Translation Prize) – and for *Fish Have No Feet* (longlisted for the Man Booker International Prize 2017).

PHILIP ROUGHTON is a scholar of Old Norse and medieval literature and an award-winning translator of modern Icelandic literature, having translated works by numerous Icelandic writers, including the Nobel prize-winning author of Halldór Laxness. He was the 2016 winner of the Oxford-Weidenfeld Prize for his translation of *The Heart of Man*. *About the Size of the Universe* is the fifth novel by Jón Kalman Stefánsson to appear in his translation.

ABOUT THE SIZE
OF THE UNIVERSE

Prelude

Let's make one thing clear before we go any further, any deeper into what we don't understand, can't cope with but desire, fear and long for, one thing clear so that we have something to cling to: we're in Keflavík. That peculiar, out-of-the-way town with a few thousand inhabitants, an empty harbour, unemployment, car dealerships, fast-food vans and a landscape so flat that from the sky it resembles a rigid sea. On calm mornings, the sun rises like a silent eruption. We see it when its fire appears behind the distant mountains, as if something huge is ascending from the deep, a force that can lift the sky and change everything; we see it when the dark colour of night gives way to fire. Then the sun rises. At first like a volcanic eruption that wipes out the stars in the sky, those friendly dogs, then it rises, rises majestically above the volcanic Reykjanes Peninsula. Rises slowly, and we're alive.

*Then destiny rolls slowly into motion, but it's snowing
on the empty streets of Keflavík, on the
unemployment and billboards*

Me and Ari's great-aunt didn't put much faith in the old ways, a polite term, perhaps, for superstition and ignorance, unless, on the con-trary, they were a kind of wisdom that kept us alive in this difficult country, on this big, lonely island. Life – neither people nor fate – had rarely shown her mercy, and she wrote just one poem about it. The poem's subject was her daughter, Lára, who died when she was only eight years old, after a grave illness. Despite her young age, Lára seemed to know where things were headed; she'd been incredibly strong, undaunted, but finally broke down, her eyes opened wide, she embraced her mother and asked, frightened, Mummy, do you think it hurts to die? Mummy, will I be alone? Our great-aunt, only ever called Lilla, smiled and said, No, sweetie. We'll always be together. I'll never leave you. It was hard for her to lie, then to smile and keep smiling for her daughter to make sure she would see something beautiful in the last moments of her life, and would therefore believe that death was just a step to one side, a momentary break from happiness, and that she needn't think it was a cruel, ugly ogre who lived on the dark mountain above the village. Lilla managed to keep smiling but not to stifle the tears that fell ceaselessly from her grey eyes. She held Lára in her arms and felt her young life fade, held her with all of love's power, which is immeasurable and more ancient than the seven-hundred-year-old lava she could see through their window in Grindavík. Held her tight, but death pulled much

11

harder in the opposite direction; it pulls everything in eventually – flowers and solar systems, beggars and presidents. Lilla felt it; she felt how love, tears, despair were useless, that no justice can be found in the vicinity of death, just endings, and then she wrote her poem, couldn't help herself, some unstoppable force drove her to write it as she held the slender eight-year-old body, having offered her life in exchange long since, her happiness, health, memories, everything, but was completely ignored. Nothing made any difference, and the only thing that Lilla could do, the only thing she could offer her daughter, was to hold her in her arms as the tears fell, one prayer after another, so heartfelt and pure that it's incomprehensible that they changed nothing; perhaps there is no justice in this world, not a shred, not a trace. Then, perhaps therefore, she wrote the poem about her daughter. That she was an eight-year-old girl with curly blonde hair, a bright forehead, clear blue eyes, a pleasantly squarish nose, and below it a mouth whose laughter could make all the world's anger subside and become a dark pebble that anyone could toss away.

Lilla's younger brother was a poet, as was her sister, but Lilla had never been able to write poetry, any more than her older brother, me and Ari's grandfather, not a word, until that moment when everything fell apart. One poem, two stanzas, and then the world died.

A year later, Lilla's husband had left her. It was as if she no longer cared about living, having more children, opening herself up to him; he hardly ever got to be with her, let alone touch her. He accused her of fanatical grief; that's how he put it, fanatical grief. I should have known it, he said angrily, nearly spitting out his words. I was warned again and again about your family: rootless, fanatical, undependable and neurotic artists. I want to go on living; is that a crime, a betrayal? Your grief is killing me.

He slammed his big fist on the table, his eyes glistening, seeming suddenly to be fighting back tears. Later he became a wealthy, nationally renowned ship-owner; he is mentioned in the *History of Grindavík*, though not a word is written of Lilla; that's the way it is – we remember wealth, not grief. She moved back to Reykjavík. With her entire life's baggage in a single suitcase: a change of clothes, four books, the snuffbox belonging to her father, who'd died the day before her Confirmation, fallen blind drunk into Reykjavík harbour, laughed as he flapped his arms and legs in the cold sea, was fished up some time later by his giggling drinking partners, because Lilla's father, me and Ari's great-grandfather, looked like a ghostly jellyfish or misfortunate fish in the water, fished up so much later that he fell ill, developed pneumonia and died. Nothing else in the suitcase: a change of clothes, four books, the snuffbox, a photograph of Lára, two sets of her clothes, her doll, four drawings and the poem that Lilla would later type up and paste beneath the photo. And, finally, the guilt of having betrayed Lára by going on living instead of dying with her.

The photograph and the poem were always the first things Lilla hung up when she moved into a new basement flat, a new attic flat, a new hovel, which she did far too often, moving a total of twenty-six times in just over forty years. Almost as if she were on the run, never staying anywhere for more than two years. The first thing she always did was hang up the little photograph of a smiling seven-year-old girl reclining against the wall of a house in Grindavík, during the years when the sun shone. The photograph hung above the little green sofa, the poem pasted beneath it and the four drawings arranged around it. Over time, the photograph and the poem became the only things left to remind the world that Lilla's daughter had existed here on earth. Early on, Ari and I learned the poem by heart, off our own bat, without really thinking about it; we'd sat countless times in the chairs opposite the sofa, drinking hot chocolate and munching biscuits, enjoying Lilla's kindness, and the poem had somehow sifted in. When Lilla, by then an old woman, her health in decline, discovered this quite by chance, she lost her composure; that steady individual began to tremble, to rock back and forth as if to calm herself, but then burst into tears, completely defenceless before us, as if that poem was the only thing that kept her daughter from vanishing into oblivion. That as long as the poem existed in the world, and someone knew it, Lára was safe in the great beyond. Someone would take care of her when the darkness was full of menace. The poem was thus a kind of message that reached across the indefinable space between life and death, that reached all the way to the eight-year-old girl waiting for her mummy, beyond our understanding, reached all the way, touched her and said, Hush, hush, it's alright, Mummy will be coming soon, soon she'll die and you'll pick buttercups together again.

Moved twenty-six times, from a basement to an attic, from an attic back down to a basement, and before going to sleep for the first time in any new residence, Lilla counted the windows, one, two, three, four, five, because then the night's dreams would come true, ancient beliefs, superstitions, old baggage, that was pretty much all she believed in, that dreams had a power that wakefulness or logic didn't recognise, and who knows, maybe she would wake up on a new morning to the smile of her daughter, who would still be eight years old even after decades had passed; nobody ages in death, time doesn't pass in eternity, its inconsiderate power turns to nothing there. Somehow, Ari and I adopted this practice of hers, to count the windows in any residence we sleep in for the first time, even if temporarily, in the belief that that simple act can make dreams come true, bend the laws of nature. I count the windows in my uncle's small, two-storey wooden house in Keflavík's old neighbourhood. In order to do so, I have to go outside, out into the snow, so dense that Keflavík has vanished entirely. I come back inside completely white, wearing an angel's veil, as if blessed; my uncle's cats hiss at me like two vipers, but I lie down after covering my uncle, who dozed off in his chair listening to Hljómar sing "it's heavenly to be alive", which is a bold claim. Covered him, bumping twice into the model airplanes hanging by thin wires from the ceiling, American fighter jets. I counted the windows, the snow melted off me, I shut the bedroom door carefully to keep the cats from coming in and scratching out my eyes, then I lie down on the bed, which resembles an old sofa-bed, and fall asleep. Through my sleep I hear the sea, which is out there, out in the snow, not far below the house, the biggest instrument on earth, the siblings Fate and Death in its sound, two opposites: consolation and violence. I sink slowly into the world of sleep, and the sound of the sea blends with my dreams. The sea that once was the home of Oddur, Ari's paternal grandfather; he stared at the sea and was free. The last thing I hear before sleep takes me, before my dreams embrace me, is my uncle talking in his sleep in the living room overhead and then laughing merrily.

I sleep.

As does Ari, up at the Flight Hotel. It's easy for him to count the windows; it's impossible to avoid knowing how many there are, just two, but they frame a considerable amount of precipitation. Everything else has vanished, the residents of Keflavík can take a break from the world for a while, it no longer exists. There are only snowflakes and the air between them. Only falling snow, that whiteness from the sky. Messages, kisses that melt on our foreheads. Everything else has vanished, the petrol station, the shops over the road, the New Cinema, Hafnargata, Hringbraut, which is a bit further away, the unemployment, the empty harbour, the Christmas decorations, the hoardings. There's nothing but snow, relentlessly swallowing everything tonight and, by doing so, connecting earth and sky, which is probably more important than we realise, because old beliefs, much older than those about count-ing windows and thereby making dreams come true, far older, from times without windowpanes or even houses, state that on such nights, calm and with so much precipitation that there's no longer any difference between earth and sky, the dead can speak to the living. The snowflakes change into messages from the dead: I still love you; Dear God, I miss you terribly; I'm fine; Very well indeed, thanks; They have great coffee here and the view will leave you speechless; May you rot in Hell; Don't waste your life in banal-ity – do something magnificent, the attempt is always worth it, and striving makes you beautiful; Remember: wrap up warm tomorrow morning, it'll be chilly and you mustn't catch cold.

Ari hears none of this; he's sleeping.

He finally fell asleep after reading Sigga's article, which was enclosed with his stepmother's letter, an article about the power of men over women, about the power that men appropriate – and then Sigrún's account of when she was raped. Ari and I watched Kári lead her away from the dance to his Lada, and we saw him rape her. She, just sixteen, he thirty-something, a father of two. Somehow, we misunderstood what happened, saw the car rocking and his buttocks appear in the rear window, hairy, white, like two

16

little imps. After reading the letter, Ari wept, though not immediately. At first, he just sat there, paralysed; then he rushed around his hotel room, quivering with rage, shame, feelings of inadequacy; threw himself down on the bed, stared, swore, rubbed his face and felt that it was wet with tears. He thought, almost in surprise, I'm crying. He cleaned his teeth. Cried. Read Sigrún's account again. Went online, typed her name into a search engine and fished up four photos from the Internet's sea. She was markedly older than fifteen in the four photos, but that didn't matter, because Ari remembered perfectly how she moved in the slaughterhouse out west, in Búðardalur, the sleepy village where a few trees grow, where laundry flaps on washing lines, people toss and turn in their sleep – that's about it. Sigrún moved in such a way that we couldn't help but love her, it was impossible not to. Ari dreamed of a life with her, we made her laugh sometimes – which would make our very bones quiver. She got into the car with Kári, who pulled down her trousers and thrust himself into her, raped her as we sat nearby in a blue Land Rover, watched the Lada rock, saw Kári's buttocks, listened to Brimkló and felt sorry for ourselves. Ari lay in bed, a bag of sweets in front of him, a bottle of whisky anchoring his stepmother's letter, mostly unread, he was going to read it before going to sleep but couldn't. Exhausted, endlessly tired, yet it took for ever to fall asleep. He didn't draw the curtains shut because it was relaxing to watch the drifting snow, had no idea that snowflakes might be messages from the dead; Be sure to tuck yourself in well to keep the cold at bay. His heart pounded, his nerves trembled, but the falling snow finally calmed him. Calmed him, put him to sleep, now he's sleeping. Having returned to Iceland after being in Denmark for just over two years, noticed the mountains like huge flowers on the other side of the sky; then had to bend over an old school desk so that Ásmundur, our cousin and old role model, could slip his broad index finger into his rectum. He's sleeping. The whisky bottle anchoring his stepmother's letter, Oddur's certificate of recognition next to it, like an important message that he has yet to decode.

Ari's last thoughts before he sank into dreams were about Lilla. Probably because he thought, Two windows, one, two – there, I've counted them, now my dreams will come true. What if I dream something bad, something foul, good God, what if I dream of someone's death, have a nightmare in which my children die? Oh, Lilla, he thought as he nodded off, and then she came to him, short, calm, she'd been lively as a child, as a young person, but sorrow stilled her. She was always calm – that's how we knew her, kind, serene – but sometimes her eyes sparkled, as if they longed for more life, happiness. She had the warmest hands that Ari had ever felt, as if she could comfort everyone with them but could never forgive herself for having gone on living when her daughter died, for having left her behind in the grip of death, not pulled hard enough, loved her zealously enough, what sort of person can't save her own child? She came to Ari as he nodded off, stroked his forehead with her warm, calloused palm, comforted him, calmed him, hushed him to sleep, her eyes kind but sorrowful because the dead, like her, are condemned to silence and so must rely on us.

It snows on Keflavík.

It snows on unemployment, empty streets, a small two-storey wooden house in the old neighbourhood and the hotel that was built on the ruins of the Skúli Million freezing plant, snows on this town that holds memories, me and Ari's tracks, it snows on the block of flats where Jakob, Ari's father, lives, but he may not be sleeping; maybe he's awake, listening to music, thinking about his life, which is approaching its end, approaching the gate of darkness. He was born out east, in Neskaupstaður, and once lay half-conscious on the beach, not even a year old; his mother, Margrét, has just tossed him aside and is rushing headlong into the sea. He lies there awake and thinks about his life, or doesn't think about it, avoids thinking about it. He can't sleep, or doesn't dare to, is afraid of sleeping, where we're so vulnerable, an open wound – where all our defences crumble.

Norðfjörður

— PAST —

How is it possible to create such deep calm? Is it perhaps the greatest gift, the peak of creation?

Years have passed.

Perhaps not terribly many but a few, and time changes everything, quickly and slowly; some have died, others have been born. We find ourselves between world wars, during a twenty-one-year interval, humankind gathering ideas that overcome the Devil. It's been a handful of years since Oddur stepped naked off the boat with the fully dressed Tryggvi in his arms. It was a starry, frosty November night; Tryggvi had jumped into the sea, was going to swim to the moon but had begun to go rigid, sink, when Oddur managed to wrangle him onboard again, sailed at full steam back to land, naked at the wheel, having dressed Tryggvi in his own clothes, every last garment, then carried him ashore in his arms, and into the village; we've told you all this before. We need to recall a few things because we forget so much, both so hammered on French cognac that not a trace of thought remained. What's more, Tryggvi was closer to death than to life due to the sea's frigidity and most likely would have died there beneath all the stars, Oddur himself being chilled to the bone, babbling nonsense, not a sensible thought in his head, had not Áslaug, a girl from Vatnsleysuströnd, a runaway in search of adventure in Norðfjörður, seen them. I saw you, she told Tryggvi later, lying practically unconscious in the arms of someone I first thought was a merman who'd come up from the depths of the sea to bring me what I desired.

She often told Tryggvi, and then their daughters, this story, that she'd awakened from a strange dream, gone out to pee, half-asleep, and seen them coming. She never grew tired of repeating this story, did so for the last time when she, an old woman, lay in the hospital in Keflavík and death came to fetch her, managed to tell it one more time, as if she wanted to leave the story behind in life, how it all began for them. She'd carried him to where she was staying, strong woman, undressed him, warmed him with her flesh, and little by little desire stirred, then love, and the rest was happiness.

Years have passed, and now the two brothers-in-law are out fishing, a hundred kilometres from home, south of Vatnajökull glacier; they've just finished setting the line and are looking forward to a rest.

A calm, gentle day, just a slight shifting breeze, as if God hasn't given the weather much thought. Or was dumbfounded by His own creation, particularly the glacier towering white over land, sea and the fishermen aboard *Sleipnir* out of Norðfjörður. How is it even possible to create such deep calm? Is it perhaps the greatest gift, the peak of creation, to create what barely exists and does nothing, barely touches anything yet changes everything? Changes the world into beautiful stillness and, on top of that, touches strings deep inside these fishermen from Norðfjörður, pulling cod from the invisible depths just outside of Hornafjörður, which is where the boats from Norðfjörður must come in mid-winter. They're here for weeks at a time, far from home, far from their beloved Norðfjörður, which must be the most beautiful fjord in the country, in the world, and what don't we do for those damned fish – for cod not least of all – we could just as well pack it all in and shoot ourselves in the head if the cod disappear. They've set the line, the effort warming them, but then the cold hits them as they listen, smiling, to Tryggvi, looking forward to resting as the line lies in the sea and collects fish. In three or four hours they'll haul up the line, wait for Rúnar the cook to prepare their dinner, and then they can rest, catch some vital shut-eye; they shuffle their feet, their cold toes, the calm so perfect and the quiet so deep that a low thud can be heard when someone farts on land, many kilometres away – if Tryggvi's to be believed. He's in fine form; he talks, the others listen, Oddur has just threatened to throw Tryggvi overboard, haul him up like a cod and gut him, if he doesn't shut up. Þórður hears his father curse Tryggvi and make this threat, but he also sees the smile half-hidden in his beard.

Oddur had brought his eldest son on board as a fully fledged deckhand several weeks earlier. Þórður had worked as a deck-hand for nearly a year on old Guðmundur's boat, the oldest skip-per in Norðfjörður, an indomitable strongman with a massive body, who, the previous autumn, had been hauling in the damned cod with his crew. Something big's biting, growled the old man, in a voice so deep that the pebbles quivered on the seabed twenty metres below. Bloody hell – that's what I call a catch! said Guð-mundur as the capstan jerked and creaked, as if complaining at too much weight, that it was unfair that it had to do all the work of hauling in the fish; Guðmundur leapt over to the capstan, grabbed the line, he'd never been one for machinery, had relied all his life on the strength in his own hands, trusted it the most, cursed the capstan, squared his shoulders, those beasts of burden, and exerted his enormous strength to haul the big fish up from the depths, though it turned out not to be a cod or even a big halibut, which people were starting to appreciate, but death itself that the old man hauled in. His heart burst just as he managed to haul death a thumb's length above the gunwale, enough to reveal its eyes, two deep, dark holes. Such were the last moments of old Guðmundur, that powerhouse – and around the same time, one of Oddur's crew moved to Seyðisfjörður, which is strange, of course, to move from the most beautiful fjord to another, much worse one; some people seem beyond hope. These things turned out to dovetail well, death and the move, and Oddur brought Þórður on board. Just sixteen years old. Not fully tried, and taken over many a fine deckhand. Oddur could easily have chosen from the cream of the crop of fishermen from Norðfjörður, even elsewhere; it was thought a big deal to join Oddur's crew, he being a bountiful fisherman, respected for his strength of will, which could, admittedly, be harsh at times.

Father and son never spoke of this between themselves, but, thinking about it now, it seems possible that they never spoke of anything but fish, the sea, the mountains, a fly on the windowsill and the importance of hard work. Which is why Þórður knew, as if it had been spelled out for him, that he had to hold his own, that he mustn't slacken or become distracted, nor work any less hard than the fully fledged deckhands, preferably even harder, and he wanted to do so; he burned with enthusiasm. They're out at sea, a hundred kilometres from home, and Margrét knows that Oddur is keeping his eye on their son. He's not encouraging him, more like challenging him. She has no say in the matter. There's too much distance between their home and the sea. When old Guðmundur died and his son-in-law inherited his boat and took it to Reyðarfjörður, she'd entertained the idea, or the dream, that Þórður would work on the land, that he would be at home more often, to everyone's delight; he could do some reading, even prepare himself for further studies, but then Oddur announced his surprising decision, that he was going to make his son a member of his crew.

They had lain in bed and it was almost a winter's night but bright because moonlight filled the fjords and made it difficult to sleep; they lay side by side and one thing led to another, as it ought to do: her left hand began roaming. It moved beneath his duvet to stroke the body she had first got to know in the fo'c'sle of *Sleipnir SU-382* countless years ago. They'd aged since then, had grown a bit stiff, they'd had their difficulties, plenty of them, yet it was still nice to lie together like this. Night, real night, is nearly upon them, and the moonlight is busy changing the world. It's pleasant to send her hand on a surveying expedition, to stroke muscular arms, sturdy thighs, to stroke his penis, feel it swell and harden in her palm. Soon after, they were young again.

It was likely around 2.00 a.m., they lay there exhausted, she lolled in warm bliss and began sinking into sleep. Oddur propped himself up and said tranquilly, mundanely, that he was taking Þórður on in place of Guðjón, who'd moved, like an idiot, to Seyðisfjörður. It'll be perfectly fine, he said. He'd made this decision without saying anything to her. Perfectly fine, he said, and meant: he's reliable. Meaning: he's an adult; he's a man now. In other words: there's the two of us and there's you. Finally, he added, He's coming south with us to Hornafjörður; it'll be a good learning experience.

Margrét had just felt Oddur's warm semen inside her, had grabbed his head, kissed him eagerly, but now she felt her heart harden, become rigid, turn to stone. Oddur had made his decision without asking her opinion, as if he suddenly owned a greater share in Þórður than she did, and the two of them now belonged to a world that she could never reach. As young as he was, albeit big and strong for his age, but still just a child. Her child. Her darling. With his gentle disposition, a warm, mischievous gleam in his lively, grey-blue eyes, and so admired by his siblings. Gunnar Tryggvi, his younger brother, an eight-year-old kid, imitates Þórður's walk, tries to keep his eyes fixed thoughtfully on the ground like his big brother, and Elín, the youngest, objects to going to bed until Þórður has told her stories that he's read somewhere or pulls out of a hat. If kindness really exists in this world, wrote Margrét once in her diary, burning with motherly love, it's definitely to be found in Þórður. How will it go for him, good boy that he is, strong yet sensitive, and so talented; in what direction will he go? Will he have the chance to go anywhere, will he get to grow up, free from these mountains – and his father?

A little over a year ago, the headmaster paid Margrét a visit, she was on her knees scrubbing the floor, Elín hanging on to her, pestering her, wanting to climb onto her back, she would make such an excellent horse, when suddenly the headmaster appeared. He had knocked, but Margrét had heard nothing over Elín's babbling, over the sound of the brush as she scrubbed, rubbed the floor, so he just walked in, said good day and turned immediately to the matter at hand, as if he wanted to conclude it as quickly as possible and make his escape: he wanted Þórður to continue his studies. Such talent must not be squandered, he said, and Margrét replied immediately, still on her knees, an awkward position to be in, angry at the man for walking right in, she with her red, swollen hands, probably red-faced from work, from exertion, her forehead sweaty, and said sharply, almost churlishly, against her better judgement, in fact, So, do sailors squander their lives?

The headmaster, who was called Þorkell, and who brought schooling kicking and screaming to life in Norðfjörður, as if out of nowhere, possesses a will of steel but gets on well with everyone, which is probably one of the most important attributes a person can have.

So, do sailors squander their lives?

Þorkell looked down at Margrét, who had lived in Canada for eight years and come to know a bigger world, with more possibilities than can be found here amid the mountains. It's both a blessing and a curse to see further and more than most people around you, to see a larger world than the one right in front of you. Þorkell rotates his hat in his hands, opens his mouth, hesitates. He knows quite a bit about Margrét, has heard the stories about her, about the extremes that isolate her, the mood swings from depression to joy, she's either bedridden or dancing, but had occasionally made herself heard at meetings about working-class matters, when she came across as having a harsher temper and sharper tongue than many of the others present – but wasn't there also, at the same time, something mysterious about her, as if she didn't reveal herself completely, concealed part of herself from the world? Knew more than most, saw through everything and everyone but kept quiet about it? Perhaps out of arrogance; she has a reputation for having a big head, there are stories about her running half-naked into the arms of a farmer, walking barefoot down to the beach and wading into the sea with a baby, lying in bed for days and letting her household go to rack and ruin. Oddur deserved better. Þorkell rotates his hat. He knows all this, he's from around here, is three years younger than Margrét, two years younger than Oddur and has always had a timid respect for the man, the other

29

a great leader when they were boys, acted like an adult when he was only ten or eleven. Þorkell rotates his hat, Margrét is on her knees, scrubbing, doesn't stop despite him walking in and standing there. He smiles at Elín, who responds bashfully, shoving two fingers in her mouth and shutting her eyes. He knows that he should have knocked harder and called out, not just barged in on Margrét. Þorkell stares at her swollen red hands. He's married, a father of three, loves his wife, yet Margrét is the most beautiful woman he's ever seen, he's felt like this since returning from his studies in Reykjavík, and then Edinburgh. Went out into the world but returned, was always planning to return, didn't want to be anywhere else. Returned, and shortly thereafter, on a gloomy, rainy day, a grey, cold day, with rain falling on the lowlands but sleet or snow on the mountain slopes, the peaks whitening, capped with blossoms of snow and ice – he'd been sunk in paperwork and was suddenly seized by a feeling of malaise, had to escape, walked down to the pier, and there stood Margrét, waiting for *Sleipnir*, Oddur's boat, to dock. The world was still so young that she would always wait for him at the pier. She'd spotted the boat coming in, dashed out without bothering to get her coat, grabbed a shawl at the last minute, it was draped over her slender shoulders. She stood there drenched and burning with love, and her hair hung in streams over her forehead and cheeks, stood there erect, noble, and he watched and thought of a leopardess he'd seen in a zoo in London, proud but uneasy in its cage. He stood above the pier, obsessed, gripped by the knowledge and sorrow that this sight would forever deprive him of perfect happiness.

Keflavík

— PRESENT —

God is an old teddy bear,
and it's a rare calm day here in Keflavík

"Say my name, as only you can say it, and then I'll know that I exist."

Ari wakes to singing that seems to come from a vast distance. It takes him some time to wake up completely, or well enough to distinguish between sleep and waking, dream and reality, which may be why he thinks, if only for a moment, that the singing is not of this world, that the night has been cut off between worlds and now the dead are singing to him so beautifully, to help him awake, cover him with softness before reality hits him. Then he is fully awake and remembers where he is: the Flight Hotel in Keflavík. It's December, it's impossible to venture more deeply into the winter darkness. In the next room, someone is singing. On the morning of the day on which Ari is planning to see Jakob, his father, who may be dying, changing into song in the beyond, or else into silence, oblivion, we don't know which one will prevail when we die, cruelty or kindness, extinction or a new beginning, don't know whether God is a starry embrace or an old teddy bear from our childhood. It's nearly 8.30 a.m. and someone is singing in the next room. Ari lies in the darkness and listens to a woman singing some sort of lullaby in English, singing as if she's consoling someone, and not even the concrete in the wall or its steel frame, those lifeless, rigid materials, can dampen the affection in her voice. She sings so softly that Ari can only distinguish one line, though so vaguely that he isn't sure if he hears it correctly: *Say my name as* only you can say it, and then I'll know that I exist. He reaches instinctively for his phone, opens his inbox, clicks on the name Þóra and writes: "Say my name" . . . Is about to send it but hesitates, ruining everything; no-one should hesitate or think twice where love is concerned. We think too much, feel too little; that's humanity's misfortune. Ari sighs, saves the message as a draft.

It's almost completely calm outside.

It's a rare calm day here in Keflavík. Didn't calm like this happen mainly in summer, when the days could be so clear that you could read messages from eternity through them? Bloody fucking calm, people said, because then the smoke from the refinery between Njarðvík and Keflavík hung over the town, the stench invaded each and every building, we felt as if we were sunk in rank fog, as if we were being punished for the good weather, and the housewives who were too slow to bring their washing in had to wash it again to get the smell out. The refinery has long since stopped refining oil from capelin; the big building has been demolished and replaced by two warehouses, one a car dealership for many years, the other built just to fill the space, which seemed like a good idea at the time, but they both stand empty today, contain nothing but silence and sunbeams that manage to sift in through the big windowpanes, their gloss dulled by salt. The car dealership went bankrupt following the economic collapse of October 2008, as did so many similar companies, though quite a few businesses still operate here in Keflavík and Njarðvík, they're on the up again; in fact, nowhere in the country has more of them per capita; it's one of the Icelandic records we take pride in. Most families in Keflavík have two or three cars, and if they're bored they sell one and buy a new one, preferably no later than the following day. The residents of Keflavík often find themselves bored these days, the fishing quota being a thing of the past, the U.S. military gone, Rúnni Júll dead, little left but unemployment and the three cardinal directions, wind, lava, eternity, which is why it's such a splendid idea to sell a car and buy another to replace it: at least then something's happening, both in our lives and in the car dealer's career, and Keflavík immediately becomes a better place.

No-one's out and about on Hafnargata, though a few cars creep past Ari, it's almost 11.00 a.m., he took his time getting out of bed, the lullaby immobilised him, he lay there and listened until the singing stopped. Then he turned on the light and saw everything, Sigga's article on the desk, his stepmother's letter under the whisky bottle, the letter he knew straightaway he wouldn't read until after he'd seen Jakob, didn't have the nerve, didn't dare; saw the photos of his three children – Hekla, Sturla, Gréta – Oddur's certificate of recognition, the yellow folder of letters, photographs, clippings, poems, fragments of poems, and the two Duty Free bags full of sweets that he'd bought as if in another day and age, as if his children were still little and awaiting at home, as if Þóra were waiting for him too, as if he belonged somewhere. The bags like a memory of what he'd thrown away, like an accusation of failure at enjoying life, of not living life to the full. Those who fail are never safe; even bags full of sweets can turn into accusations.

A big pickup comes down Hafnargata, slows as it approaches Ari, the driver gives him a long look, curious, almost hostile, as if Ari has done something awful to him or spoken badly of Keflavík. The pickup skids on the icy road, as if the driver has stepped on the brake, intending to stop, and Ari, a bit flustered, continues approaching the next door but hesitates when he sees the sign:

Massage. Desire flows through him like an electric current.

He shuts his eyes.

Why do we have to be so vulnerable to the sex drive; why can't we just shove it in our pocket and take it out when it's convenient? It has happened, when the perpetual-motion machine of the sex drive starts up within Ari, as it regularly does, of course, in everyone, rarely taking account of what we're doing on any particular day, of where we are in our lives, infusing our blood with desire for something enticing, exciting, something coarse or sensual, that Ari has gone online and typed in the search term *erotic massage*, and this is why that innocent sign, *Massage*, has such an uncomfortable effect on him. He opens his eyes, reaches for the doorknob, hears the pickup accelerate abruptly, as if fleeing the scene, as if its driver has no desire to witness what's happening, and disappears down Hafnargata. The door is locked. Oof, thinks Ari, relieved, but then a hoarse male voice breaks the silence:

Do you have an appointment, my friend?

Ari turns and sees a man standing in an entrance two doors further down, staring at him, and adding, when he doesn't reply, She's not there, my dear Snæfríður, but I can ring her if necessary, if – the man stops, glances down, as if searching for the right word – if you need to let off some steam. A deep silence grips Hafnargata, as if the road can barely stay awake, despite the cheerful Christmas lights blinking eagerly here and there, as if Keflavík were sending a message to the world, to Santa Claus himself, to bring a gift that might actually matter: three hundred jobs, a fishing quota, an aluminium smelter, a waste-disposal facility in Helguvík; or that this Snæfríður would wake up and come with her soft, comforting hands.

Ari approaches the man, walking quickly to keep him from

36

shouting anything else, drawing attention to them, and says, as he comes closer, No, no, absolutely no need to call, I haven't made an appointment, I didn't know this was a massage parlour, and, to tell you the truth, I don't know why I tried to open the door. The man watches Ari approach, narrows his eyes as if he's thinking and moves his lips in a way that makes it difficult to tell whether he wants to spit or smile. Well, you think it was your love of books that steered your hand? he says with a wide grin, baring his teeth, all those long, yellow teeth, as big as those of a horse. Fuck me, says Ari, stopping in his tracks, is that you, Svavar!? The man gives one of his horse-laughs – it's Svavar, with whom Ari and I worked salting and drying fish at Drangey in Sandgerði between early 1981 and the autumn of 1982, a little over thirty years ago, how time has passed. Bloody hell, how quickly it passes, is there any way to slow it down a little? Yeah man, says Svavar jovially, tall as ever, hair as black as it was, his neck as long, with its big, bustling larynx like an independent creature at the centre of his throat, a small animal that he couldn't swallow completely; always so skinny that the women at Drangey were constantly worried about him, whether he was getting enough to eat, whether his packed lunches were sufficient; he ate like a bird – It's incredible you're still alive, they said worriedly. Some of them finally managed to convince Svavar to eat more, but perhaps they were too persuasive, because he's got quite a paunch on him now – it stretches his white T-shirt with its sunset image of an empty Keflavík harbour and the question beneath it: *Have you been to Keflavík?* Yeah man, repeats Svavar, rubbing his big hands together, as if wanting to add, Now we're having fun! Yeah man, it is I, as bloody daft as ever, and here's my kingdom, office and shop! He makes a sweeping gesture as if to draw Ari's attention to the windows full of puffins, lava rocks, photographs of Reykjanes, the Reykjanes lighthouse, the Blue Lagoon and the band Hljómar: "The Icelandic Beatles, only better!" What I wanted to say was that Snæfríður rarely gets up before noon during the darkest months; she likes to say that the Devil invented winter mornings. What do you think of the massage parlour's name? It was my idea, actually; I thought of you when it came to me, and I've thought of you ever since, don't know why, just expected to see you standing there below the sign; but bless you forever, old friend, it's glorious to see you again, you haven't changed except for being a bit uglier – as if you weren't ugly enough before!

Svavar smiles broadly, giving a little laugh, and Ari smiles back, happy to see that smile from the past, those teeth, this man, and then turns to look up at the sign jutting out above the entrance to the massage parlour: *Snæfríður Íslandssól: Massage Parlour.*

Crazy how the years have blown by us, man, continues Svavar, and you, you're so famous now, yes, the only famous person I know, to tell you the truth, which is, of course, why I should shoot you here and now, stuff you and put you on display in the window as a famous person from Keflavík. What the hell, I'll make you a coffee, he says, turns on his heel and goes indoors without checking whether Ari is following him, which he does, of course, after looking down the street, in the direction of the New Cinema, glancing at the Christmas lights blinking eagerly, as if trying to stay awake.

After settling into a little room behind the shop, Svavar brews some coffee and tells Ari about his friend Snæfríður, whom he met when she purchased the place, intending to turn it into a massage parlour. She had no difficulty getting a loan despite it being shortly

38

after the economic collapse, when society seemed to be dead broke, except of course for the fishing industry; the quota kings could fill swimming pools with cash while the rest of us were left to eat whatever froze on the streets. Flaunting her charm, however, Snæfríður managed to wrestle herself a loan and rent the place dirt cheap, yet always had trouble with the name.

Then, for some reason, I thought of you, says Svavar. I'd just seen your picture in the papers – they praised you as an ambitious publisher, even went so far as to call you a national treasure, and a poet to boot, and I recalled that the last time we met, so unforgivably many years ago, you were absorbed in Kiljan's *Iceland's Bell* and had a major crush on Snæfríður Íslandssól.[1] You'd even written a poem about her, calling her "the blonde dream of spring". The name for the massage parlour came to me out of the blue: Snæfríður Íslandssól – Massage Parlour. Since then, everything's gone Snæfríður's way; she's busy as a bee and flourishing. Jogs seven kilometres three times a week, is pushing fifty but still slim as a model and so radiant with that long blonde hair of hers that it's like eternal summer being around her. That is, after she's had her five cups of coffee in the morning. The only thing missing is a good man, though there's no lack of suitors; she's always looked great, been so attractive – the Yanks up at the Base fought over her when she worked there. Literally fought; love letters awaited her when she came to work, they asked her out on dates, they offered up their lives, one tried to hang himself with a power cord when she turned him down but was saved at the last moment, and consequently demoted. A soldier is allowed to kill everyone but

1 Kiljan: Iceland's Nobel Laureate in Literature, Halldór Kiljan Laxness (1902–98). His historical novel *Iceland's Bell* (*Íslandsklukkan*) was originally published in three parts (1943–6). Snæfríður Íslandssól ("Iceland's Sun") is the novel's main female character.

himself. Dammit, that Snæfríður can be hot-tempered on winter mornings – you can't go near her without a bulletproof vest and hard hat.

Here, however, is some real coffee, straight from Haiti, says Svavar, pouring pitch-black liquid into a cup for Ari and shoving an open pack of Homeblest biscuits across the table, Gullbylgja radio buzzing in the background, classic pop songs, I love you, where have you gone, it's raining, hold my hand. The songs, the confessions of love, the regret, regularly interrupted by the station I.D., which resembles a desperate cry to its listeners: Don't turn me off! Don't change the dial! Ari takes a sip of the strong coffee, shuts his eyes momentarily and sends Þóra a mental S.O.S.: Don't turn me off!

Keflavík

when the Berlin Wall held the world together,
and split it apart

Telephone line, first breasts, fireworks, airplane fuel – and someone shouts hooray!

January, most of the Christmas lights have been taken down, and the days are waggons filled with darkness.

Five days, or six, since the residents of Keflavík menaced the sky with their fireworks and drunken shouting – so excited as the New Year's comedy special finished and the clock approached midnight, approached a new year, approached the future, the moment when our entire life seems somehow to change into the past – as if they'd resolved to blow up the sky, and by doing so exact revenge for how distant it was from this blackest place in the country. Some were so drunk that they set their jackets or trousers on fire, almost as if they longed to shoot themselves into the sky and thereby transcend the mundane, the grey repetition.

Jakob was in charge of the fireworks at home, with help from his cousin. They set them off with a great deal of shouting, but the stepmother had shut herself up in the windowless study; she never could bear fireworks, their racket and the money that went into them, not just at home but across the nation, which, of course, complains constantly about how tough life is, about low wages, high prices, how it's barely possible to live a decent life, yet set off fireworks for dizzying sums, perhaps to have even better reasons to complain about cash shortages in the new year. The stepmother cursed. She shut herself in. Frightened by the ruckus, can't help it, angered by the waste, the folly, as she called it, even angrier about Jakob's drinking, gulping down booze during the comedy special and shouting hooray every time a new rocket went whizzing up.

Ari was in his room, listening to music on his headphones, the turntable spun with the Beatles, E.L.O., Mannakorn. He fled there before the clock struck midnight, the moment of timelessness, a meeting of past and present, the magic moment when even enemies embrace. Jakob was so drunk that it wouldn't have been surprising if he'd tried to embrace his son and say something to him, maybe My son, my man – better to hide in his room, disappear into his music. Between shots, Jakob shouted hooray, but his cousin tried to reposition the bottle that had shifted from the shock of a firework hissing up out of it, and from Jakob's overexcited clumsiness in stuffing a new one into it; he tried to prop it up in the snowdrift so that the firework shot into the sky, not straight at them or, even worse, in the direction of their neighbour's garage. Two years earlier, Jakob had tripped over himself or some bump or hole in the yard just as he was lighting a fuse, resulting in the bottle tipping over and the rocket shooting not upwards but exuberantly towards the garage, smack into one of its windows, breaking it and getting snagged in the glass, where it remained stuck and whizzing as if an effervescent life were being suppressed. The neighbour came rushing out, screaming at Jakob, so livid that you couldn't understand a single word he said. Jakob regarded him silently before saying loudly, yet calmly and clearly, Shut up, you fucking Yankee whore.

Then he bent over to prop the bottle up again and shoot off a new rocket.

I should have you arrested! shouted the neighbour, hurrying into the garage; it's unclear what he wanted Jakob arrested for: calling him a Yankee whore, shooting off fireworks while drunk, or breaking one of his garage windows and in so doing endangering the entire neighbourhood, since that garage was always full of aircraft fuel from the Base, intended for the fighter jets that roared regularly above the rooftops of Keflavík. What a bang there would have been if the bottle-rocket had managed to break into the garage, an ebullient display as fire encountered a hundred litres of aircraft fuel. The sky truly would have been menaced, it would have had an earful, and Jakob and his cousin, and perhaps numerous others, would have soared straight to eternity.

There's precious little interaction between these neighbours, never has been very much, partly because both the stepmother and Jakob look down on the debauchery and smuggling connected with the Base, perhaps also because of Icelanders' instinctual annoyance with their neighbours, a deep-rooted intolerance, as if we still aren't accustomed to living in towns and cities, the demands made by such places when it comes to respecting others are a veiled attack on individual freedom. In short, the neighbours on Kirkjuteigur don't communicate very much. Fucking Yank-lickers, says Jakob when he's pissed off at them, perhaps on a fine day as father and sons polish their fleet of cars with the music cranked up. The stepmother once got into a heated argument with the wife about their cat, which uses the opportunity to snatch redwings when they're focused on pecking at the breadcrumbs the stepmother feeds them. Cursing and wielding a broom, she'd chased the cat across the neighbours' drive, where the wife was getting out of her car, and it kicked off. Otherwise, the woman rarely shows herself outdoors – although two years earlier, Ari had caught a glimpse of her white flesh as she sunbathed in her back garden. He was raking grass after mowing his lawn and edged closer to the thick hedge in order to get a better look, pretended to reach for something on the ground, but then a cloud drew a veil over the sun, the temperature dropped, she swore, abruptly stood up, looked at the sky, likely to

45

estimate how long it would take the sun to reappear, put on a pull-over, went inside. Those moments – from her standing up, looking at the sky and then putting on her pullover – created an unbreakable bond between her and Ari. She had no top on, Ari was kneeling by the hedge, saw her in her entirety through the tangle of branches, stared mesmerised at the first breasts he'd ever seen in his life, smaller than the ones in porn magazines but far more significant, somehow more intimate, and apparently just waiting for him. He stared, hardly daring to breathe. He'd never suspected that anything could be as beautiful and arousing at one and the same time. Bare-chested, she put on her pullover, and that's how he always saw her in his mind's eye, bare-chested beneath a pullover, jacket, coat, whether he saw her hurrying out to her car, ran into her at the shop. Her small, beautiful breasts rested bare beneath her clothing, like a secret message to Ari.

But New Year's Eve is a nightmare for her and her husband, who drives a truck, delivering, among other things, fuel for the fighter jets up at the Base when the tanker ship docks. He makes regular trips to the pipes up there, siphons several hundred litres into fifty-litre canisters, puts them in his boot, is careful to go on days when one of the two policemen who buy fuel from him is on duty and can wave him through the gate. It's been years since he had to buy fuel for his family's fleet of cars, neither have his parents or his siblings; the policemen, the leaders of Keflavík's two political parties and a number of acquaintances get fuel from him for half the petrol-station price. A substantial bonus – but then New Year's Eve arrives and Jakob changes into a cursed devil in the eyes of his neighbours, hammered on alcohol, fireworks whizzing in every direction, brushing the rooftops on their way to the sky, shooting upwards with hissing power like life bursting at the seams

46

to be lived fast and to the absolute fullest; Jakob shouts hooray as his life creeps along, no showers of sparks, no fiery flight, no heading towards the sky. He shouts hooray, but his stepmother shuts herself in the little study, cowers there, her arms wrapped round her knees, becomes a knot that life has tied in haste, a double knot, and Ari has shut himself in his room, has disappeared into a song, "Telephone Line" by E.L.O., "Starting Over" by Lennon, the music is a refuge, an escape, new possibilities – Jakob shouts hooray in the garden when a firework shoots off and the clock strikes 12.00, it's midnight, the moment when the years lock together, a few fractions of a second when the past is the future, the future is the present, and the present is the past. Jakob slaps his cousin on his back, then turns to look for Ari but sees no-one, looks around for his stepmother, but she's nowhere to be seen and his cousin has gone inside to ring his elderly parents, leaving Jakob standing there alone, beneath the gaping black sky, the fireworks finished. He lights a storm-proof match and watches it burn.

The 5th or something of January, a Trabant stuck in a snowdrift, someone has a huge bottom – and then we drive out of Keflavík

It's the first day of work for me and Ari at Drangey, the fish factory in Sandgerði. Ari's stepmother makes porridge for the three of them in the morning, makes a packed lunch for Jakob, who reads *Morgunblaðið*, harrumphing at the paper's politics, his views have always been more in tune with *The Will of the People*, though *Morgunblaðið*, unfortunately, is richer in content and has con-siderably better sports pages, and it's good, more than good, to immerse yourself in descriptions of matches in the English and German leagues, immerse yourself in a world in which boundaries are clear and numbers eliminate uncertainty. Ari eats slowly, impatient for his chance to read the sports pages. The Polish military loiters menacingly. There's unrest, the labour leader Lech Walesa is threatening socialism, two bartenders at Hotel Esja are in custody, suspected of embezzling funds by watering down the drinks. Jakob is so shocked that he reads the story out loud. Looks up, is about to add something, but notices the stepmother's expression, buries himself again in the paper, and silence returns. Ari stops waiting for the sports pages, wolfs down his steaming porridge so quickly that it burns the roof of his mouth, wants to go up to his room to listen to a song or two on his headphones. Jakob flips through the paper; there's a programme about Tómas Guðmundsson on the radio. "Thomas at Eighty", about one of our greatest-ever poets; Ari reads upside down, but then Jakob flips back to reveal two other pages covering Icelandic politics, crouches over that wasteland, those strangling weeds. Tómas Guðmundsson, thinks Ari, storing the name in his memory; he's going to go to the library tonight and check out a book by this poet. He vaguely recalls the name from school, gets up, rinses his bowl, grabs his lunch and is about to go up to his room. Where are you going? asks his stepmother. Up to my room, he mutters.

Stepmother: Up to your room? That's not where you work. Jakob stops reading. They both look at him. Now it's the two of them, he thinks.

Ari: I know.

Stepmother: Máni won't put up with you being late for work.

I'm just going to, he begins to say, before stopping and simply standing there. You're going to what? asks the stepmother. He shrugs. There's something wrong with you, says Jakob, almost as if

48

he's suddenly pissed off, yet at the same time as if he feels more relaxed, because now it's the two of them, he and the stepmother, they're together, they've met somewhere. Ari looks at them, they look at him. Jakob turns back to his newspaper, she eats her porridge, Ari puts on his coat and walks out into the dark morning. Cloudy, 3 degrees centigrade, it rained so much in the night that the snow that covered everything shortly before Christmas is almost entirely gone.

Máni, Drangey's owner from Strandir district, had driven over in the Trabant the night before. The world had been different then; it was snowing, everything was white, as if Keflavík were changing into a frigid heaven. Máni let Ari drive around in the Trabant while he sat silently in the passenger seat, staring straight ahead, arms folded, back straight, tall, unshaven, a red-chequered cap on his head. Where should I go? asked Ari. You decide, Máni had said, after staring out of the window for several long moments, as if surprised by Ari's confusion. Ari started the car, drove off. It had only been a month since he'd got his driver's licence, and he had trouble distinguishing between first and third gear, repeatedly found himself in trouble when he had to stop at an intersection, twice killed the engine when he tried to drive off while in third. Máni stared straight ahead the entire time, said nothing, didn't move. Ari tried to fish through the man's silence for some help, at least to get a response, muttering, after killing the engine the first time, I'm having a bit of trouble knowing if I'm in first or third, but Máni didn't reply. Ari thought he detected a tightness in the left corner of Máni's mouth, as if something had got seriously on his nerves. They drove on in silence, sometimes in fits and starts due to Ari's clumsiness or nerves. Finally, Máni cleared his throat, which startled Ari so much that he drove off the road and got the Trabant stuck in a snowdrift between the church and the Yank Building, which was located on a corner some 30 metres from the church. The Trabant's tyres spun, the engine died. Máni folded his arms, stared into space, said nothing. There was no need to say anything; his silence said it all: Ari probably couldn't even take a piss by himself. Ari restarted the car, his face burning with shame, from stress, his coat was way too warm, his hands were sweaty, and things got even worse when he couldn't manage to find fucking reverse to try to rock the car back and forth to free it from the drift. He tried to put the Trabant in first, but it slipped into third and the engine died. Ari hastily got out of the car to escape Máni's heavy silence and oppressive presence but also to attempt to free the car; he started digging with his bare hands, sweeping snow from around the tyres, worked frantically on all fours, with almost feverish intensity, and finally leaned against the car, sweaty, out of breath, with ice-cold hands, and met the eyes of the priest, who stood smoking on the church steps. Ari automatically said hello and bowed his head, the priest nodded, then looked away when a large family car with a "Jo" plate – signifying the Keflavík Airfield – drove up, turned left and parked in the Yank Building's car park. A woman got out of the car; that she was American was clear from her clothing, her face, pink make-up, heavy rear end, presumably due to her diet, in those years they ate greasier food than we did, calorie-rich fast food, but that difference has been erased – almost as if we're all turning into Yanks. She got out of the car, opened the rear door, grabbed two carrier bags stuffed with food from the PX, the biggest shop on the Base, shut the door with her rear end and then caught sight of Ari, of Máni in the front seat and of the priest on the church steps and stood stock still for a few moments, as if she'd been startled. They all looked at her. Six male Icelandic eyes. She tightened her grip on her bag, laden with products that residents of Keflavík covet and smuggle off the Base, for themselves or to sell on the black market, tightened her grip on her bag – before hurrying in. Nearly ran, seemed to flee, as if she was afraid that they were going to ambush her, had lain there in wait and intended to profit from her appearance, make use of her, that they were greedy for the foreign goods in her bags, the dollars in her purse, the English in her mouth. She hastily put the bags down at the door, opened it and hurried inside, on the run from the three men. On the run from Keflavík, from Iceland, hurried inside, safe for the moment behind her American furniture, with no need to fear exploitation by that defenceless little nation.

Ari got back into the Trabant, managed to put it into first gear and spun its tyres out of the snowdrift as Máni repositioned his wad of chewing tobacco and said out of the corner of his mouth, Huge bottom on that one. Ari shifted into second.

The priest was on the church steps yesterday too, you might well think he lives there, says Ari as we slink past the church in the morning darkness, and the priest, who appears to have just got up, leans against the doorjamb, looks down the road towards the blue-black sea as he pulls a cigarette out of a crumpled pack, sighs, feels a twinge in his lower back, sees us driving slowly by and thinks, perhaps, Not you again, takes a drag of his cigarette, inhales the thrill and the poison, then exhales. His wife says she can't love him anymore. She says that he's betrayed his ideals, including his life, including his family. He smokes. Sometimes life seems too long and too difficult for ideals. I wish I were as young as you lads, he mutters at the Trabant, as Ari shifts from second into third. He succeeds on the first attempt, and shortly afterwards, the Trabant comes to a stop outside a house on Skólavegur. We have to wait a while before a short woman comes up from the basement, her lunch and coffee in a worn carrier bag, at 7.42 a.m. I move into the back, the woman sits in the front, Máni and I say hello, she says nothing, reaches into her coat pocket, pulls out a pack of Camels, lights one, takes a drag, her eyelids droop momentarily, her expression almost happy. Her skin is greyish, her face spotted with freckles and set with delicate wrinkles, her eyes small but lively, as if they're always on the alert, as if there's a taut string deep within her. She exhales, finally says hello, and the Trabant crawls out of Keflavík. The woman smokes silently. Her name is Linda, and she's so short that Kári, the skipper of the 248-ton fishing boat *Drangey*, rarely calls her anything but The Sample – How's The Sample today? he asks when he comes to the fish factory, and she replies, You're so bloody fat, Kári, that I could squeeze all of me inside you!

We drive out of Keflavík.

The new cemetery is on the right, about two kilometres outside town, on open land, dead residents of Keflavík buried there as if to punish them for having chosen to spend their lives in this windy place, this semi-American town.

Ari has been to the cemetery twice. The first time was when his stepmother's father was buried. An old farmer from up north in Strandir who moved here with his wife when old age began to slow them down, when their vision began to dim, and the man became little more than a good-for-nothing, as he called himself, short but so stout and tough that he seemed to be made of stone. Weathered after nearly fifty years of farming on a fjord where the wind can be so cold that it kills birds in flight. He never suffered an injury, was never ill, he'd hardly ever had a cold his long, hard life, farming and fishing in cold weather – but one morning almost a year ago he was sitting at the kitchen table with one of his daughters, sipping coffee from his saucer, reading *Morgunblaðið*, humming softly as he often did at such moments but suddenly fell silent, carefully put down the saucer, looked up, said, Goddammit – and collapsed over the table, dead.

It isn't flashy, the old man's grave. A white cross, a black plaque inscribed with his name; that's it. Just the name, and of course dates: 1900–1978, his entire life compressed into a single dash. Sufficient space, however, has been left on the plaque for his wife's name when night draws over her; she's still alive despite experiencing poor health throughout her long life. Ari had never seen the old couple touch each other, let alone flirt, but she wept at his funeral. That day, the wind blew cold and damp from the sea; the priest's voice trembled with the cold and he instinctively began speaking faster in order to return to the warmth of home sooner than later. He had to read the poem "Shark Hunting" by the dearly departed Jakob Thorarensen, who was from his district and one of the very few poets he felt that he could justifiably spend his time reading.[2] It was a long poem that somehow became even longer in the chill wind, the cold that penetrated the living but left the dead in peace.

Just this past Christmas, Ari had gone with his stepmother and her mother to put candles on the grave, to let a gentle light shine over the man we love and miss, but the wind immediately blew out the match. Ari's stepmother lit a candle inside the car, but as soon as she got out, the wind blew the flame off the wick and into the

2 Jakob Thorarensen (1886–1972) was a poet and carpenter. "Shark Hunting" ("*Í hákarlalegum*") was written in 1900.

blue yonder. They were forced to abandon their plan and left the lightless candle behind like an apology at the foot of the cross.

Kenny Rogers plays at a dance

The Trabant crawls along. At times this East German product struggles against the Icelandic wind; Ari strains the feeble engine in his fight to shift from third into fourth, to gain some speed, to get the car above 40 kilometres per hour, and accidentally shifts into second. The Trabant lurches as if punched, Linda drops her half-smoked cigarette onto the floor, they approach the turnoff to Miðnesheiði. A sharp 90-degree turn; it's a well-known game, a competition, a test of manhood, to take it at maximum speed; Gummi, Linda's 21-year-old son, holds the record. He made the turn last autumn at 68 k.p.h. in his big American car, a magnificent vehicle, red and glossy, his weekends went into polishing and waxing every square centimetre of the car at his brother-in-law's garage, listening to The Yank, Kenny Rogers or Johnny Cash, and that's where the car is now, in fact, on this dark Tuesday morning, though not newly waxed and glossy but so banged up that it looks more like a person crying his heart out. During a short-lived thaw just before Christmas, Gummi had attempted to beat his own record, with two passengers as witnesses. They'd approached the turn with "Coward of the County" cranked to the max on the powerful stereo; Kenny Rogers' warm but slightly hoarse voice filled the car as he sang about Tommy. Everyone in the car sang along wholeheartedly to the song that everyone in Keflavík knows, shitfaced, with goose bumps, every boy or man imagining himself as Tommy, loving the sweet, kind Betty. Gummi took the turn just as they sang the final line along with Kenny,

Sometimes you gotta fight when you're a man, they were going 71 kilometres per hour – which proved to be a bit too fast. Or Gummi was too drunk. The car rolled twice. Stopped upside down; one passenger had a broken arm, the other four cracked ribs and a dislocated shoulder, but Gummi himself, who was barely scratched, crawled cursing out of the car and kicked a rock – so short, according to him, only a single centimetre taller than his mother, and such a lightweight that he evades injury.

Ari takes the turn at 31 k.p.h. Linda glances over at the speedometer, grins and smokes her third cigarette on the heath. I'm pale and sweaty, feel like throwing up, Ari can barely see out of the window anymore and finally ventures to open it a crack, the north wind slips in, bringing us clean air, its tidings of a long, cold winter. Are you trying to kill me, boy? mutters Linda, hunkering deeper into her coat. Sorry, mutters Ari, as he reluctantly rolls the window back up; it's 7.51 a.m. So dark on the heath, it's as if the sky has turned out all the lights, though in the distance, to our left, gleam those of the military, our protectors, close to five thousand soldiers behind a fence, heavily armed yet vulnerable to the wind, the unbearable boredom. The fresh, cold air had managed to diffuse the tobacco smoke a bit, we can breathe again, my carsickness eases for the time being and we crawl past Rockwell, the radar station that scans the sky day and night for Soviets. Damn, it would be nice to have a radio in the car, I say from the back seat, always good music on The Yank between 7.00 and 8.00 a.m. Bloody Yank, says Linda in her hoarse voice, We shouldn't listen to their fucking radio. We should boycott the bastard, she adds, taking a long drag and holding the smoke in for a few moments, until she begins to cough, then exhales and continues: . . . boycott the bastards but squeeze what we can out of them, because we won't be getting rid of them. They shit money, those fuckers. I open my mouth to defend The Yank, the Base's radio station, its music, which is certainly better than bloody Steam with its endless screeching symphonies and sawing violins, but the cigarette smoke makes me carsick again, shutting me up as I lean my forehead against the cold window.

The cold sea air feels good as we get out of the car outside the Drangey fish factory in Sandgerði. Máni is waiting in the old cafeteria; the new one is upstairs, furnished just a few weeks ago, a steep staircase, seventeen steps, but little used, the women prefer the old one, which is also Máni's office; a 10-square-metre room with a single table screwed to the floor, two backless benches, an old radio that's never turned off though no-one seems to listen to it, except for the weather forecast and catch sizes, when suddenly every word comes through loud and clear, but in between, the device is full of incomprehensible jabbering, endless readings, a hundred Beethoven symphonies. Máni is sitting at the table with an open notebook in front of him, a pencil stub next to it, the walls darkened by cigarette smoke and dust, his insulated Hagkaup coat zipped up halfway, a blue cotton shirt underneath it; that's how he's always dressed, except that the shirt is sometimes red; he does various chores at the factory, drives the lorry down to the pier for fish, to Keflavík for foot-ropes or all the way to Reykjavík to meet with Iceland's stockfish producers in fancy hotel conference rooms, in his coat, a red or blue shirt underneath it, parks the lorry, with its lingering smell of fish, among his colleagues' Range Rovers and Mercedes Benzes.

As we walk in, Máni says, Well, Linda, which means, as we would come to learn over time, Hello, Linda, and Happy New

Year. She replies immediately, having suddenly become chatty and cheerful after her silence on Miðnesheiði, Yes, Happy New Year to you, too, Máni, and thanks for the old one! Máni looks at us, says nothing, just looks, glances down at his open notebook with its empty white pages, then looks back at us. Linda looks too, and it's as if they've come to a tacit conclusion that we're worth no more than those empty pages, that we're insignificant, barely reliable, taking turns at 30 k.p.h. For a moment, we feel like maybe we should start smoking, because anyone holding a cigarette automatically seems more important, more capable, more confident, as if the world takes such people more seriously. Finally Máni opens his mouth again, we can see his crooked, tobacco-stained teeth, and says, without taking his eyes off us, blank pages that we are, Well, Svavar. We look round to see Svavar standing in the doorway, tall, slim and panting. He'd got up late and dashed the entire kilometre to work, stuffed two slices of bread into his mouth as he ran, his woollen jumper covered with breadcrumbs, butter at the corners of his mouth, panting, his big Adam's apple rises and falls in his slender throat like an animal searching for a way out. He quickly wipes one corner of his mouth, nods, turns on his heel, goes into the room adjoining the cafeteria, hurriedly puts on his coverall, because clearly, once again, *Well, Svavar* meant Hello, Happy New Year, thanks for the old one, but also: You're late, now get to work.

Máni tucks a wad of tobacco under his lip, glances at Ari and me; barely a minute later, we've started scraping and scrubbing fish tubs along with Svavar. Preparing for the winter fishing season. Svavar had looked at us, then held out his hand and said with a grin, I'm Svavar – hopefully you're not too boring! Árni arrives half an hour late. Saunters in calmly, as if time doesn't matter this far north in the world and in life. Máni walks in, says nothing, just raises his arm, taps his watch. This is Árni, Svavar says, the professor, bloody hell you're late. I overslept. I thought your mother usually woke you. Yes, she used to, but it didn't work, I always went back to sleep. Árni hesitates, glances over at Ari and me, appears to weigh us up, judge us, before adding, carefully, probably because what he was going to say possessed considerable explosive power, I didn't want my dream to end. What were you dreaming? asks Ari – the first words that pass between them. Árni smiles, and his pale, almost feminine face shines: I dreamed I was changing into Einstein's equation $E = mc^2$. What's that, and who is this Einstein? asks Svavar, but Ari and I exchange glances and I say, That's a good dream, I completely understand why you wouldn't want it to end. I don't understand a single bloody thing, Svavar says with a snort, but that equation of yours sounds like the title of a totally great rock song.

How many days do we have on this planet, in our lifetimes, that really matter, in which something has truly happened, in which the synchronisation of planets, the circulation of our blood, causes our lives to appear brighter, fuller, in the evening than in the morning – how many days?

Nothing remarkable happens that Tuesday at Drangey. Of course it doesn't. We're in Sandgerði and the fishing season hasn't begun yet. Hands move slowly, drowsiness pervades the village, we've nothing with which to address the world. Just us four, scrubbing and cleaning fish tubs, and two women scraping and painting the planks in the stalls: Linda with her pack of Camels, and Andrea, a red-haired woman who lives in Sandgerði but is from the same fjord in Strandir as Máni and Ari's stepmother. A strong woman who moves quickly and with such determination that the air quivers a bit more around her than around the rest of us. Máni is bent over the forklift with a screwdriver and pliers, the radio dozes off in the little coffee room, it's cold in the building, the January darkness and a distant sky outside. An unremarkable day. Except for the unrest in Poland, and two bartenders at Hotel Esja on their way to jail for watering down alcoholic drinks – otherwise, one of those bland Tuesdays with nothing to remember them by, which do nothing but bring us one day closer to the end. Not even a comma in the big script. Except for us four. In our world, it will be one of the few days that we set aside without hesitation and keep for viewing later, when everything has slowed down and the blood in our veins has begun to get an inkling of death. That's the way it is: the history of the world goes in one direction, the history of the individual in an entirely different one, which is why there must be at least two equally correct versions of human history.

It's time for coffee.

The women go to the little room with Máni, they smoke, Máni vanishes in a fug, the radio announcer coughs, but Árni and Svavar lead me and Ari up to the tidy new break room shunned by the women, Svavar reaches for a worn deck of cards, we play whist and watch Árni take out his lunchbox and his bottle of milk. Svavar shakes his head and says, Just as well the women can't see you. Only grannies and babies drink milk; where's your coffee? Coffee makes me queasy, explains Árni, and Svavar shakes his head again, looks at us and chuckles. Ari and I smile, happy to be in such company, we look out at the flat, nearly barren landscape resembling a dumb beast in the morning darkness. A few lights in the box-shaped houses, a one-eyed Datsun drives past, a housewife

59

yawns at a kitchen window, Árni gulps down his milk. He's two years older than us, has finished one and a half years, three terms, in his physics course at Keflavík Comprehensive School, and people in Sandgerði call him either "the professor", for his personality, his helplessness and his schooling, or else "the biddy" due to his delicate feminine appearance, so pale and weak-looking that the merest sharp comment would probably propel him to his sickbed. Árni had aced his exams before Christmas, had no trouble with the material, had never shown much interest in work, bent over his books and music, and seemed right at home at the comprehensive, was finally in the right place, nevertheless announced just before Christmas that he was leaving school. Gave no explanation and responded with silence when his worried mother pressed him with questions, just shut himself in his room and listened to music, his eyelids drooping as if he hoped that Ian Anderson's next flute solo would carry him off in its arms.

Árni's mother always puts care and thought into preparing him a nutritious lunch, about which he always seems indifferent: a banana sandwich, two slices of bread with cucumber, a biscuit, crullers, raisins, a thick slice of marble cake. Árni eats a third of his sandwich, we get the biscuit and crullers, he breaks the marble cake into quarters and hands each of us our own piece, like a covenant of friendship. Árni's fingers are delicate, so narrow that it's as if the daylight shines through them. Earlier, when he was at Sandgerði Primary School, his lack of energy and eccentricity seemed to rile his schoolmates; they tied his hands and feet, shoved him into cupboards, under staircases, into the rubbish bin – once, they hid him behind the shed, where it snowed on him; he was forgotten but found four hours later, completely blue with cold and exhausted from sobbing – those days are behind us, and his dreams sometimes transform him into the most beautiful mathematical equation in the world.

From History of Sandgerði

"Sandgerði is a village at the western tip of the Reykjanes Peninsula. The Sigurvon rescue team, one of the country's oldest rescue teams, is stationed there. Not much happens in Sandgerði; television reporters and other members of the media have had trouble finding their way there in the few instances when something newsworthy has happened: when the rescue team was successful, when someone shot himself, when a dog adopted a lost, ragged seagull chick. The winter sky over Sandgerði can be beautiful, packed with stars, ornamented with Northern Lights, and on spring mornings it can be so tranquil that you can hear the fish breathing deep down in the sea, which stretches as far as the eye can see . . . the grass in Sandgerði has been likened to green knives where it pokes up through the black sand, spreads out and livens up the surroundings. Some of the villagers keep a few sheep in memory of the countryside they came from, and when they lie outside chewing their cuds on fine summer days, a certain level of contentment seems achievable. There are frequent storms; the village is exposed in every direction, with nothing to tame the wind. It blows hard, the houses shake, the sky quakes, the boats knock against the pier, a cat flies into the sea or up onto the heath, depending on the wind direction; the gusts tear up the grass and blow it away. When the storm slackens, the grass is gone, everything has turned black around Sandgerði, and the daylight is so dim that it's as if the night will never end."

The sawblade cuts the head off, and the rest of us who are damaged set course for Hallgrímur Pétursson

"You will always be / my endless love" sing Lionel Richie and Diana Ross that year, each and every day, somewhere in the world, London, Los Angeles, Copenhagen; it's the slow-dance song at dances in Sandgerði, along with "Reunion" by Upplyfting. The four of us go to two dances there and see the girls we dream about disappear into the arms of others, and the entire hall hums or sings along with the songs of heartbreak, those shameless declarations of eternal love, as if life were first and foremost a long kiss, as if love never fell to pieces or wound down, as if it resolved all problems. Sailors, baiters, the women on the fish-processing line, electricians, lorry drivers, counter girls sway to "Endless Love" and "Reunion", close their eyes, kiss, whisper things that the songs, the night and the wine blow into their hearts, about immeasurable happiness that endures. "You will always be / my endless love"; "because I love you so much that I could almost die / for just this one night in your arms." Outside, the grey armies of mundanity are waiting with their weapons, dirty underwear, burnt porridge, disagreements on how well and often they should clean the house, money worries, too much drinking, too little sex, insomnia – everything that seems to have it so easy laying love across its knees and disgracing it. "You will always be / my endless love" because I love you so much; Ari and Árni and I never sing this song. Not a chance; we would never let on that such sugar-sweet sounds could affect us, but Svavar both sings the songs and plays them on the organ at home, even when the rest of us are around, gets totally caught up in them, shuts his eyes, opens his mouth and sings with such conviction that we find ourselves face-to-face with his big horse teeth.

*

That's how it is; such are life and the galaxies above Iceland in 1981 and 1982. The world and its events rolled along; the throats of two hundred people, children, women, men, were cut one night in Guatemala, the military in Poland is still restless, Mr Brezhnev, the Soviet Union's highest official, is growing angry, and Ronald Reagan, the President of the United States, the world's most powerful man, has the I.Q. of a small dog and the emotional capacity of a pistol. Each morning, we drive out of Keflavík and make four stops, the number of passengers increases when the fishing season begins, we drive over the heath to Sandgerði, then out and back over the same heath at noon, not in a Trabant but in an eight-passenger Toyota, the fish-drying racks are filled and emptied, the saltfish stacks grow higher. Every coffee break, we four play whist; old Kristján and two or three others join us at the peak of the fishing season. Kristján is glad to be one of us, a part of life, but once in a while, often out of the blue, the joy seems to be sucked out of him and he changes into a dull rock tossed away by life.

The galaxies revolve above Iceland, but here the universe revolves around fish.

Fish is the beginning and end, the alpha and omega. Máni drives down to the pier, the *Drangey* has docked, its helmsman, Jonni, stands bare-armed on deck in blowing snow and piercing frost. The lorry has to make several trips from the harbour to the fish factory, sometimes filling all three stalls, which means a dreadfully long work shift ahead. Stalls full of glistening wet cod with fixed, empty eyes. Ari grabs a cod and remembers the East-fjords, all the way to Norðfjörður, to his grandfather Oddur, who fished for decades and reaped appreciation and respect, as verified and confirmed by the certificate of recognition hanging in the most prominent place in the living room at Kirkjuteigur. He fished for decades and never felt better than when he was at sea, where all of humanity's problems were solved, he fished to survive, fished so that the nation would gain full independence and break free from poverty and primitive ways. Here stands his grandson, decades later, on the other side of the country, holding a freshly caught cod. I feel something, Ari says to me, and I know it's important, but I just can't put it into words; they keep escaping. Yes, I say, words can be timid birds. Maybe you need to change into air to touch them.

Árni's usual place is in the holding area. He's most efficient there, shovelling fish onto the conveyor belt with his gaff, generally works hard, infected by the rhythm, but is distracted now and then, some thought takes him away and he stands stock-still, his boots submerged in cod, lost to us, the conveyor belt at the end of the middle stall conveying nothing but air, no more fish are carried up to Svavar at the heading table, where he toils like a hyperactive foal, trembling with the joy of exertion and his ambition to keep pace with the women at the processing table, entirely focused on grabbing the fish, slapping them onto the heading machine's conveyor belt, tugging slightly at the head, thumb and forefinger in the eye sockets, a monotonous task like most others in the fish business, especially when it's like this, the holding stalls over-flowing with fish, tons more waiting, thousands of fish to head, always the same motion, for hours at a time, no-one to talk to, not if you're at the heading machine, your world the noise of the machine, the whine of the saw. Nevertheless those hours can be good and meaningful for Svavar when he breaks the monotony by imagining the cod as one of his bullies at primary school, where he was teased constantly, nicknamed The Horse because of his teeth and his horse-laugh, the name stuck during his early years, hung there like a curse – humanity's imagination is almost nowhere as fertile as in cruelty. You're Goggi, he mutters to a big, fat cod, slapping it onto the belt and relishing the cry of the sawblade cutting off its head.

Of course he grabs only empty air when Árni is distracted, when some thought distracts him and he stands there bent over a cod, poking with the gaff at its glazed, empty eye, or just stares into space, a euphoric smile on his lips, as if life were bloody good. Oh, now the professor's thinking something wise, says Andrea when the processing table has been cleared, no more fish come from Svavar, they're able to catch their breath, and Linda, who cuts the stomachs, has lit a cigarette, takes a long drag and rocks back and forth to rid herself of the pain in her hips. Four women at the processing table, one to cut the fish's stomach, the next to gut it, the third to separate the liver from the roe, the fourth to slide the fish into the splitting machine, four different women, all of whom were brought up in fish processing and toil, working full days on top of tending to their homes, cooking for their children and husbands, preparing lunches, doing the laundry, tidying up; life is work, they can't tolerate slothfulness yet say nothing at first, just stand at the processing table as Árni pokes at a glazed cod eye or stares idly into the distance, perhaps glad to have a moment's rest, they stare at Árni almost affectionately, as if they appreciate his delicacy, his obvious lack of toughness, firmness, determination, perhaps find it beautiful, perhaps because he gives their existence – the fish is all it is sometimes, the long hours spent processing it – an unexpected softness. But the conveyor belt continues revolving, grabbing nothing but air, and so far no-one has been able to live on that, and there stands Árni, staring into space like an imbecile, a smile on his lips. I've hardly ever seen the professor look so stupid, says Andrea finally, reaching for a handful of livers and tossing them at Árni, startling him back into action.

Where do you go? I ask him once, when you space out like that in the stalls, stare into the blue as if you're seeing something truly beautiful and good; where do you go?

It's a Saturday afternoon, wind and rain at sea, which is why there's no overtime, a moment's rest from the empire of toil, and we four, the misfortunate, drive around in Árni's airy Saab, which is our world apart, a solar system outside of life. We drive back and forth over the heath, in the dwindling light and into the darkness. Sometimes to Garður, the village that's so spread out it hardly exists, often to Hvalsnes church, where the poet and priest Hallgrímur Pétursson lived out his depressed days many hundreds of years ago. A poor backwater pastor in a place where the wind seems to blow straight from Hell, but where, on good days, the ocean can be so blue that it seems to embody happiness. Here is where he lost his daughter, she was just three years old yet had already composed some verses of her own; she was sharp as a tack, precocious, and so filled with joy that for a time Hallgrímur thought that injustice and cruelty would cease to exist, and her smile would always be stronger than the darkness. Then she was snatched away. When she had only just begun to live. Her small, soft fingers which had often stroked her father's rough, ugly face, stroked it tenderly and transformed it into a beautiful hymn, into a lively piece of music, were down in the dark ground, her laughter silenced. The only thing that Hallgrímur could do was write a poem, like our great-aunt Lilla, centuries later, in the hope that it

66

would alleviate the sorrow, the piercing pain, and somehow brighten the impenetrable darkness. Which it simply didn't do, not one bit, a nearly four-year-old girl was just as far from life as before, happiness just as distant from humankind as before, all laughter broken. Justice usually took a detour around Hallgrímur, and poverty, then leprosy, sucked the life out of him. We still read his poems, many hundreds of years later, most often, perhaps, his hymn to his daughter, the little girl who long since became polished bones in the earth, no laughter there, no happiness, her grief-stricken father has been dead for nearly 350 years, but the poem lives on. It nestles into us like beautiful music, a bit dark, very melancholy, yet bright with a beauty that seems able to move the atmosphere. Sprung from love that survives the centuries, humankind, even religion, yet is so utterly useless when death begins pulling; timeless poetry that comforts everyone but the person who composed it, and the person who died.

Old Kristján often tells us about Hallgrímur, naturally getting no work done while he does so – he leans against the saltfish stack, resting his tired old body, resting his old bones, which always seem so terribly weary, even in the morning, after a decent night's sleep, as if he'd reached a place where no rest was possible but that to be found in death. It's good, however, almost nice, leaning against the blessed saltfish, breathing in its smell, watching the young men work, telling them stories about Hallgrímur, reciting the poem about the little daughter while we listen, not letting up for an instant, interested because the poem was written nearby, it hadn't occurred to us, perhaps not to anyone, that literature could thrive here, which it does, of course, because literature thrives everywhere. We're also moved by Hallgrímur's story: his poverty, struggle, sorrow; he comes across as someone so damaged yet is

still important, which is why we take the long detour out to Hvalsnes church, where the road ends – not far from the other side of
the church are the fenced-off grounds of the American military,
which prefers fighter jets to hymns. We drive there in the smooth
Saab, and I've just asked Árni, Where do you go when you space
out like that in the stalls?

Árni smiles as if he's remembered something beautiful;
his thin, feminine lips part, but he says nothing, just turns up
the stereo, which spins and spins with forty-five-, sixty- or ninety-
minute cassette tapes we've filled with music, sometimes entire
albums or else mixes we want to play for each other, Led Zeppelin,
Jethro Tull, Bowie, Utangarðsmenn, Pink Floyd, the Beatles. Svavar
sometimes has trouble hiding his enthusiasm for R.E.O. Speedwagon and Upplyfting, but we put up with his questionable taste,
forgive him because he's truly one of us. We're all damaged in
some way, don't fit in and consider ourselves lucky to have all
started working at Drangey around the same time, for Máni, that
silent man from Strandir, as silent as the moon he's named after, as
aloof as its surface, yet something inspired him to hire us, as well
as old Kristján, slowly being pushed aside by life, time or old age.
He who always used to stand at the heart of the work stream due
to his diligence and experience but who has become completely
useless, a wasted sack, nothing left but memories, an exhausted
body and a vast stock of poems.

The poems are quite good; they can be used as blankets when
the world is cold, they can be caves outside of time, with strange
symbols on their walls, but have so little to say if your very bones
are tired, if life has rejected you, and your cup of coffee is the only
thing that warms your hands at night.

Keflavík

— PRESENT —

What are poets for if they can't help us live?

Ari sips his coffee, takes a biscuit from the packet on the table, Svavar reaches his long arm to turn up the radio a bit, "Staying Alive" by the Bee Gees; he was incorrigible when it came to music. He organises trips around Reykjanes – "Discover the magic of lava" – sells lava rocks, cuddly puffins, photographs, Hljómar albums, 20-centimetre replicas of the Reykjanes lighthouse, each of which is inscribed with one or two verses from Hannes Sigfússon's "*Dymbilvaka*", a long poem composed at the foot of the lighthouse in the winter of 1949: "Thus does the cello drag a heavy sorrow ashore."[3] This is my kingdom, Svavar had said as they walked through the shop; he puts sugar in his coffee, stirs it and smiles happily because Ari is with him. You knew of course that our Árni got married – who would have expected that? says Svavar, shaking his head; he's never been seen with a woman! It's my understanding that his wife just stuck him in her pocket; that was the extent of their courtship. Except that they had a lovely boy, who moved to Denmark to work in computers; everything seemed rosy, but then he just walked out, his only explanation being that he needed to find himself! What a task that is, old friend, finding yourself! Personally, I never bothered about such things; I wasn't like you, brooding all the time; I just enjoyed living. Anyway, my life turned upside down. It all began quite innocently, although I did change course now and then, gave up a steady job to go back to school,

3 Hannes Sigfússon (1922–97) was one of the so-called Icelandic "Atom Poets", modernists active in the 1940s and '50s. His "*Dymbilvaka*" ("Passion Vigil") is considered one of the finest Icelandic modernist poems.

but there was nothing behind it, or so I thought, except a desire for something new. Slowly but surely, I realised that in a certain sense I'd lived without, well, without thinking, and that I'd probably stopped loving my wife long ago. Despite having once been absolutely mad about her. Life, man; it's not the rock song we thought it would be.

I've often, says Svavar, grabbing two biscuits and squishing their chocolate sides together to make a sandwich while regarding them regretfully, all those calories, pondered these questions – when are you really alive, and why does love change into a habit providing security instead of happiness? Yes, and why does it become difficult, over the years, to distinguish between love and habit – isn't that downright awful; are we just supposed to accept it? If anything should be clear, shouldn't it be love? Isn't this something that you poets should be helping us with – even explaining, if only in passing, why it's so hard for people to be happy? I mean, what are poets for if they can't help us live?

And then eternity comes to earth

Snæfríður Íslandssól's lights are on when Ari emerges from Svavar's room, trembling from the strong coffee, and the neon sign in the window of the watchmaker's shop over the road is blinking. It's past noon and Gunnar's Watch Repair and Jewellery Shop broadcasts an announcement, or distress call, to the residents of Keflavík and the world, Open, open, open, I'm open, come in for God's sake, I have so little to do, come and I'll fix time for you, I can repair anything, I can set your watch to the past, how about 1981, long before the Internet, what freedom to be rid of that distraction; I can reset time to zero if you prefer, which means a new beginning, a chance to start all over again, so many possibilities!

It's calm in the sky, perhaps everywhere in Keflavík except here on Hafnargata, it's as if the town's barren high street manufactures wind, repeated attempts have been made to plant up the area, but the salt suffocates any growth – and if anything survives the salt, the wind beats it down. The only thing that grows here is people. And, in recent years, unemployment. And obesity, diabetes, digestive disorders, stress, biscuit packets, chocolate – it all grows and expands. Everything has become *king-size*; king-size Snickers, Prince Polo, king-size beds, armchairs, flat screens, king-size happiness. King-size penises. It's all advertised on the Internet and in the media; Ari read *Fréttablaðið* over a hearty breakfast at the Flight Hotel and saw an ad promising a longer, broader penis – it was even possible to expand it to king-size! I saw that ad, too, after waking in my uncle's old wooden house and having a breakfast of muesli with *AB-mjólk* as my uncle sat hemming and hawing over his script, *Memories of a Base Rat*; I read *Fréttablaðið* and noticed Bathmate promising king-size happiness:

> Bathmate.is, a quick and efficient way to enlarge your penis: gain up to 7 centimetres and up to 30% more thickness. Many women say that a thicker penis gives them more satisfying orgasms. *No woman says no to a better, thicker penis.* Studies show that a larger, thicker penis improves men's confidence and well-being. Bathmate thickens your penis right from the first use!

The wind blows round Ari on Hafnargata. He's standing in the same spot, outside Svavar's tourist shop, and doesn't feel so well, not having a particularly thick or long penis. It's obvious who uses

Bathmate! A bigger penis improves confidence and gives you more of a glow, helping you advance in your career, earning you better wages; you can afford a bigger house, a holiday home, a nice S.U.V. – the claim that God is shaped like a penis is most certainly correct! Women want a thicker, longer penis; it gives them greater, deeper pleasure, helps them approach the divine.

Snæfríður stands at the window of the massage parlour, looks out, down the empty road, her gaze brushes against Ari like a wing. A blonde dream of spring – she's so blonde that it would probably be possible to write an entire novel about her, a dreamy piano concerto; she has such difficulty getting up on these short winter days – and what can you do about that? The wind blows cold; it doesn't give a thought to happiness, isn't worried about cancer, excess weight, a penis that's too small or not thick enough, doesn't think about breasts sagging lower and lower, like tired people, let alone Ari, who finally rambles off down the road, happy that Svavar didn't see him, probably too busy Skyping with his grandson, babbling and making faces at the four-year-old who hiccups with laughter, otherwise he would certainly have come out and asked worriedly, Huh, you're still here, is everything alright, my friend? Svavar, who's loved Snæfríður for years but never dared to say anything, hint at anything, afraid of destroying a precious friendship, but dreaming of her, desiring her. From love it's exactly the same distance to happiness and unhappiness.

Ari walks off, composing and sending me a text as he does so: "Met Svavar, unchanged, except 30–40 kilos heavier, the same questionable taste in music, the same warm eyes."

The same warm eyes – Is everything alright, my friend? Concern for others is in Svavar's blood. He can't help it; can't bear to see someone hurting without trying to console, fix, help that person, so guileless that he always asks straight out, is incapable of skirting the issue, it occurs to me that this was the explanation for the bullying in primary school in Sandgerði: it wasn't his big teeth, as if he'd accidentally been given those of a horse, a manufacturing error, no returns, and, on top of that, sounded like a horse when he laughed; that wasn't the reason, the trigger, but rather, his innate concern for others, which causes him to empathise when he's around people who are vexed. He felt the kids' sadness, powerlessness, distress, fear and terrible worries, they sensed it, felt his big eyes – yes, they're also a bit like a horse's – gazing compassionately at them, and shook him off, made him the schoolyard punching bag before he could ask whether everything was alright, because maybe nothing was alright, maybe the whole family feared their father's hands, his knuckles, his temper. Feared that he'd come home tired, grumpy, drunk, his wife a fucking nag with enormous thighs and lifeless hair, her body as exciting as a fish that's been dead for days. Is everything alright? No, not at all, Dad beats me, Mum is drunk when I come home, Grandpa died the day before yesterday and I cried my fucking eyes out: best to punch you and call you names before you ask, before you blow my cover.

Is everything alright; how was Ari supposed to answer? By lying, like most of us do? By saying, What, no, yes, goodness me, everything's great, I'm a bit spaced out, you know, having just returned to this country and all that. Or, just tell it like it is: No, hardly anything's alright. Snæfríður's unhappy, longs for someone to put his arms around her, you love her but don't have the guts to do anything about it; and I miss waking up next to the woman I love, with whom I lived for twenty years, whom I betrayed because my heart split in two, because I loved two women, is that a betrayal? I don't know, but instead of facing up to the difficulty of loving, I fled from my wife, fled from life; I find it unbearable not to see my children every day, not to participate in their daily life. No, old friend, hardly anything's alright because my wife saw to it that yesterday, my cousin Ásmundur, none other, our old hero and role model, stuck his index finger up my rectum, probably searching for my betrayals; and last night I discovered that just over thirty years ago, I witnessed a rape but did nothing, realised nothing, just felt sorry for myself; and I bought a porno magazine at Kastrup Airport, suddenly felt horny seeing the cover photo and looked forward to checking out the magazine in private, but the woman on the cover turned out to be a girl of about the same age as my daughters and I felt like I'd wronged them somehow, agreed to the notion that their bodies were commodities meant for men; how can you ask if everything's alright when you have two daughters in a world designed by men; society, culture, religion tailored for them and God in the shape of a penis; and my grandmother, Margrét, never got to live the life she desired, so never got to know herself properly; I don't know what kind of life her son – my father – dreamed of when he was young; my father, who might be dying. I'm on my way to visit him, we haven't seen each other in almost three years and have probably never talked about things that matter, and I fear that nothing will change that now; but one time we hid behind some curtains, the sun baked us, we didn't move because we were certain her life depended on our not being found. Svavar, this is the situation: We're hiding behind some curtains, it's summer, the sun is quivering in the sky, which is so blue, it's as if eternity is on its way to earth.

About the size of the universe

— BACK IN THE DAY —

Endless happiness!

This all began with a death. It's July, Iceland's gentlest month, when the moon is held up by birdsong and the warm sun is an important message from happiness – at such times, where is there room for death? How can darkness assail anyone when the sun stretches out in the sky and ice-cream shops in Reykjavík are filled with people? Boundless happiness; children skip rope, play hopscotch, football, they shout, shriek, laugh, run around the block of flats in Safamýri, the one at the top of the road, the one that towers highest on the hill and thus is slightly nearer the sun than other blocks of flats. Thirty to forty children around the block, sun-baked mothers on the balconies, tobacco smoke drifting up like a sigh, raucous laughter carries from a flat on the third floor to the left of the central staircase, it's the summer holiday, the balcony doors are opened wide, opened to the sun, the shouting, this wonderful day that's like a blessing in every way, like all the things we desire. Sweaty glaciers, sun-baked housewives, children who run screaming with joy, so steeped in vital energy that it's as if the sky has moved closer, as if God has moved closer to Iceland to take a photograph of this happy slice of life; moved closer with a movie camera to project this day onto the screens of heaven when winter darkness has fallen over the world. Projects it to a packed auditorium, popcorn and angels' wings crunch, the darkness of the universe is outside, but God is showing the film "Joy – Why the World Exists". The stars: laughter on the third floor to the left, the block of flats itself, Safamýri 52–56, thirty-nine children, bright with joy and games, the shopkeeper Söbekk smiling outside his shop, and, much further away, magnificent glaciers that sweat like gloomy aunts, except for Snæfellsjökull glacier, which is an ice-cream cone for the sky, God and his host of angels in a jam-packed cinema of heaven. "Joy – Why the World Exists".

Director, screenwriter and producer: God. Cinematographer and assistant screenwriter: Jesus.

God and Jesus.

Two blind chickens.

Seeing nothing but what's right in front of their eyes, what everyone wants them to see. Not seeing old Þórólfur on the third floor to the right, the old grump feared by us kids, lying in the master bedroom with the curtains drawn, his wife in the kitchen, smoking by herself over the cooling coffee and a serial on the radio, Jón K. Magnússon concludes his reading of his translation of a story by Wilkie Collins, "The Dream Woman".[4] She'd looked forward to the reading yet didn't catch a word of it. They both miss the mountains to the north, miss the sheep shed, the sheep, the dog, the chickens. They haven't always been so old; once they were young and had the world at their feet. One night while they were fast asleep, time took a big step, and they woke up old. Suddenly a nuisance. Unfit, too rigid for life. Ended up here, in this block of flats in Reykjavík, a farm to the north with mountains and a livelihood for a three-bedroom flat and a garage for the Land Rover. Þórólfur has drawn the curtains against the sun, the day, the joy, the cine camera of the sky, because sometimes he misses the mountains and the countryside so terribly, the mountains he grew up with, and that were there right in front of him for seventy-four

4 "The Dream Woman" by the English writer Wilkie Collins (1824-1889), was originally published in 1874 (a revised version of an earlier story, "The Ostler", published in 1855).

years. He lies there, heavy and sad with longing for mountains that have forgotten all about him.

Two blind chickens flapping about with a cine camera, they film the world, say, Well now, there on the third floor to the right, the curtains are drawn, someone rushed out into happiness so quickly that he forgot to open them. The camera pans down the block of flats, two housewives on the balcony on the second floor to the left, both topless, "Let the Sun Shine In" by The 5th Dimension is playing on The Yank. Let the sun shine in, the light, the warmth. Good idea. "Let happiness in; it can't get through a locked door," said one of the *Ten Tips* books that Ari would edit in Denmark forty years later; let it in, don't let the day's worries, stress, your career ambitions, shut it out; let happiness in and it will reward you generously. Of course, yes, we'll do that, no question, any time; but the camera is pointed at the first floor to the left. Oh, says Jesus happily, look, two boys hiding behind some curtains! What fun, says God, and then the camera pans down to the field, showing children running among sunbeams. What fun, says God again. Yes, splendid, agrees Jesus. Two chickens, blind as bats.

It was my idea.

Hey, I said, let's hide behind the curtains in the bedroom; they're so long in front of the balcony door, and heavy, that they stop the light, no-one will see us, no-one will find us, if you slip behind the curtains, the world changes into two blind chickens and you're safe. Great, said Ari, and that's why we're there, within the happiness of the day, the swollen sun turns slowly through the blue sky, we hear the laughter, the sounds of the songs from the balconies above, we hear Jakob, his sister Hulda and my uncle, with whom I would later stay in Keflavík, all calling Ari. We stay silent. We shut our eyes, hold hands tightly, barely breathe. We absolutely mustn't be found. Everything will be ruined if we're found. They came and got Ari's mother yesterday. Now it's his turn. That's why we're hiding behind the heavy curtains, our backs hot from the dim rays of the sun.

Reykjavík

— EARLY 1980S —

Someone needs to change his way of thinking, but
God still reigns!

The '50s, Presley is on the verge of becoming something bigger than just himself, the Soviets launch one spacecraft after another, sending them to snoop around beyond the earth's atmosphere. Laika the dog, a three-year-old stray, is aboard one of the spacecraft. She growls and barks fearfully at the stars shortly before she dies, alone, far from life, for the advancement of science.

Ari's mother moves in with Jakob.

It's an autumn morning. He reads *The Will of the People* and is looking forward to eating his toast. First, though, he drinks two cups of coffee to wake up, establish contact with the world, reads the paper, war rages in the world, as always, somewhere, but it's only 7.00 a.m. here in Iceland. This afternoon, G. A. King, from the international organisation of the Seventh-Day Adventists, will deliver a talk entitled "God Still Reigns!" Unfortunately, the announcement doesn't mention who could possibly have come close to threatening or snatching power from God: British warships in Icelandic waters, the President of the U.S., the Devil, sin, Elvis Presley perhaps. The point, of course, is that God hasn't lost his kingdom. Still, it's shocking to learn, so early in the morning and still dark outside, that things were touch-and-go with God on the power front, and that there's a struggle – because the word *still* tells us that even God doesn't hold everything in his hands, and that something or someone could potentially threaten him. It's difficult news that, when all is said and done, we're stuck with an imperfect God who, in addition, appears to be extremely concerned about power and overly sensitive to what's said about Him, to criticism, afraid of not being viewed as sufficiently strong, is vengeful, pedantic, barks fearfully at the stars. But if we change our ways of thinking, we can change God.

What? exclaims Jakob as he takes a bite of toast, because she's been talking, Ari's mother, and he's barely awake; the morning is dark and life moves slowly, barely crawls, inches its way cautiously forward, which is the best way, anyway, read the newspaper slowly, say little, drink a hell of a lot of coffee, smoke two cigarettes, and you're ready to go: Life, here I come! She's very inconsiderate, she talks and talks, he can't make sense of it all, isn't ready for such heavy discussion, dammit, it's not even 7.00 in the morning! What he does catch is that someone barks, and someone has to change his way of thinking. Which would be that bloody Brit, wading up to our border in trawlers and warships, he says with his mouth full, looks up, is about to swallow – but she's naked. Has slipped out of her nightdress, exposed her slender shoulders, her small, firm breasts, and the day is just beginning. His bricklaying job awaited him, and the bus up to Vífilsstaðir Hospital, where she works in the kitchen, stops at Skaftahlíð in twenty-one minutes – but maybe life is too short for this sort of wisdom. At least she doesn't listen to what he's saying, that she needs to hurry up and get dressed, she hasn't eaten yet, she eats far too little, the bus will be there soon, the morning is dark, he's only taken two bites of his toast and hasn't finished reading the paper, hasn't even got to the sports pages. She doesn't listen. Sometimes it's as if she can't tolerate wisdom, will do anything she can to challenge it. And, unfortunately, knows how to arouse him: he follows her into the living room. She who laughs at him. She who is now on the sofa. She, who says, flippantly, We've got to be quick – and opens her legs.

Which flips his switch.

He rips off his trousers, throws himself on top of her, enters her, she gasps, and he's quick, too quick, is unable to contain himself.

Afterwards, he lies there exhausted, his heart pounding. But he's also a bit shocked by all of this, can't help it, as she wipes hurriedly between her legs, then puts her hands there, inserts two fingers, inhales deeply, closes her eyes, enters her own world, disappears into the bliss – and moans.

And then has to catch the bus!

Jakob had never suspected that it could be possible to be so happy, that something so big could fit inside him. It's both liberating and frightening how easily this slender girl can turn everything upside down. One minute he's looking forward to reading the sports pages, biting into lukewarm toast spread with cheese and jam in the dark, drowsy early morning, the next minute he's in the living room, halfway on the sofa, halfway on the floor, his trousers round his heels, her expression so wild, so insolent and she so hot and so wet that he has to shout. He who's never shouted except when drunk, at football matches, and then with others, among others, certainly not at 7.00 in the morning, having barely swallowed his bite of toast, jam still coating his teeth, absolute silence in the house, on Skaftahlíð, in the world. The mountains are barely awake, the sky is heavy with sleep, and then his shout in the midst of all that silence! A shout they surely hear, the couple upstairs, both in their early seventies. Jakob has rented from them for two years and they're so happy with this sweet, polite and hardworking boy from the east that the wife irons his shirts, but then that filly moved in, turning the peace and quiet into clamour that's disturbed them on other occasions – though never at 7.00 in the morning. It's unheard of! They are awakened by the voice of the girl, who apparently can't keep it down, hear her laughing or giggling, dashing from the kitchen to the living room – and then Jakob shouts. Shouts!

The husband has got out of bed. He fetches their broom and pounds its shaft on the floor. Jakob hears it and feels bad, embarrassed, but she of course hears nothing, pretends not to hear, or just couldn't give a damn, two fingers between her thighs, moving them quickly, the old man pounds on the floor again. She's approaching climax, tosses her head side to side and moans to avoid exploding, almost out of her mind with pleasure – yet still feels, deep beneath everything, an infinite sadness at being solitary in her bliss. Alone. And shortly thereafter, thinks, as she runs down Skaftahlíð, red-faced, dishevelled, Why can't happiness follow me there, too, all the way, why do I feel so alone in the midst of pleasure, as if Jakob were far away, unable to reach me despite being right by my side? Does happiness never go all the way? Is love, after all, never enough? If it isn't, will I die alone?

If it isn't, will I die alone?

We will back away from this question.

Ari's mother is on the living-room floor, with two mad fingers, her head jerks back and forth, she bares her teeth, moans and makes other sounds, some of which resemble suppressed barking, and the broomstick pounds repeatedly on the floor above her.

The husband pounds the broomstick harder on the living-room floor. Such things should be forbidden, he says irritably, in his pyjama bottoms, no top, his body worn out by sixty years of hard work. He's no feast for the eye, hammering the broomstick on the floor, his skin slack, his chest more like breasts, his heavy paunch hanging like a dead reptile. They're both bleary-eyed, stirred to her raucous voice, awoke fully when Jakob sprang up from the breakfast table, followed the laughing filly into the living room, something fell to the floor and shattered, a cup, laughter, a lustful cry. Living above love isn't necessarily desirable; it could be described as a hidden flaw in a piece of real estate. Such things should be forbidden, he repeats, once again pounding on his living-room floor, though we don't know exactly what he means, whether love should be forbidden in general, or merely from its place among human beings, certainly not in a block of flats, it's impossible to get love to respect tenants' regulations, rules of polite behaviour – or perhaps he means that people should be forbidden from ageing because once, you were young, quivering with energy, possibilities, no-one doubted your role, your body wasn't so bloody treacherous, waking you with back pain, sore knees, an upset stomach, but then you're old, you've got goddamned women's breasts, you're out of action, no-one asks your opinion anymore about anything, and the only thing you can think to do is pound the broomstick on the living-room floor.

A powerful protest.

As if anyone would notice.

Except, of course, the broomstick and your wife.

Yes, the years have made her skin pasty as well, pulled down the corners of her mouth and her breasts, which once were big and plump, a feast for the eyes, other men had eyed her up, unable to help themselves, had ogled her, envied him, couldn't refrain from mentioning in his hearing that she looked like a film star with those breasts, but now they hang like crumpled, half-empty rubbish bags. She looks away when he bends over, complaining about his right knee, pretending to have to bend over further in order to protect his knee, but doing so only to hide his embarrassing and unexpected erection, to hide how he, this old man, this overstuffed, frayed burlap sack, this burned-out life, grandfather, great-grandfather, how he gets an erection at 7.00 in the morning because of young people moaning in the flat below. Because that goddamned filly makes immoral noises and he, the grandfather, the old lout with a sagging paunch, senses the energy beneath his feet; the soles of his feet vibrated, the vibrations ran up his stiff old legs, slipped through his half-useless knees and into his wretched thighs, and then, to his horror, he felt the blood pouring impermissibly warmly into his crumpled penis. He hardly remembers the last time his old companion managed to stand up straight. He bends lower. Is alarmed. Terrified that his wife has seen this; what a disgrace, an old man with an erection because of some goddamned horny young people – she would never forgive him. Would never let him live it down. Fucking bloody hell, he mutters to himself as he pounds the broomstick on the floor once more, as if that would fool anyone. He senses his wife looking at him, feels her eyes on him, angry, shocked. Once upon a time, everything was better. He remembers how she could laugh, and dance, remembers how no-one danced like she did.

Below him, the filly moans.

No, it was closer to a scream.

Dammit, he thinks, and pounds the floor with the broomstick. His wife says something.

What? he exclaims. *What?* He feigns frustration, looks up. She's on her feet, is on her way to the bedroom and says over her shoulder, Come on then, you old oaf, if you dare! Says it with the titillating, wonderful humour he thought she'd lost ages ago. Lets her nightdress slip off, as if she were still young, lets her nightdress slip coquettishly, old as she is, almost shameful, very embarrassing, but he couldn't give a fuck and gets up, carefully and eagerly, carefully because of his knees and his heart, lets go of the broom, lets it fall, and follows her. Proudly takes off his pyjama bottoms, almost falls over in his eagerness, she lies in bed and smiles as if time doesn't exist, as if that envoy of death hadn't been invented yet. He lies down next to her, draws closer, enters her just as Ari's mother opens her eyes and says, Dammit, fucking clock! Dresses, hopping on her way out, gulps a cup of coffee, then runs down Skaftahlíð. Jakob watches her go as the teen idol Tab Hunter sings "Young Love" in his head: "They say for every boy and girl / there's just one love in this whole world / and I know I've found mine."

Young love and the sentences transform into solar systems

Jakob sings "Young Love" at work, and the sky brightens. The light comes from the east, illuminating the sky, gently covering the stars with its light, drawing forth mountains, conjuring up the sea.

"They say for every boy and girl"

He grabs the shovel and envisions her running down Skaftahlíð, always nearly missing the bus to Vífilsstaðir, the hospital originally built for TB patients, far up on the heath, far from the sea, which the light has just found and drawn forth for us to admire.

"There's just one love"

She runs down the street, she runs in his mind, she runs inside the song "Young Love", hopping from word to word.

"In this whole world"

Pulling on her jacket as she runs, bare-headed, tousle-haired, red-faced, having just had an orgasm; can there be a better way to start your day? He puts down the shovel, watches the mixture turn in the mixer.

"And I know I've found mine."

The day passes slowly. Inches along at a snail's pace, and Jakob gets home before her, which rarely happens, he being so terribly busy, many buildings rising in this young city that's crawling rapidly over heaths, gravelly ground, moors and fields. The nation streams here from the countryside as if fleeing its past, the toil on the land, the airless turf houses, hundreds of years of stagnation. Most often, Jakob works until 6.00, 7.00, 8.00 p.m., whereas she comes home between 4.00 and 5.00, and waits for him. Impatiently. An unbearable wait. Seconds turn into minutes, minutes into hours. An excruciating wait if it weren't for the books she regularly takes out from the library on Þingholtsstræti, poetry, novels; some books seem to make life expand, containing sentences that change into solar systems. She reads, she scribbles a few sentences and thereby survives the wait; otherwise, her impatience would drive her mad. When she hears him coming, she tosses everything aside. That's also how it should be; that he comes after her. Today, he seems distracted, confused by love, his brain a radio station incessantly broadcasting that one song, "Young Love", in between envisioning her running down Skaftahlíð, irresistibly red-cheeked, irresistibly tousled. During his coffee break, some-one had been talking about the Pyramids, how they rise up, five thousand years old, and tower over the desert, perfect in form and engineering, but he had thought, Oof, a load of rubbish compared to her in the morning! If she went to Egypt looking tousled and red-cheeked, the Egyptians would rise up and demolish every one of those fucking Pyramids!

Sent home.

Are you ill, Kobbi?

Yes, dammit; I feel like crap today. I think I'm developing a fever.

He goes home.

Arrives at their basement flat three hours ahead of her, the good old flat is empty, impoverished, silent, completely incomprehensible how he managed to live before he met her. He sits down. He stands up. He sits down. He paces. He throws himself on the bed. He turns on a faucet. He turns it off. He shaves. He sits down with pen and paper, he addresses a letter to Neskaupstaður, hasn't written for three months, but in the meantime received three letters from his mother, Margrét, she's in the east, growing older. Dear Mother! Everything's fine. I'm very busy at work. I often work until 8.00 in the evening. Also on Saturdays. I've also been playing quite a lot of bridge.

He puts the pen down. "Playing quite a lot of bridge" – doesn't that sound as if he's slacking? Just to be sure, he adds, I mean, when I'm not working. We actually have a tremendous amount of work. Ágúst, my boss, is pleased with me. He's been encouraging me to take my journeyman exam, says I'd make an excellent bricklayer. How do you like that? Last week I bought some jeans. I no longer live alone. I met a girl who's really great. I'm sure you'd like her. She reads a lot, like you, and her uncle, her aunt as well, in fact, have written books. Mostly poetry, I think. Her grandfather is a famous singer! Or was, anyway. How do you like that? Though I'm not sure Dad would have considered it a plus! I haven't told him. She works at Vífilsstaðir Hospital. I have nothing else special to tell you. I'm also tired from work.

Jakob puts down the pen.

Yesterday, the last thing she asked him was if the mountains to the east were extremely broad-shouldered. Should he add that? No, it wasn't worth it. It probably wouldn't make sense. Nor is he really sure that mountains can be broad-shouldered.

He gets an envelope. He writes: Margrét Guðmundsdóttir.

Norðfjörður

— PAST —

They conquer mountains and then descend to Hell

It's utterly useless to hate mountains, thinks Margrét as she gazes at the ones that rise over Norðfjörður. Sometimes in summer, they capture the sunlight, transforming them into a song, but today they capture nothing – the sky regards the earth pessimistically from between greyish clouds. No sunshine, no music, but the postman is talking to a woman at a house down the slope. They are laughing. Margrét sits at her frosty kitchen window, as if she doesn't want a clear view of the world – just its outline, nothing more – but then she presses her finger to the pane and lets its warmth melt the frost, as if to convince herself that she's still alive, and sees the woman and the postman through the clear spot. They talk together, laugh together. She never goes out to laugh with the postman. She lets a baby die inside her; she still dreams of the boy stillborn ten years ago, he comes to her at night sometimes, with his pure face, his blue, accusing eyes . . . She's boring. Depressed. Lets trivial things get to her. Too big for her britches, even though she has almost nothing, has nothing to brag about. She lifts her finger again, writes *failure* in the frost on the windowpane, and the daylight sifts over her through the word. The front door is pushed open, and Elín shouts something in her bright voice as she kicks off her shoes, both eager and impatient with anticipation because the postman, happy to save a few steps, had handed her a letter from Þórður. In she walks, red-cheeked from the cold and so wonderfully five years old that the frost melts from the window-panes of life, the sky cheers up, starts looking around for the sun, grabs a few birds and sprinkles them over the earth – and Elín kicks impatiently in the embrace of her mother, who has thrown her arms around her like someone drowning. Mummy, she pants, read the letter!

The letter is thick and chock-full of infectious energy. The fifth one Þórður has sent them; they become thicker and thicker, and Margrét can see Þórður sitting on a damp bunk down in the fo'c'sle, the air cool and damp with seawater, smelling of salt, fish guts, toil; or in the chilly, damp fishing huts; perhaps the only one awake, filling one page after another, using his knees as a desk, describing his surroundings, the people, their ways of speaking, the glacier that fills the horizon. They've had excellent catches, have hauled in the most fish of all the Norðfjörður boats and have no intention of stopping. They set sail so early that it's still night, after stocking up on bait, preferably capelin as it swims up the estuary, set sail and don't return until the boat is loaded with cod, unless they have to flee back to land, escape ragged storms, sail into Hornafjörður, probably the most dangerous approach in the entire country, requiring real skill, experience, patience to make it unscathed through those breakers. Þórður describes it all: the weather, the height of the waves, the approach, and how they watched another Norðfjörður boat vanish in the churning surf of the approach, watched a breaker tear the mast apart, two crewmembers were thrown overboard, one was saved, the other was found three days later, entangled in the line that had gone overboard with him.

Some evenings, it's as if Þórður can't stop writing. As if he can't hold back. The words are like a volcano inside him, magma that must find an outlet. He can't stop, stays up and writes instead of sleeping, getting some rest. He tries not to wake the others, but it's hard in such tight quarters, and one time Oddur wakes up, barely manages to tear open his slumping eyelids, it was as if the sound of the pen had scratched his sleep to bits, and he's furious, completely over the top, seeing the boy hunched over, scribbling on a sheet of paper instead of sleeping and resting, refuelling. He fumbles for something, grabs a hook, throws it at his son, says something, so hoarse that it's impossible to distinguish his words, but their meaning is unmistakable. Oddur turns onto his other side, falls asleep in mid-turn.

Þórður doesn't mention this in the letter but says that sometimes, his dad can't help but grin, or smirk, when Tryggvi starts talking about poetry as they work on the line or bait it, or as they gobble down their food. Tryggvi is good at making the crew forget their fatigue as he talks about Kristján the Mountain Poet,[5] who occasionally wrote as if the language were made of darkness – or retells the great poem that he and Áslaug bought last spring from a travelling bookseller, by an Italian poet called Dante. The poem, which Tryggvi read in a Danish translation, tells the story of Dante descending to Hell with a dead poet as his guide. They travel through all of Hell, thread their way through each level, through the nine circles that comprise it, as Dante gives detailed descriptions of the punishments suffered by sinners, some for thousands of years or more, without hope of redemption; the punishments are their eternity. No discounts. It's a spectacular story that captivates the crew of *Sleipnir* for weeks; exhilarating descriptions of how the poor wretches are punished relentlessly, with great ingenuity, for sins large and small. The sinners are not even granted

5 Kristján the Mountain Poet: the late-Romantic Icelandic poet Kristján Jónsson *Fjallaskáld* (1842–69).

the peace of sleep, because the dead need no sleep; there went their dreams – you're damned without dreams. Those in the outermost circle have it the worst: the souls that are shunned by both Heaven and Hell, those whom no-one wants anything to do with and who suffer eternal punishment, not the slightest hope of relief, not a whiff of an indulgence, a moment's rest, because those poor wretches had lived completely *"uden Skam og uden Ære"*, as the poem says.[6] Died without having lived, never made an effort, hesitated constantly, lived in a state of hesitation, had no dreams or, even worse, had them but never dared to follow them; you can't help but pity these poor wretches. That's how it is: you can't change the facts, neither by force nor with money; he who lives without dreams and lets himself be carried along by the stream deserves neither the grace of Heaven nor the torments of Hell. Both God and the Devil reject him.

So you're best off living life to the full, writes Þórður – but sometimes the hauls are so huge and they're so worn out from exerting themselves and weary from lack of sleep that they just work, saying almost nothing. Just work, and try to stay sane. Haul in so many cod that they start seeing stars. They totter, babble nonsense, burst out laughing, snarl at each other for no reason; on three occasions Oddur and Tryggvi have had to tear people apart, hissing, cursing, kicking, spitting men. But it's worth it; fish is money, and money means opportunities for this thousand-year-old nation that has independence in its sights after seven hundred years under foreign control. They haul in fish for themselves and their families, of course, but also know that the nation's

6 *"uden Skam og uden Ære"* (Danish): "without blame and without praise" (see *Inferno*, Canto III, line 35). The translation that Tryggvi read is by Danish writer and translator Christian K. F. Molbech (1821–88): *Guddommelige Komedie* (1865).

future depends on it. Accordingly, Þórður gives it his all, knowing that if they haul in enough fish, it will be possible to build more schools, better ones, more hospitals, bigger ones, lay more roads, smoother ones. There's no road to Norðfjörður, not yet, they have to catch more fish, a road is desperately needed over the dizzyingly high mountains that have killed people for a thousand years, led them astray in storms, exhausted them, consigned them to death by exposure in choking winds, blinding blizzards, crushing snowfalls. Oddur has stood up at a rally in Norðfjörður for workers' rights, against the disgracefully unfair distribution of wealth, and declared his rock-solid conviction that the purpose of fishing in Iceland should be to enable the nation to rise up out of poverty and the darkness of history – so that men and women need not die of exposure in the mountains simply because there is no road there for them to travel on. This was the dream, the vision, behind every fish. Better times. Oddur and Margrét shared this dream; she had also stood up to declare her views on the subject, although a skipper's words carry considerably more weight. It's a simple fact, has nothing to do with common sense, derives its power from tradition. *Dream* and *vision* are beautiful words, but words and beauty are of little use without a steadfast will to back them up. And a huge amount of work. Which is why one should rest when time permits. Sleep. Renew oneself. A tired man works less. People should sleep, not waste time writing absurdly long letters, let alone to people they'll be seeing in a few weeks' time. Even Tryggvi realises this; his letters to Áslaug and the children are short, two pages at most. We've caught this many fish, my shoulders are stiff, I'm sick and tired of eating nothing but fish, doing nothing but hauling in fish, I'm probably changing into a fish, almost certainly a cod, you won't recognise me when I come home. Oh, what a big cod, you'll say, then you'll grab a knife, slice me open and toss me in a pot to boil.

Absolutely wonderful, this word: later

Elín has grown impatient. It's been so long since the postman handed her the letter from Þórður, and her mother just reads and reads it silently – she doesn't get to hear anything! She'd dashed home with the letter, excited to hear more of the story that Þórður has been telling her and Gunnar. Mummy, she says impatiently, *Mummy*, she repeats for probably the hundredth time, stamping her foot impatiently. Margrét is finally finished reading the letter but unfortunately can't tell Elín what happens next in the terribly exciting story of the clever, good but somewhat hot-tempered mouse who works so hard to save two siblings, who, by pure chance, are named Elín and Gunnar and have got lost in the mountains, pursued by cruel but indescribably foolish trolls. Elín has to wait until evening to hear it, these are Þórður's clear instructions, and she shortens the wait by sitting down at the kitchen table with her doll Rósa in her arms, drawing a picture for her brother and writing in big, clunky letters with countless errors: Every evening I must sing for Rósa because she misses you so much that she cries and can't sleep. Why do you have to be away for so long?

Why do you have to be away for so long, why do you have to die, the world isn't anywhere near to being as good a place since you left, after the mountains separated us, the wasteland of death, the darkness into which we cast our questions, the doubt and bitter despair, without getting anything back?

Why?

Hush, hush, you'll understand later.

Absolutely wonderful, this word: *later*.

We can throw almost everything into it. Dirty underwear, promises, uncomfortable questions, the unsaid and, finally, your death, sweep whatever it may be into it, so that everything is spick-and-span when our guests arrive, so that we ourselves are shiny.

Why do you have to be away so long instead of staying at home and telling us stories, letting us ride on your shoulders, turning us upside down?

Being here for us.

Being here for us – might that be the gold standard upon which our lives are based?

Hush, hush; you'll understand later.

Here's an explanation that might do splendidly in the meantime: Because in the winter months, it's a much shorter route to the fishing banks from Hornafjörður than from Norðfjörður, the centre of the world, which is why the Norðfjörður boats sail there and stay for weeks, during the moodiest months, when low-pressure systems stampede us like a herd of temperamental giants – which is why *Sleipnir* rises and falls with the breathing of the sea and the nearby glacier. They sail and they fish, they process the catch, they fish for bait, they bait the lines, and sometimes they go without a proper night's sleep for weeks. Then even Tryggvi, like the rest of the crew, falls silent, they take every opportunity to sleep, greedily snatching those moments, sitting, standing, leaning against anything reasonably steady, close their eyes and are gone. Steal a minute here, a few seconds there. Even fall asleep with food in their mouths. Their jaws slacken and they just manage to wake up in time to suck the half-chewed bite into their mouths before it leaks out of them. Suck it in fast, glance around furtively, as if having done something wrong. Þórður has never been so tired in his life, which, admittedly, has not been long, just sixteen years, and the men treat him kindly when Oddur's not around, wake him up last, try to protect him, but he's also quicker to recover than they are, young as he is. This new experience, being one of the adults, far from home, in a new environment, gives him energy. His world expands with new experiences, new perspectives, but missing home makes the distance so hard. Þórður misses his mother, her presence, hearing her warble while doing her chores, Icelandic lullabies, songs from America, even something made-up, misses being able to share his new experiences with her properly, and misses his siblings terribly. Especially the younger ones, Elín and Gunnar. Missing people is painful. But this glacier – doesn't just looking at it make life possible? Some days it seems more like air than land. The air here can be transformed in a flash, the clear skies of the last few hours disappear, and the glacier suddenly becomes a big, filthy heap, horrifically heavy; I'll crush you, it says to the mountains beneath it. At such times, it's impure, menacing, and it howls at the boats that sail out to sea, towards fish and waves, toil and deepening waters, howls at them, casts curses and threats out to sea, howls inside Þórður, shakes him to his core, he has to grab hold of something just to stay standing. When Jónsi, one of the deckhands, asks, Are you feeling ill, kid? he answers, No, no, it's alright, it's nothing, it's just the glacier howling inside me.

Keflavík

— PRESENT —

That we can do, we here in Keflavík!

December is the earth's darkest month. Above Keflavík, the clouds are nearly white and so expressionless that it's as if their minds have gone completely blank. Ari has stopped at the corner of Hafnargata and Tjarnargata, expecting to see the Hljómalind record shop, but it has clearly been gone for a while – its empty, dirty windows gape at him.

No more record shop in Keflavík, and nowhere on the Suðurnes Peninsula, no ex-Hljómar singer slipping young people Mozart's *Requiem* or rock albums. Where is he now, with his swinging hips; who's going to enrich the lives of the youth here in Keflavík and the vicinity, hand them folded angels' wings, Peter Green's poignant guitar solos? Maybe the Internet has taken over from him. It's much bigger, of course, wider-reaching than an old singer from Keflavík, but neither YouTube nor Spotify change the fact that the empty windows resemble a gaping wound on the corner of Tjarnargata and Hafnargata.

Tjarnargata is quite long and boasts Keflavík's tallest building, the savings bank built in the mid-'80s, having previously been a two-storey stuccoed building overlooking the Keflavík Botanical Gardens. A beautiful, friendly looking building – but money never sits still; it has more energy than we can comprehend, and it wants to grow, that's in its nature, wants more space, both in concrete and in our lives, ceaselessly aims for power and slips easily into people, changes nerve impulses into krónur, dreams into stacks of banknotes. Hence the new savings bank building, five times bigger than the old one, Keflavík's biggest building, our pride and joy for more than ten years before the bank declared insolvency, and its dizzying debts were divided up in brotherly fashion between the nation and the residents of Keflavík.

Ari removes the green fleece cap that his daughter Gréta sent him in Copenhagen as a birthday present last year, puts it into his shoulder bag and recalls the erotic magazine he bought at Kastrup in a flash of arousal, saw the cover photo, the beautiful face, the bold, seductive look, the enticing headline: *Hot, naked girls are waiting for you!* It had turned him on unexpectedly, robbed him of his self-control; he bought the magazine in haste, grabbing a copy of *Rolling Stone* and a magazine about astronomy, *The Universe*, and slipping the erotic one between them, trying to hide "hot, naked girls" within the universe. Naked girls; so true – impossible to express it better, naked girls, because the woman on the cover is not a woman but a girl, likely the same age as Gréta, or Sigrún when Ari was in love with her at the slaughterhouse out west in Búðardalur; you remember, you mustn't forget, her right eye was "Here, There and Everywhere", her left "If I Fell". The girl in the magazine is called Jane, and she wants to be a veterinarian. There are nine photos of her in various poses; in the largest two, she's on all fours, raising her ass to show her vulva and anus, because studies show that this is the pose that men find most appealing.

Ari had flipped the magazine open to this photo at Kastrup and felt hot blood gush into his penis; he had to buy the magazine, couldn't help himself. Forced himself to open it again this morning and there was the girl, her ass in that pose, revealing everything, although her expression, which yesterday appeared so bold, aggressive and saucy, as if she found it exciting that sons, fathers, grandfathers, great-grandfathers throughout the world would masturbate to her photos, wasn't the same anymore. Ari had looked into her eyes and found them empty.

He quickly shoves the magazine into the rubbish bin, shoves it in deep, rids himself of it, relieved, pleased with himself, makes it disappear, it's a good feeling, as if he's accomplished something, won a moral victory, shoves it down, gets rid of it, makes it disappear, what we don't see no longer exists. His hand feels sticky after brushing against something: a banana skin, a half-eaten sandwich, Gréta's genitals. He rubs his hand on his leather jacket, and it's as if his shoulder bag has shed a load of kilos – in it are just his cap and scarf, a volume of poetry by Szymborska and a small notebook. Ari hurries across the car park, past the Eymundsson Bookshop, previously called the Keflavík Bookshop, run by the same devoted couple for more than forty years, so devoted that they died just two days apart; three weeks later, the Eymundsson chain had bought the shop from their children, just as it has bought up all the other bookshops in the country; the market seems inherently aimed at uniformity, which is why it feels at times as if there are fewer possibilities in the world now than thirty years ago, as paradoxical as that sounds, thinks Ari, shaking his hand and turning towards the retirement home housing his father; the huge savings bank building overshadows the Community Cinema, the sea, the horizon. Ari crosses the road, glances sharply at that temple of materialism, temple of debt, and notices the recently added sign above the main entrance, sees the seven letters that form one of the most beautiful words in the language: *LIBRARY*.

Ari is so surprised that he stops abruptly in the middle of the road, barely avoiding being hit by a car tearing down Tjarnagata; the driver, a middle-aged woman, has to slam on the brakes, the car skids on the ice, the woman struggles to regain control of the car, which spins in a semicircle, just manages to swing past Ari, its rear wheels hit the curb and the car stops. Behind the wheel, the woman takes three deep breaths, slowing her pounding heart, the violent coursing of her blood, and then rolls down the window, looks at Ari, who is still in the middle of the street, torn between shock at having nearly been run over and joy at how the sign with seven letters can transform a big building, turn greed and insolence so effortlessly into optimism and care, knowledge and searching. My dear man, says the woman, not rebuking him but as if she is worried yet remarkably calm, I almost ran over you! Ari looks at her, uncertain of her age, whether she's over forty, or fifty, or even sixty, but then she smiles, perhaps at his expression, the helpless aura he sometimes gives off. Her smile creates deep wrinkles that radiate from her eyes, and dimples that make her more beautiful, more profound; she's scarcely over forty, he thinks. So it's you, the writer, she says. My sister rang last night and said, You'll never guess who I drove from the airport down to the Flight Hotel, with a stop in Sandgerði! Naturally, I couldn't guess, and just imagine the crime I'd have committed if I'd run over the writer in front of the library!

Then Ari remembers her, recognises her, her name is Linda Rós, and she's the older sister of the taxi driver who drove him from the airport yesterday, a former beauty queen, in fact still is one, so beautiful that she should be awarded prizes every day, begin each new day that way, hopefully someone is doing just that, her husband, children, life, with a kiss, a smile, kind words. Linda Rós wasn't as beautiful, and kept to herself, but was a good student, always with the highest marks in science; the last Ari had heard, she was studying physics at a renowned university in the U.S., and there she sits, smiling, calm, despite having nearly run Ari over, barely managing, by split-second decision-making, to save him, spinning the car more than 180 degrees and hitting the curb. She smiles. I wasn't paying attention, says Ari apologetically, after taking a deep breath. I'd just seen the library sign; I had no idea that the residents of Keflavík were capable of transforming the savings bank and all of its debts into a library! Yes, she says; that we can do, we here in Keflavík – we can change loss and crime into shelter and joy. You should write about it, poet, she says, blowing him a kiss, such a sexy kiss, as she drives off, that for several seconds Ari feels weak at the knees, like a vulnerable, inexperienced boy.

I would write about it if I were still a writer, mutters Ari to himself as he turns onto Kirkjuvegur, with the kiss she'd blown him still inside, it rests in his knees like a happy butterfly.

Ella just died?

Ari walks up a low hill, catches sight of the block of flats where his father lives, each step brings him closer to the building, closer to Jakob, they lived together for twenty-two years, father and son, experienced death and difficult times together. Together, but at the same time distant from each other. "Expect a package," his father had written to Ari in Copenhagen several weeks ago, and a package arrived, containing Oddur's certificate of recognition and the photo of the two of them: Ari's parents, Jakob and she of whom they'd never spoken, never mentioned after death came to fetch her from the hospital at Vífilsstaðir, took her away from it all, saved her from her hell of pain. Dying, she left behind nothing but silence. If we can't speak, if we dare not, the silence that death leaves behind can, over time, become larger and heavier than life itself.

There are about forty flats in the building, and a pile of junk mail in the lobby. Ari finds his father's bell but hesitates before pressing it, regards his finger on the bell, looks at the name: Jakob Oddsson. The son of Oddur the skipper, a legend out east, renowned among the elderly, forgotten by the young. One can read about him in the second volume of the history of Norðfjörður; he has five mentions, and there is a photo of *Sleipnir SU-329*, in its original configuration. Oddur the sea hero. Stories were told about him, stories that Jakob grew up with. Some of them towered over him, as huge and imposing as the mountains surrounding Norðfjörður.

Ari decides not to ring the bell. He's never thought of his father in this way, as a son in the shadow of his own father. The obvious can become invisible if we're too close to it. He looks at the bell again, then the entrance door opens, and an old woman struggles to get through it with her Zimmer frame, which is good, not that she's so old, can't go anywhere without her Zimmer frame, but rather: now Ari doesn't need to ring the bell, hear his father's voice on the intercom, because what's Ari supposed to say? Hi, it's me. Who? Jakob would ask gruffly, and what was he supposed to reply? Ari, your son – is that a satisfactory reply, and is it a given that Jakob would buzz the door open, too tempting to pretend that he hadn't heard, too tempting to hang up, unplug the intercom?

Ari makes it to the entrance while the old woman is still in the doorway, struggling to fit herself and the Zimmer through it, going so slowly that she barely seems to be moving, on her way out into the cool, half-lit December day. Ari holds the door open for the woman, she looks up, her blue but blurry, slightly glazed eyes are playful. Say hello to Cary Grant, she says, patting her Zimmer, my rock; he could be a bit more lively, the old darling. Then she inches her way out into the day, which is dimming, losing its light, sinking into winter's darkness.

Ari has entered the building. It smells of old people and bygone things, smells of what barely moves and is, in a way, closer to death than to life. He walks down the ground-floor corridor, flat 109 is at the end, that's where he's headed where he's been heading, perhaps, in one way or another, for a long time, maybe forty-five years, at least since he ran away one night from a big house way up on a heath. Yet he doesn't go there, not right away, he puts it off, heads up the stairs to the cafeteria on the fourth and top floor instead.

It's good to take the stairs, the effort feels good, oxygenates the blood, it will take longer to stagnate, climbs the steps and ends up in the cafeteria with its unexpected view. Big windows all around, the building is on a hill and nothing obscures the view, he can see in every direction, sees as far as the half-light of this December day allows him to see. Having gone straight up, he stops for a few moments to catch his breath, looks out over the houses of Keflavík, all the way up to the old Base, where the American military spent more than sixty years on a nearly barren heath, exposed to the wind. The soldiers' strict training, perfect weapons, proved no match for boredom. Thousands of them lived there with nothing to do, no enemy in sight, just endless dart games, T.V., beer, one or two Icelandic women who found happiness with some of them or lost themselves in misfortune, alcohol and drugs. Otherwise: nothing. Except for the wind and the darkness, which can be so dense during the heaviest winter months around Keflavík that soldiers died of exposure when caught short outdoors, wading through the darkness like a snowdrift. Their main battle involved killing time, a non-stop defensive struggle against life-threatening boredom – their commanders had to send quite a few letters west-wards across the sea to America: Dear Madam, Sir, We regret to inform you of the death of your son. He died of boredom, found it impossible to defend himself. He met his death bravely, served the United States of America until the bitter end.

Ari turns slowly, enjoying the view. There's the sea. It's so incredibly huge, and the lights of Reykjavík have begun glittering beyond Faxaflói Bay. Ari is so taken with the view that he doesn't notice three people sitting at one of the tables, two women and a man. The man is staring out to sea, sipping coffee through a sugar cube caged between his teeth, seemingly lost in his own world, while the women chat. Ari has a strong, almost uncomfortable feeling that he knows one of them, but he's unable to place her until she says, Yes, yes, she just died behind the wheel, as I'm sitting here! Then Ari remembers her – the jerking of her head, the shock of hair that used to be red but has faded to reddish-brown, and the way she smiles out of the corner of her mouth: it's Andrea. Andrea with whom we worked at Drangey in the early '80s, a strong woman with broad shoulders, thick, powerful arms, firm but invariably calm and apparently immune to fatigue, to difficulty, so serene that it was as if life couldn't mess with her. She did, however, have her challenging moments; existence had punched and kicked her – the heaviest blow coming during our second year at Drangey, when a huge wave snatched away her only son. His shipmates watched him vanish like a bit of flotsam grabbed by the sea, sweeping away his thoughts, memories, eagerness, the watch he'd been given for Confirmation and wore on his left wrist, his comb in one pocket, and in the other, his wallet, holding a few banknotes, the logo of Liverpool football team and a photo of Agnes, his fiancée.

He was buried on a Tuesday in February; it was Andrea's first day off work in twelve years – since giving birth to his sister. She took a day off work – and was back at it again at 8.00 the next morning. In the cold morning darkness. Stood there at the fish tubs with me and Ari; we pulled the fillets from the ice-cold, heavily salted water, tidied them with our knives, cleaned them, the frost tightened its grip on the building, slowed the flow of water, blood, life, the roof creaked, as did the sky, she bent over and grabbed the fillets, one after another, silently, never looked at us, and Ari and I said nothing, made shy by her sorrow, shuffled our feet as we worked, the cold slipped easily through our boots and wool socks and gnawed at our toes, Lúlla laughed at something as she stood there with another woman, salting roe in barrels. Time barely seemed to move, and Ari gave the clock a furtive glance. Andrea saw him push up his sleeve, stiff with cold and salt, straightened her back, looked sternly at us, almost harshly, grabbed a fresh fillet, tidied it in a flash, said, It's crossed my mind to hate God.

Then she fell silent, continued with her knife work but twice as fast, which rather frightened us, the violence in her movements. She grabbed the steel lying nearby, sharpened her knife, stuck her hand into the tub, pulled out a white fillet as if she were pulling a drowned angel from the salty water, aimed the knife, cut, said, But for what? What use is hatred? I very much doubt that God would have felt my hatred, though I would certainly have felt it, it would have burned inside me, because you can be sure, lads, that hatred is stern and uncompromising. I'd lost more than I could endure and felt as if only hatred gave me the strength to stand. Which made it easy to get up yesterday morning and get ready. They were sitting on either side of me in church, my lovely Sóley and Agnes, and Agnes held her belly as if it ached, her beautiful belly, seven months pregnant. I knew they both needed me, and then it dawned on me, stupid woman that I am, as that vile pastor spouted his obligatory drivel about God, that there is a much greater, better, stronger power than the one we find in hatred. Just so you know, she added, abruptly bending over to grab a fresh fillet and shooting us a look – and we noticed the smile at one corner of her mouth, as if partly apologising for what she was saying, because such a thing had likely never been said before at Drangey. Tidying the fillet, she said, Anyway, you lads are alright. Our hearts blazed, the compliment made us feel nervous and bashful, we were so bloody lucky to stumble onto the exact right response, the one question we had: When is Agnes' baby due? Andrea smiled at us, as she does now, at the table, smiles at Ari in another era, the then unborn child now in its thirties, and the first woman to become head of the primary school in Sandgerði, her grandmother's pride and joy.

Andrea smiles at Ari, but the other woman stares into space and says, as if deep in thought, Ella just died.

Andrea: Died behind the wheel, as I'm sitting here! What a life, Lára! She was driving down Hringbraut and died behind the wheel; just fell asleep. The car kept going, went through a red light, took a sharp left, ran over a poor old arthritic cat, took down Ágúst's rubbish bin, you know, Gugga's Ágúst, actually it was a recycling bin, they're careful about sorting their rubbish, they've always been outstanding citizens, the paper was scattered everywhere, golfing magazines, *Seen and Heard*, dirty magazines belonging to poor Ágúst or his sons, the wind blew them all over the place, even onto the grounds of the primary school; they live right by the school.

Ella just died?

Yes, my darling, as I told you. Died behind the wheel. You

remember what she was like, such a love, so kind-hearted but useless really. Had a child with a married man, a real loser, from the Base, then dies driving down Hringbraut at 50 k.p.h., runs a red light, takes down a recycling bin, dirty magazines, *Seen and Heard*, golfing magazines, all sorts of other paper blows onto the grounds of the primary school, and . . .

Seen and Heard?

Yes, my darling. *Seen and Heard* is no less harmful to innocent children, though I was thinking more about the dirty magazines. But then, what do you know, a police car happened to be in the right place at the right time, driving down Tjarnargata and turning onto Hringbraut just as Ella ran the red light without slowing down, so it turned on its lights, its siren too, just for a second, but naturally she didn't pay any attention and drove straight into Ágúst and Gugga's yard, right over the poor cat, took down the recycling bin and was finally stopped by a twenty-year-old rowan tree.

Ella just died?

Yes, but at least she wasn't slapped with a traffic fine. The fine for running a red light is really high these days, but you can't really fine the dead, no matter how badly they behave. That's something the dead have in common with the rich: rules and regulations don't apply to them.

Where did Ella go?

Good question, my darling. I've always liked the notion of Heaven, and I assume it's big enough for all of us, even old bats from Sandgerði. I hope to make it there myself someday, even though I don't deserve it; in fact, not at all.

Andrea strokes the back of the woman's hand, as if in consolation, as if to say, Everything'll be alright, at the same time turning to look at Ari, who sees her nearly invisible smile at the corner of her mouth and knows that's her way of acknowledging him. The other woman, Lára, gets awkwardly to her feet, goes to the window that looks out over the heath. Will spring be here soon? she says into the darkening day; afternoon is approaching Keflavík with bags filled with darkness. The man clears his throat, removes the sugar cube from between his teeth, announces crisply, Spring doesn't come for everyone. He puts the sugar cube back between his teeth, and there it stays. Lára, who seems not to have heard him, presses her forehead to the windowpane; I've stopped seeing anything, she says, almost cheerfully, as if amused, as if it's better to see less. What I mean is, spring always comes to those who know how to live well, says Andrea. What do you think, Gummi, do you think we've lived well? The man, Gummi, reaches for the coffee pot, refills his cup and says something, but keeping the sugar cube between his teeth, which renders him unintelligible, he sucks the black coffee through the sugar cube, sifts darkness through sweetness. Maybe that's a kind of answer, thinks Ari, smiling at Andrea, hoping she sees it, that he's smiling hello, doesn't have the guts to stay there, has to go downstairs, immediately, right now – and knock on his father's door.

He wastes no time going down the stairs, stands at the door to flat 109. Inside is his father, the past. Raising his right arm, he makes a fist to knock on the door to his past, when suddenly music starts up behind the door and comes flooding through it, through the wooden boards between father and son. Ari instantly recognises the song: Megas, "The Old Petrol Station by Hlemmur": "I owe the bank a million and my roommate brings me treats / of old-style wooden troughs filled with pickled meats . . ."

Ari drops his arm and shuts his eyes. Imagines everything too clearly. Kirkjuteigur, the little house, him in his bedroom, his stepmother in the kitchen, in the laundry room, keeping herself busy, Jakob in the living room, in the high-backed red swivel chair, having just put on Megas, and then they know what's coming. The vodka bottle hidden behind the living-room curtains or in his wide pocket, a glass of juice or cola, and when he's certain that neither of them can see, Jakob stands up, reaches for the bottle, pours himself a glass. He and Megas. Ari in his room, his stepmother somewhere and nowhere, the two of them pretending not to notice. Hoping that he'll fall asleep in his chair, go out to meet someone, which was what usually happened, though Ari had to wrestle his father to the floor three times after Jakob hit his stepmother, tore at her hair, screamed that she was ugly, that she was the worst ever, that she'd destroyed his life.

Jakob. Megas. The vodka bottle.

An inseparable trio. And, of course, the explanation for Ari's delayed entrance into the peculiar world of Megas.

He stands at the door to flat 109. Inside is what he needs to address, the silence that needs breaking. Megas sings undisturbed, hoarse, cynical, absolutely not at a loss for words. He sings like someone who's come to an important conclusion about life but isn't that impressed.

Ari curses softly.

He knocks on the door.

Now something will begin.

Norðfjörður

— PAST —

Þórður wrote a poem.

Which is no big deal, of course.

For centuries, people here on the far-northern Atlantic Ocean have written poems, sometimes with zeal, without letting the toil, the monotonous food options, the dark, damp dwellings, the narrow-minded community inhibit them. Written poems as if their souls depended on it, as if writing were a matter of life and death, at least of dignity. Written so many poems and verses here in Iceland that it is no news whatsoever when a seventeen-year-old boy writes one. He's written quite a few, of course, but at the moment we're talking about one particular poem that was published in the weekly *Eastfirthers*. It's about the sea, and has a bird in it. The paper's editor singled out the poem in his editorial, noting the young age of the poet, who was a member of the crew of *Sleipnir SU-382* from Norðfjörður: "truly one of Iceland's spring men".

Good of Þórður to put a bird in his poem. Birds are more closely akin to air than to land. Þórður had shown Tryggvi the poem, shyly, yet without hesitation; you rarely have to hide anything from Tryggvi, you can let down your defences, allow yourself to be ridiculous, a failure, what's more, his and Áslaug's house is a large part of Þórður's world, a place where he can waltz around as if he were at home, take food from the cupboards, lie

---

7 A "spring man" (Icelandic *vormaður*) is someone who takes on work in the spring (for example, for the fishing season). The term also applies to high achievers or go-getters, harbingers, in a sense, of auspicious periods in the nation's life.

down on one of the beds, joke around with their three daughters. Perfectly understandable that he goes there with his first successful poem. He'd realised immediately, as it was coming into being, that it was a real poem. A poem about the sea, the waves that form such a strange landscape, and the only thing that recalls the land is this bird, which is, as we said, more akin to air – God's draft of an angel. Three verses, the last, the strongest, is about the bird. Þórður had been sitting on a rock on the mountain above Norðfjörður when the poem came to him, and experienced such a strong sensation of flying as he described the bird that he shut his eyes and raised his arms, convinced that he could fly himself. When he opened his eyes, he turned out to be just as incapable of flight as the rock on which he was sitting. That was his first lesson, possibly his hardest one, but among the more important ones: a writer never succeeds as well as his writing.

Tryggvi had read the poem in the couple's reading nook, a corner they'd agreed they needed at home, occupying valuable space in their not-especially-big house, a place to go when they needed some peace, an escape from the everyday, their obligations, the hustle and bustle; in other words, a 2- or 3-square-metre cubbyhole packed with books. Tryggvi read the poem, then sat for a while with it on his knees, staring at nothing. For so long that Þórður became worried the poem was bad enough to disappoint Tryggvi, that it had been a waste of time, there's nothing worse in the world than wasting time, spending time on things that didn't matter a jot; it was unforgivable. Tryggvi was silent because he felt so moved, he felt like racing over to his sister's house, just 50 metres away, to tell her that Þórður had written a poem that proved he was a poet. Just think, a poet, in the family – if only Mother could have seen this! Þórður fidgeted in his chair, Tryggvi cleared his throat, and three weeks later the poem appeared in *Eastfirthers*.

The poem caught people's attention, as did the editor's statement that the poet was "one of Iceland's spring men". People knocked on Margrét's door to congratulate her on her boy, and the priest, a young man, mentioned the poem at mass; Our poet, he said. There's the poet, there goes the poet, people said when they saw Þórður. Margrét clipped the poem out of the newspaper, hung it up in the kitchen, Gunnar and Elín memorised it, never forgot it, and it became a tradition of Elín's, almost a ritual, to sing the poem to herself, set to a homemade melody, as she prepared Christmas dinner. Almost as if the sacredness of Christmas came with the poem. But no-one congratulated Oddur. Two or three people mentioned the poem to him hesitantly, as if testing the waters: There's a poem by your boy in *Eastfirthers*! So I've heard, was all he replied. The others said nothing.

Then all falls silent

Don't misunderstand me. Of course it's important to know how to write poetry with substance. Yes, and definitely worthwhile to know how to describe the sun, which will soon be inching its way up the eastern sky to wake us, dispel the darkness, illuminate it as it shines its light on the Norðfjörður peaks, transforms them into flares that God abruptly set aside, but the fishing economy here in the Eastfjords is a shambles, the individual and company debts out of control – as they are all over the country, in fact. What's more, the roads in the Eastfjords are inadequate; some places have none, or what's there doesn't live up to the name. Why in the world are there cars, why is there progress, if there are no roads to pave the way? We're repeating this so you don't misunderstand, it's definitely worthwhile to be able to do what we mentioned, transform the sun's struggle up the eastern sky into words, and how lovely it is for newspapers to publish poems about the sea and a bird; but Iceland has seen, and continues to see, so many difficult days that we can't let anything distract us from our struggle with uncertainty. Iceland's been a sovereign nation for just over fifteen years, and its chances for full independence almost certainly stand or fall on how well we cope on our own, whether we manage to build roads through the wilderness of our difficulties. If we dream too much, and for too long, we'll die, or never grow out of poverty and hardship into independence. In short, if we forget to haul fish out of the sea, the fish that matter more and more, and soon will be even more important than agriculture, as unbelievable as that sounds, it will become ever more difficult to survive, and our dream of independence will never come true. Þórður has started to lose track of himself. It's so obvious. He stays up late to read that Italian poem of his, or to write long letters, instead of gulping down vital rest, loses strength every day as a result, and is so exhausted that his concentration fails. Sometimes, he stands there motionless, holding his gaff, his job being to gaff the fish as the capstan winds in the line, to hit the head in precisely the right spot, either on the cheek or beneath the jawbone, something that Þórður had done quickly and consistently at first, but recently he's been missing the mark far too often and damaging the fish, which is a bloody disgrace, or else he doesn't pay attention, which is even worse, just stands there holding the gaff, staring into space as if he's being paid to do just that, as if that were precisely what the nation needed – to stare into space. Dream into space. Read instead of resting its exhausted body. O.K., let's shove the nation's future to one side, to hell with it for the moment; it's so airy-fairy and far removed from us out here on the open sea, amid the waves and troughs, in the midst of toil, of fatigue; anyone who stares into space instead of striving falls prey to distraction because he's too tired, sleep-deprived, misses his mark and damages the fish because he prefers reading to resting – he is plain and simply betraying his crewmates. Threatening their cohesion. Diminishing the output, frustrating the crew. For sleep-deprived men, such frustration is downright toxic, pure and simple, and a drain on their energy. Oddur attends to his duties while keeping an eye on Þórður, his son. He knows that the other men have started noticing his son's sluggishness, have seen him damage some of the fish with his gaff. They say nothing, just glance at him sometimes, and yes, maybe a word or two down in the fo'c'sle or in the fishing huts at night, telling him to get some rest instead of lolling around with those damned books of his, writing bloody long letters, as if there were anything to write about besides fatigue and fish. They say these things calmly, as if to no-one in particular, but Oddur detects the frustration behind them. Þórður, on the other hand, detects nothing; he ignores it all, just reads and writes, "one of Iceland's spring men". If only that bloody poem had never been published; it's gone to the boy's head. Led him astray. All the congratulations, the priest's blather, that pale man who's little more than his cassock and sermons. Yes, and then of course there was the headmaster's visit, which lit a vibrant fire under Margrét's fantasies about education, a future far from the sea – and Tryggvi's enthusiasm for plying his nephew with books. All of these things. Oddur's frustration grows. Frustration, impatience, anger. They're raking in fish, the crew is working feverishly, the capstan hauling in the line, loaded with fish, but Þórður just stands

there, motionless, his head in the clouds once more, his gaff
hanging idle, he's quite tall, nearly a head taller than his father,
straight-backed, with beautiful brown eyes, a sharp nose, has
perhaps never looked as much like his mother as now. There – he
bends over, gaffs a fish, a fine-looking cod, but hits it badly, just
behind the pectoral fin, and Guðjón, the crewman working next
to Þórður, changes position, partly turning his back to him. The
day before yesterday, Oddur had finally grabbed Þórður's arm
and said to him, softly but sharply, Don't let those damned books
and poetry swallow you up; here, what matters beyond all else is
to make sure you do your job! Þórður had blushed, said, Yes,
Dad. Yet there he stands, as if he can't be bothered with this for
one more minute, immune to the others' glances, to how Guðjón
has turned his back because he can no longer bear to witness
such slothfulness. Oddur exhales. Walks slowly over to the fish
that Þórður has just damaged, examines it, then grabs it by the
tail, walks straight over to his son, who turns, distractedly, still
wearing that smile – and Oddur smacks him with it. With all his
strength. The heavy fish slams into Þórður's cheek and cheekbone,
so hard that the fish's flesh is torn, it bursts open, so hard that
Þórður drops his gaff and is nearly toppled overboard. Then all
falls silent.

About the size of the universe

— BACK IN THE DAY —

Jakob strikes without thinking. Is it better, less serious, a worse crime, to strike without thinking, without taking a conscious decision? A blow struck due to stress, tension, fatigue, insomnia, which mess with your head and can transform your feelings into tears or fists – sometimes there's just the tiniest distinction. In such cases, the blow isn't as significant, making it possible to forgive it. But can a blow really be forgiven, especially if it's struck by a father, a husband? Anyway, who says that it should be forgiven? It may be that an unintentional blow is, after all, much stronger because it's been inside you forever, in your blood, a taut string, some kind of anger, a huge imbalance, forever in search of an outlet, meaning that there was never a question of if, just when: Jakob sweeps the curtain aside, he shouts something and he strikes.

Jakob had searched the entire flat, this three-bedroom flat in Safa-mýri, the topmost block of flats of four, searched everywhere, with his sister Hulda, his older sister from the east, and an uncle, who, at the time, was young, about thirty; the three of them had searched for Ari for a long time, calling out his name. For so long that we two became convinced that the world had lost track of us, while we were safe behind the curtains with warm sunlight on our backs, the high-spirited, excited shouts of the kids in the field below, and two young mothers sunbathing on their balconies above us. Two bodies in their early twenties, warmed and glowing in the sun. Life should still be an adventure, a string of discoveries, but these women are at home from morning to night; that's how it's been, and that's how it will continue to be. They exist in part outside society, and everything they have inside them, their strength, abilities, ideas, lie unused deep beneath their skin, so deep that they themselves are hardly aware of them, perhaps aren't aware of them at all. Except that sometimes they feel restless when something moves them unexpectedly – a wild rock song, a sentence in a book, a glance in a shop. A restlessness that can turn abruptly into irritation, as if their suppressed energy is searching fervently for an outlet, but they just tremble for a few seconds, and then it's gone, then it's nothing. No outlet, no crack in society to provide their energy with an outlet, energy that's lost, beauty that suffocates.

They listen to The Yank, Mick Jagger is singing, he sings with his genitals, lets them rip, they're both topless, one of them suddenly starts giggling, slips off her panties and spreads her legs slightly, as if between them is the only crack where the suppressed energy has an outlet. God, what if someone sees you, says the other, smothering a giggle; Oof, no-one can see us, replies the one who's completely naked, glowing with sunshine, suppressed energy, and Jagger sings, he's a waist-down singer, she spreads her naked legs, her blonde, curly hair damp with sweat or something else – Jakob sweeps the curtain aside, shouts and strikes Ari with his open palm. A heavy blow. The universe reverberates, planets are knocked out of their orbits, two blind chickens look round in surprise, and Ari is nearly knocked off the ledge we're standing on, I just manage to grab him.

We were prepared to stand behind the curtains for a long time. Hulda had searched the bedroom, looked under the bed, in the clothes cupboard, moved the bedside tables, as if she thought we

132

could hide there, as if we were scarcely taller than 20 or 30 centimetres; it never occurred to her to look behind the curtains. We'd been there for so long, the sun had been baking us for such a long time, that we'd begun to believe that the world had passed us by, making it possible to change everything. That she would stop being ill, would come back, would tell stories and sing in the evenings, boil fish but forget to put water in the pot, put Ari's trousers on him backwards, which meant that he could unzip them, fart through the gap and make everyone laugh. The two of them could go to the bakery to buy two pastries from Böðvar the baker, who sings with her in the polyphony choir, and once said that her eyes were the most beautiful thing he'd ever seen.

It's because of her that we're hiding behind the curtains.

Yesterday, they'd come to fetch her again. She'd been home for four weeks. Too weak to sing for Ari, they just lay together, he listened to her breathing, Böðvar sent her opera music on 33- or 45-r.p.m.'s, along with a note containing beautiful words, as if beautiful words do any good. Ari crawled into bed with her as soon as Jakob left for work, she moaned, she's being devoured from within and nothing can help her. Ari is as useless as beautiful words and God. Someone should put him, God and the words out with the rubbish – then they came and took her away.

That was yesterday. Now it's Ari's turn.

He's supposed to go too.

Away from the flat that contains her clothes, record albums, coffee cup, books. Something tells me and Ari that her life depends on his remaining in the flat, drinking from her cup, opening her books, listening to her records, touching her clothing. Which is why we hid and had begun to believe that it would work – but then Jakob sweeps the curtains aside, shouts and slaps Ari so hard that the universe reverberates, so loudly that the planets are knocked out of their orbits and God flaps his useless wings.

For how long do you remember the blow? And when does it start? When do the nerve impulses rush off with a signal about a blow, how far back does it go, does the blow live on in your blood, perhaps, pass from one generation to the next, thus ensuring that the striker's identity is never coincidental – nor that of the person who is struck? Oddur lashes out with the fish, he strikes, and Jakob's hard palm slams into Ari's cheek – and Ari sweeps everything off the breakfast table. Then he raises his fist and pounds on the door in a block of flats in Keflavík, inside which Megas is singing.

These are the questions. Where are the answers?

Interlude

Did Ari go to see him?

Night approaches Keflavík like a giant dark bird, and Uncle has prepared meatballs, cabbage and potatoes for dinner. He boils the meatballs and cabbage to a pulp; that's how he cooks all his food, boiling it until everything is definitely done. He whistles one of Hljómar's songs as he fishes the mostly flavourless but filling meatballs out of the pot. The contemporary infatuation with food, innumerable cooking shows, recipes that the media publish like prayers, consolations, hymns, have completely passed him by. I spoon a big glob of rhubarb jam next to my meatballs; Uncle puts the Heimur male choir on the gramophone, the men sing "I Look into the Spirit of the Past, Forward into the Quiet of the Heaths",[8] and I'm on the verge of tears – because the songs remind me of a bygone era, a bygone atmosphere, and because my uncle seems to have no idea that recipes have replaced prayers, chefs have replaced priests and psychologists. Have you lost God? If so, then cut a chicken into eight parts, brown it in oil in a pan, season it with salt and pepper, sprinkle a bit of flour on the pieces and then roast it – more later.

Uncle serves me seconds, turns up the male choir, opens the living-room window, opens it to the night, where there are beautiful things like stars, Northern Lights and silence. He pours *brennivin* into milk glasses, half filling them, takes a sip, stares at nothing, and I see a trace of sadness in his eyes. Afraid it doesn't look good for Jakob, he says, stroking one of his cats. You said

8 An Icelandic version of the American song "Home on the Range", set to the same tune.

that Ari visited him today, how did it go? I know that Kobbi waited for him, a long time, and looked forward to it, though he didn't dare show it. Did Ari go to see him?

Yes, I say, he went.

Ari went. And tapped "shave and a haircut / two bits" on the door to his past.

Keflavík

— PRESENT —

"Shave and a haircut / two bits"

Ari knocks. Twice. The second time firmly, automatically tapping "shave and a haircut / two bits" out of habit and cursing himself; it sounds absurdly cheerful. As if he was standing there quite happily and enthusiastically at the door to his past, not stiff and strained, since the presence of Megas means his father is drinking – Tell us, anyone, preferably you over there: what words can we use here? What are the right words to describe alcoholism in such a way that it's no longer possible to hide from it, escape it, ignore it? What words describe the selfishness, the cruelty, the weakness? Describe the lie inside him. That makes you harm those you love, whom you ought to protect, makes you inflict wounds on them, wounds that never heal? That's the situation: Ari taps "shave and a haircut / two bits" on the door to his past, Megas sings from the bottle, we're in Keflavík. Shave and a haircut – two bits.

Now the universe is flowing through us

I was expecting Death, not you.

Says Jakob as he opens the door, as the happy tapping finally reaches him through Megas and the tobacco smoke filling the flat. Happy tapping – is that how Death announces itself, "shave and a haircut / it's Death", to calm the person it has come to fetch, some poor old soul, a young person, a small child who is terribly frightened, to calm and comfort: It's alright, I may be the darkness into which everything seems to vanish without a trace, but behind me are sunshine and birdsong.

141

*

I was expecting Death; father and son look at each other. They haven't seen each other in nearly three years, have barely had any contact apart from Ari's receiving Jakob's peculiar package three weeks ago, which contained a photograph of him and Ari's mother, Oddur's certificate of recognition – and, shortly thereafter, when Jakob sent Ari a devil-may-care e-mail about death coming; it was on its way. The tobacco smoke is so dense that Ari can barely make out the living-room window of the two-bedroom flat or the two heavy bookcases, whose top shelves are loaded with awards from bridge tournaments over the past decades. They look at each other. Not for long, I mean not for long according to the time by which we measure everything and that passes here on the earth's surface and among the stars, that is measured by clocks; for them, that short space of time equals many heavy minutes, rocks that time is struggling with. At least it does for Ari; we know nothing about Jakob, he's just there, doesn't open the door for us, is drunk, wearing a bathrobe, leans against the doorjamb because of his drunkenness, or because he is dying, death is slowly but surely sucking away his strength, his vital energy, the only way he can stand upright, to face his son, is to lean against something. It's unclear which is more difficult for him, to die or to face his son, but there they are, having both lived fairly long, gone through different times, experienced life, experienced death, read this and that, Ari knows his way around Kierkegaard, has read vast numbers of novels, he knows how far it is to Pluto, how black holes form, and Jakob knows a thing or two himself, having lived for more than seventy years, he's seen the world change, men conquer the Moon, yet there they stand, face to face, and have no idea what to say; nothing comes to mind, as if they're both experts in silence and have met to compare notes.

One time, they were by her side, the three of them stood at a window of the hospital up on a heath, looking together into the sky, across which the moon sailed in the semi-darkness of spring, two months before Neil Armstrong and Buzz Aldrin hopped onto its surface, cautiously, as if they feared that the lunar crust might crack. They stood at the window, she so thin that death would cut itself on her a few months later, but there they were, alive, a young couple in their late twenties, with their five-year-old son, standing at the big window. The universe is flowing through the three of us, she said, and that's why we'll always be one.

One of the few instances involving her that Ari remembers clearly – and the only words of hers that he remembers with certainty. She'd held him in her arms, lightly stroked his cheek with her right thumb, said this and hugged him close, tight, as if to say, That's why the two of us will always be together.

Now the universe is flowing through us.

The only words that Ari remembers. The only words of hers that are still here on the earth's surface, and for forty-five years he's kept them in the safe-deposit box of his memory, taken them out countless times, like priceless rubies or an old teddy bear to fall asleep with. The most sacred words, but fearful, deep down, that it never happened, is a false memory woven out of elements of fiction, regret and sorrow. He never dared to ask his father whether it happened, whether the three of them actually stood together in the rays of the universe, perhaps afraid that Jakob would deny it, shake his head, wave him away, that her words had never been spoken, the rubies just fool's gold and no teddy bear left to be fetched from his memory. He'd never dared – and besides, asking such a thing would have been out of the question – to broach such an emotional issue with Jakob. She died; forty-five years have passed and she's never been spoken of. As if even her name was dead, as if she had never existed. Too much for either of them to say her name out loud. Ari because of the pain, the wound that was never allowed to heal, Jakob because of something else, perhaps we'll discuss it later, if we deduce it, if we manage to open him up. They never spoke of her.

In fact, they haven't spoken at all for forty-five years, except to ask each other to pass the milk, the remote, the trowel. Jakob has never said, My son; Ari has never said, My father. Experiencing anything emotional together has never been easy. Perhaps they were watching the news on T.V., the weather forecast, followed by an American series in which someone said, I love you; my life would be nothing without you; you're the oxygen I breathe; kiss me, kiss me, kiss me again; father, mother, son, daughter – I love you so much! The two of them sat on the sofa like lost souls in front of the T.V. Which is why Ari always tried to remember to check the T.V. schedule before sitting down, which wasn't that difficult, with just the one station, and its programming rarely interesting; he had to be ready to get up and out of there if Jakob sat down on the sofa and there was something on beside the news, "The Latest in Technology and Science" or a show about how paint dries. Life is unfortunately not as considerate as television stations, however; it doesn't publish programme schedules so you can choose your moments, which is why it isn't always possible to avoid difficult ones. For several summers, Ari worked with Jakob at bricklaying. One summer's day they were working at a new retirement home above the Keflavík Botanical Gardens, built there so that the town's elderly residents, wearied by the strain of life, worn out from working, could gaze out over green grass, watch the plants grow, the flowers spring up colourfully from the nearly

144

black soil, like a miracle, a message from God, that life and its colours can penetrate the darkness. A brilliant idea on the part of the municipal council to build the home there, but unfortunately it was built by amateurs, and that summer Ari and Jakob worked for weeks repairing it, only five years old. On some days the sun shone, the weather was fine, as if God had suddenly remembered us here in Keflavík, the old folks sat on their balconies or walked slowly, some with difficulty, through the Botanical Gardens where the grass was green, where there were all sorts of flowers, and the crooked, salt-scorched evergreens resembled tuberculosis patients who relish life on sunny days. It was a summer's day of the beautiful kind we sometimes get here, boats sailed out onto the mirror-smooth sea, the sky was blue, people walked down Hafnargata, then up Suðurgata, past the retirement home, some walked hand-in-hand, which was unusual at the time. Ari couldn't recall seeing adults walking hand-in-hand except when they were drunk; it was a bit awkward for the two of them, that intimacy, seeing couples in the prime of life pass by, hand-in-hand. Jakob decided that it would be better to go round to the other side of the building and wait with the repairs to the side facing the road, they had more than enough to do on the south side; here there were too many unnecessary distractions. Yes, said Ari, and gathered his trowels and levels. They moved round to the building's west side, where nothing was happening, the space being constricted, shady and where the rubbish bins were kept. As soon as they rounded the corner, they saw the old woman. Laden with tools, levels, they saw her sitting against the wall, legs straight out in front, a crutch lay on the ground with its grip turned away from her, as if it no longer cared about the old woman, who was crying vigorously. Not vigorously enough to make her tremble; her tears were bitter but silent. Her wrinkled face was wet with them, and she cried more like a child than an old woman with life-experience, defenceless, abandoned by the world, by happiness, cried inconsolably. She didn't stop when they appeared round the corner; as they walked past, their eyes met. She clearly couldn't stop, tried to compose herself, even attempted to smile but couldn't, absolutely couldn't, her face was contorted, became a wet, open wound, and as they passed, Ari caught a faint whiff of urine. He hurried to make up a new mortar mix, though there was no need for it yet, but it was a relief to be busy with something, to shovel black sand and cement into the mixer, watch it rotate, mixing different materials into a significant whole. It's impossible to make demands on workers who put effort into what they do, impossible to expect them to have time to notice life's pain, have time to discuss sensitive topics, because we can hardly mix concrete with pain and tears; we can't construct a windowsill out of feelings. Jakob grabbed a level, placed it to check that everything was correct.

Now there's no level for Jakob to grab, and Ari can't mix some concrete; they just stand there, looking at each other, perplexed by their hesitation, as if they've both lost the scripts to their own lives and have no idea what ought to come next. The tobacco smoke is dense, the smell of alcohol overwhelming, and Megas has started a new song, singing as if he knows all of these things, the world having long since ceased to surprise him, as if he has the answers in his hand – without them helping him at all:

> No need to curse the coffin maker,
> who's got himself for his best mate,
> fills orders from the Undertaker
> and never once delivered late.

146

No need to curse the coffin maker, though he's working for Death
– the tobacco smoke in the flat is as dense as the Austfjörður fog
that has swallowed up mountains for centuries, swallowed them
silently, without any effort, swallowed and erased the sea with its
boats like flightless seabirds on its back. Swallowed the houses
in Norðfjörður so that Margrét could barely see her neighbours
through her kitchen window; the world just disappeared, after
which she may have written a few thoughts about life in her diary,
after recording the everyday details: Hulda and Ólöf went down to
the saltfish-drying lot at 7.00 this morning, Gunnar and Elín are at
school, Jakob is messing with his cards, as usual, is drawn to that
world. Plenty of things need doing, "but I can't be bothered to
write them down, it can be so boring to do them that I'm not about
to put them into words as well". She stood up, did the chores that
we won't weigh down with words, thereby showing solidarity with
Margrét. Did her chores, looked after Jakob, felt the effects of time
when she straightened up, it nestled in her lower back. Then she
poured herself a coffee, gazed distractedly out at the fog and was
startled when she felt something touch the back of her hand; it
was just Jakob, who had looked up from his cards, or his toys,
and been frightened by the fog that made everything vanish so
completely that maybe everyone was dead except the two of them.
He stood up, sought refuge with his mother, laid his slender
child's hand on the back of her work-weary one, she smiled at him,
bent down to kiss his soft hand, the same one that lets go of the
door almost seven decades later, old and withered.

Jakob steps back as if to invite his son in, lets go of the door but
is clearly in some difficulty with his hand, with what he should do
with it, it's hanging limp by his side, seems useless. Ari notices that

it has withered, that his father has withered all over, as if Death is whittling him down to make it easier to carry him over. Ari thinks, So he's dying – and the desire to say something nice, something relevant that shows that they belong to each other, impossible to ignore it, fills Ari with such zeal that it may be visible in his face. Jakob steps back and repeats, with a crooked grin: Yes, I was expecting Death, not you.

Ari: I'm not dead.

You never know what form that crafty bank director and stockbroker will take, replies Jakob, giving his withered arm a purpose by lifting it up and to the side, as if to say, Well, since you're here you might as well come in.

Ari goes in.

Steps over the threshold into his father's flat, into Megas, the tobacco fug, shuts the door and sees the police baton concealed by the open door, hanging there like a memory of my summer with Ari working as police officers at Keflavík Airport. Ari never returned his baton, and it ended up here, on a wall in Jakob's flat, right by the door, as if he expected to have to use it on an unexpected, unwelcome guest. May I open a window? asks Ari, not waiting for an answer; he walks into the flat, opens the balcony door to the cold air. Damn it's good to have some fresh air, says a woman's voice from the sofa, you really feel it, and frankly I'd forgotten that something called fresh air even existed. It helps you think more clearly, though that's not necessarily an advantage, I mean, who wants to see the world as it really is? The woman lights a fresh cigarette, as if taking a stand, declaring that it's better to muddy the view, that there were two things a person couldn't endure seeing or facing: God and a naked picture of the world. I'm Anna, she adds, smiling at Ari, who instinctively smiles back, both unhappy and relieved to have the woman there; he'd been so worried about being alone with his father. Or how, thinks Ari, as soon as he sits down in the red chair, the same colour as the sofa, might it be to talk to him like to anyone else? Some people have stated in my hearing that he's interesting, even rather funny, and, what's more, a man of strongly held views; why am I unable to see that person?

What's your name, honey? the woman asks, squinting through the tobacco smoke, she seems roughly the same age as Jakob, but with hair so blonde that it must be dyed. She's put on lipstick and make-up, styled her hair beautifully, made an effort to tidy herself up, done some primping, but is wearing a baggy tracksuit; she doesn't take her flint-coloured eyes off Ari. Her face, which is slightly swollen, cut with deep runes, is like a vague memory of considerable beauty.

You're drinking, says Ari, after Jakob introduces them: Ari, this is Anna, Anna, this is Ari – my son, he added, breaking the silence that descended unexpectedly between Megas' songs. My son. Said it like a man lifting a very heavy rock. You've been drinking, Ari said reflexively, looking at the near-empty vodka bottle on the table, two beer cans, and his temper flares suddenly at the thought of the tobacco smoke pervading his clothes, lets himself feel irritated, focuses on his irritation; it's easier than the debilitating sadness that assails him. Anna waves at one of the speakers; she has long, white fingers, nail varnish that's almost pink, Oh, honey, turn your friend down a bit so we can hear each other. Jakob, who was preparing to sit down on the sofa, because that's how things were for him now, even sitting down required preparation, stops, curses as he walks over to turn Megas down. Ari swallows his rage, his anger, his shock, at hearing the woman use the same term of endearment – honey – for both him and Jakob, as if they were one and the same, father and son, so close that it would be natural to call them by the same name. What were you saying, honey? asks Anna, and Ari repeats drily, You've been drinking, but looks at his father, looks Jakob right in the eye, apparently startling him, whether because Ari looks him right in the eye, or because he said that about the drinking, mentioned the elephant that's always been in the room, the elephant, the blue whale, the dark planet. Jakob's head bobbles slightly, as if he barely has the strength to hold it up any longer, as if all its memories have made it too heavy, all the heavy, unspoken words, but then smiles that crooked smile of his and says, Yes, we've been drinking, we're probably too old to do anything else. An easy escape, says Ari in a strained voice, anger and disappointment simmering within him at how badly this is going, at how far they are from being able to talk to each other, don't know how, can't, don't dare to. Forty thousand years between them. Certainly, agrees Jakob, preparing once more to sit down on the sofa, certainly it's an escape, but it's also impossible to dispute the fact that many a man has managed to save himself by fleeing!

About the size of the universe

— BACK IN THE DAY —

Then. Comes. Night.

On the heath above Reykjavik stands a big house surrounded by lava. It's on the banks of a lake that gets bigger the younger you are. Shallow at the shore, it deepens quickly, and in some places is very deep indeed.

It's a two-storey house. Although it's not as big as our block of flats in Safamýri, it's big enough to make Ari feel even more vulnerable when he's told to get out of the car that drove him up onto the heath. It's sunny, but the house casts a dark shadow.

Jakob had found us. He took Ari but left me alone behind the curtains, and it's definitely July. The sun is so high in the sky that it can't get much higher, and it's good to be alive. Ari gets out of the car. A woman tells him to follow her into the house. The days pass. Followed by the nights. Ari has one friend, called Einar. My name is Einar because I'm always alone,[9] he explains to Ari on the first day, after Ari has snuck away from the kids playing outside, five women sat against the wall of the house and watched and laughed a bit because the sunshine was warm, the day endless, and the children played on the large lawn. Some threw stones or bits of lava rock into the lake, and it's pleasant to watch their dark shapes disappear into the blue water. If only we could cast grief, sadness, fear into the blue water of life and see it all sink like those black stones, never to surface again.

Now go and play with the others, there's nothing as good for a sad child's heart as playing with other children, my little

9 The word *einn* in Icelandic can mean "alone"; the name Einar reflects this.

sweetheart, the woman had said to him, the one who led him into the big house, showed him where he would sleep. Put your bag under the bed, she said, and then they sat for a while on the bed in the big dormitory whose windows faced the lake, they could hear the children's laughter and shouting, and God is a blind chicken pecking at the universe. The woman stroked Ari's head gently. Would you mind, she asked, giving me some of these curls of yours? For a moment he thought he might cry, but then she said what she did about games and a sad heart, took him outside, called out to three children nearby. This is Ari, she said, he has just arrived, can he play with you? Yes, yes, they said, but he slipped away as soon as he could, when no-one seemed to be watching, found himself a place in the moss-grown lava, sat there alone, perhaps in the hope that the world would forget him, but suddenly there was Einar, looking at him inquisitively before turning away to pee, after which he said that his name was Einar because he was always alone. Then days pass.

And nights as well.

I mention this in particular, and demarcate the two, because days and nights are not akin at all, each is its own world, and they have almost nothing in common. Days, for instance, are all different. Some little more than sunshine, the sky, birdsong, others grey with rain and leaden clouds that the sky struggles to hold up, then it's cold inside the big house, on both floors, in both wings. Sometimes the food is good, sometimes the children get milk and biscuits, sometimes the food is bad, and then it takes an eternity to clear your plate. Sometimes the place is joyful and the games are so much fun that the children almost forget about death, illness, drinking, heavy fists, hard hands, they're just alive and the light reaches from the ground all the way up to the sky and the women who look after them give them warm cuddles and have a lovely woman's smell. Then comes night.

Then. Comes. Night.

All falls silent.

People. Birds. The sky.

First comes evening, with its hint of darkness in the distance, and anxiety settles over the big house. They're all in bed, under the covers, and they say their prayers together, led by the women, thanking God for the day and the world and the birds, the sun, the rain, all of it, what an awful world it would be without God, probably nothing but darkness, cold and wickedness, we thank Him for the sunshine, the rain, our lives, to be able to lie here in the large dormitory far up on a heath, we thank Him for Daddy being dead, Mummy being funny in the head, for Daddy drinking too much and hitting Mum, me, my big brother, we thank Him for Mummy being in the hospital, for me being here where Stepmother can't hit me, we thank you, God, for your creation, the work speaks for its master. Amen. Good night, say the teachers.

The door shuts.

They hear the teachers' footsteps fade down the corridor, then everything falls silent and night comes with sleep and dreams, releases them over humans, animals, the world, even the rocks doze. The silence deepens in the dormitory. Then someone starts sobbing, trying, perhaps, to stifle the sounds in his pillow, and then someone else starts sobbing, then crying. His first night there, Ari lay awake a long time, listening to the crying wane and wax, but little by little, the children fell asleep, the sobs were hushed. Their heads sunk sleepily into their drenched pillows, they all fell asleep, except for Ari, who lay awake, staring at the ceiling; his head rested on his bone-dry pillow, he couldn't cry, he'd left all his tears behind with me, hiding behind the curtains.

His prefrontal cortex is in uproar

Jakob rips open the curtains, curses, slaps Ari and then drags him out of the bedroom, leaving me behind with my tears. I rush into the kitchen and am standing by the window as Hulda and Uncle lead Ari to an unfamiliar car, Jakob stands on the pavement, and the sky, the whole world, quivers with sunshine. Definitely the best day of the summer, almost as if God had issued an order that everyone was to be happy that day. Jakob clenches his fists, Ari turns to look, Hulda says something to him, Uncle says something to him. We can't get very far without words; they can make us happy, sad, change the world, and it's nice of them to say these words, express their affection, the beautiful shape of their hearts, yet so useless that Ari is filled with hate, which is why he doesn't say goodbye, doesn't look at them, as if they don't exist, and is almost grateful to his father, standing there on the pavement a good distance away. No, never mind, Jakob has got into the Trabant, starts it, backs out of the drive, turns right, accelerates, curses, he's been away from work for two hours, had thought it would only be one, max. He drives down Miklabraut, upset, his hands shaking as he lights a cigarette, inhales deeply. His mind races.

The human brain is an enormously complex organ, and there is much about it that we don't understand. It's divided into two parts: the cerebrum and the cerebellum. The cerebrum is divided into left and right hemispheres. The cerebellum is the centre of information about balance; it controls coordination, stores information about learned movements, such as how to ride a bicycle, light a cigarette, hit your son. Lower down in the forebrain and prefrontal cortex is an area that has to do with memory, emotions and cognitive functions – controlling one's behaviour with reference to judgement and foresight. It was thus the prefrontal cortex that made the decision to hit Ari, but poor Jakob – the same area controls judgement, emotions and foresight, which don't go well together; this should probably be classified as a design flaw, because judgement, emotions and cognitive function each inhabit their own planet, are barely in the same solar system, no wonder we have so much trouble getting our bearings, are befuddled, that the world has been mistreated. No wonder Jakob makes a detour, stops the Trabant in a car park outside a block of flats in Reykjavík, smokes another cigarette there, regards his trembling hands.

His prefrontal cortex is in uproar.

He slides his right hand beneath the seat, it's his neocortex, the youngest area of the brain, that sends his hand there, but what area was it that made the decision to keep a vodka bottle under the seat, and to take a drink from it now? Jakob drinks, he shuts his eyes, this is pretty good, it's relaxing, is an entirely different life. Jakob opens his eyes, takes another drink, puts the bottle back in its place, his hands are on the steering wheel, he takes a good look at them, they're calmer now. He flexes his hand. Remarkable that the hand can be both a palm and a fist. What is warm, strokes and comforts, and what is hard, can hurt, enable the unforgivable. My fist, my brother-in-drink. He puts the car in gear, drives off to his bricklaying, the everyday, the future that will be without her who once ran, tousled and ruddy-cheeked, down Skaftahlíð, nearly missing her bus up to Vífilsstaðir, but caught it and is lying there, exhausted by pain and sluggish from morphine when Jakob arrives.

That is, when he makes it there, when the two-gear Trabant manages to work its way up the hill, higher, closer to death.

Jakob parks the Trabant outside a building in Norðurmýri, gets out, his working day continues, he grabs his level, he has strong hands like Oddur, his father, strong fists, my brother-in-drink – and the summer crawls along. She's up at Vífilsstaðir. A dark-haired woman visits, brings her flowers, two marble cakes and something that might be called excuses, something that might be called defencelessness. The flowers are placed on the table beside the hospital bed, there's also a photo of Ari and a little notebook that she hasn't been able to write in for days. The last entry is from the early summer. Then came a short poem, it just came, she didn't ask it to, but the pain became bearable for a while, she was filled with optimism, with more enthusiasm for life, and wanted to write about the sun that she soon will lose, which will soon go out for ever, leave her behind in darkness, but nothing came about the sun, all that came was the fist, my brother-in-drink.

Reykjavík, Miðnesheiði

— AND WELL INTO THE CENTURY —

But, oh, my darling, I love you still (he loves you still)

They lived on Skaftahlíð for nearly two years. In the basement, below an elderly couple who at first seemed not to like her, even stopped saying hello to Jakob, who was afraid of losing the flat, that they would be evicted, given how hard it is to find a rental in this rapidly growing city, but for some reason, their attitude suddenly changed. One afternoon when he came home from work, the couple was sitting in the basement, with a cake that the woman had baked, and afterwards everything was just as it had been, even better, and sometimes they called Ari's mother their naughty angel. A bit awkward, and what exactly do they mean? Jakob always looks away when they say this, pops something in his mouth, pretends to be busy chewing. Their second autumn together, she unexpectedly leaves to work in the herring industry in the Eastfjords – as a sailor!

Gets a job as a cook on a herring boat out of Eskifjörður, without saying a word about it to Jakob, a snap decision, and it sparks their first serious row. Jakob's temper flares; he kicks the fridge twice, forbids her to leave, I forbid you to leave! She hisses, her eyes wild, how dare he speak to her like that, as if he thinks he's in charge of her! She leaves disgruntled.

A little over a week later, a long letter arrives from her, from the east. Smelling of fish and the sea. A letter with a thousand kisses and apologies: "Oh, I miss you dreadfully! I have no idea how my little heart will survive!" Her missing him does not prevent the letter from welling up with joy, she describes the crew in such a

161

vivid, colourful way that he hates each and every one of them. The older ones know Oddur and find it delightful, if not exactly an honour, that his daughter-in-law-to-be is their cook. Jakob doesn't find it delightful at all, in fact is irritated down to his bones. They ask her to say hello to the young Jakob, ask how he is doing, why isn't Oddur's son at sea, too, "as if I would let you go there! I don't want those big waves to swallow you up! My God, I didn't know the sea was so big!"

They ask after Oddur, say his name respectfully, she is proud to be known as Oddur's daughter-in-law, as if the old crewmembers respect her, and forgive her for being a woman at sea. So proud that she sends Oddur a postcard. "Why have you never told me these stories about him? I can hardly wait to see him again, I'm sure I'll see him in a completely different light. I have to close now, the boat's pitching so badly that it's hard to control my pen, I don't know whether my words will just rush away, and when I look outside, I can barely tell what's sky and what's sea, what are fish and what are birds. Write soon! I miss you so dreadfully that sometimes I just start bawling."

Bawling, thinks Jakob, yes, yes, and they take the opportunity to console her, for example that Davíð, whom she describes as an "amusing idiot". Jakob envisions this, envisions Davíð coming upon her crying, knows how a shithead like Davíð comforts girls, the older crewmen wonder why he isn't at sea, too. Yes, yes. And Oddur gets a postcard from her – from the sea. Damn. Damn. Damn. She's away for seven weeks. Writes him eight letters. Full of sea, the rolling of the boat, herring, rattling pots; letter 3: "God oh God how I miss you! I never would have imagined that missing another person could be so painful."

I never would have imagined – and amusing, mischievous

Davíð pops up in all her letters. By her second letter, Jakob is expecting to see his name, and his whole body seizes up like a clenched fist when it comes. As if I can't see through this, Jakob mutters to himself, says, Three hearts, and only writes her a single brief letter, shortly before her return. Brief but dripping with irritation, guilt like black slag in his heart – he'd gone up to the Base to play bridge, a short tournament. He said, Three hearts.

It's good to play bridge. Few things are as beautiful as a new deck with its fifty-two cards, four colours. You hold your card and it's as if the world becomes more secure, gains in harmony, organisation. God deals the cards, it says somewhere, and it's no use to cry over your hand; you won't be dealt a new one. God deals the cards, it says somewhere, yes, certainly, but everyone plays the hand they're dealt, that's what's meant by free will. There's no such thing as fate, just free will – and the cards God deals you. Some are dealt only dogs, others nice sets of face cards and large numbers of trumps, bridge shows you that the cards themselves are only half of it, or even less; the other half is you. Alertness, memory, the ability to read others' cards, the knack for playing yours in accord with the situation, and, last but not least, to learn to know your partner – it's even possible to win with almost nothing but dogs. There are very few situations other than bridge where you're quite as alive. If life is a card game, the game is called bridge.

Jakob has played bridge for many years, participated in tournaments, won awards and tried at first to teach Ari's mother, to initiate her into the mysteries, but she had no patience, just became irritated in the strategic world of bridge. He said, Two spades, but she said, I think the night is a mysterious girl from Africa. That might have been their first conflict, the first test of their love, that

163

she could never feel comfortable in the world that he loved best. It hurt Jakob. He looked at her as if she'd betrayed him, failed him, but she stroked his head, kissed his blue eyes, wrote some nonsense on his lips with her tongue, said, Sorry I'm so stupid. She whispered, Come into the bedroom and trump me there.

She always seems to know how to soothe his anger, erase it, but now she's too far away to whisper anything in his ear, there are deserts between them, and he's angry because she's at sea, because she's surrounded by all those goddamned men, one of whom is called Davíð. Jakob envisions them together as the porridge boils, as she fries eggs, envisions them together on the floor, the table, going at it and moaning – sometimes he wakes in the night boiling with anger. But then he says, Three hearts. They're up at the Base, he and Siggi, his bridge partner, a workmate and friend of many years, they met the winter Jakob was sixteen, having just arrived from the east and working at the Base thanks to Tryggvi, much to Oddur's bitter resentment; he didn't speak to his son for two years. Ever since then, he and Siggi had been close, Jakob was Siggi's best man when Siggi got married, and frequently having dinner with the elderly couple before Ari's mother came into his life like a bomb. He and Siggi are excellent bridge partners, connecting so well that it's downright beautiful. Almost marvellously beautiful, feels Jakob, who's got goose bumps and felt himself filled with an intense, almost painful affection for his partner when they probed each other with their bids, thereby coming to know what cards the other was holding, then playing as if of one mind. He'd never imagined it could be possible to connect with another man so strongly, at the same time so subtly. How they could sit face-to-face, cards in hand, and communicate with their eyes, giving their all to win. Jakob says, Three hearts. They're at the Base, at a bridge tournament, six weeks since she went to sea, which is full of herring, that silvery fish wriggles in the nets, fills the boat, wriggling herring that turns into money and again money and even more money, a whole bloody lot of it, transforms entire communities, transforms society, herring and the American military make us rich, yank us for good from the stagnant world of turf farms where buttercups grew on the roofs and spoke to God. Who never replied. No more than Jakob has answered her letters, despite receiving seven: "Write to me, dear, I'm starting to worry. Have you stopped loving me? You absolutely mustn't stop, because what choice would I have then, but to die? Maybe you're just too tired to write? You're such a hard worker! But such a damned slacker when it comes to writing! It's getting dark now, the evenings are growing darker and darker, I've always felt as if God gets tired in the autumn, that the darkness is God's sleep, the stars His dreams."

God's sleep and His dreams hang above Jakob and Siggi as they walk with their arms slung over each other's shoulders, having just got out of the big American car in which they were given a lift from the club where the tournament was held, eight Icelanders, twelve Yanks, Siggi left his car outside the club. It'll be good to walk there tonight, he said, walk off the beer. They're outside the flat of the officer who organised the tournament, are happy, they won, played perfectly as a team, one mind, one soul. You're world-class, damn it all, the officer had said, pissed off about being beaten by Icelanders but impressed by their playing, their unanimity, their harmony. Fucking hell, he'd added, and invited the two of them to his place, along with a few others, and now they're together in the autumn night beneath the dark sky that may be the Lord's heavy sleep, while the stars, bright or faint, are His dreams. It must be a comfort, a relief, that light shines from God's dreams; it must mean that there is hope, after all. The friends stand in the car park on Miðnesheiði, the windows in the officer's flat have been opened to let the tobacco smoke escape, and Elvis Presley is spinning on the gramophone with his fame, his alluring hips, his growing unhappiness and his voice we can never get enough of. Their arms are slung over each other's shoulders as they gaze at the sky; they're young. Jakob is twenty-three, Siggi two years older, at an age when friendship can be the purest, the most zealous, almost like love, and when nothing seems able to cast a shadow over it, ever. They just gaze, perhaps feeling greatness emanating from the heavens, which we sometimes give incomprehensible names like God, eternity, purpose. Siggi inhales deeply, tightens his grip on Jakob, and Jakob has perhaps never felt so fond of another person as he does of his friend at that very moment. His affection grows so strong that he has trouble breathing and has to blink to hold back his tears; maybe that's why he says, quoting her letter, that the night sky is God's sleep, the stars His dreams, and adds, somewhat apologetically, when Siggi says nothing, has no response, that it's in a letter from her; she is, as Siggi knows, of course, a cook on a herring boat out east. No lack of intelligence or beauty in that girl, says Siggi, releasing his grip on Jakob, dropping his arm off his shoulder, off the warmth, the closeness, abruptly making Jakob feel lonely. Let's go, lights a cigarette, opens a beer he'd stuck in his pocket before they went out to the American car, takes a big swallow, hands it to Jakob. What fucking genius to be able to stand here in Iceland at night and drink beer like a classy guy in a different country, drink beer that's been banned in this country for more than four decades; the friends sigh, empty their cans, enjoy the beer, the friendship, the calm that visits us now and then down here in the south, almost as rarely as Christmas, but when it does, it lies above Miðnesheiði and Keflavík like a dream. She isn't lacking in intelligence. Or in beauty. Jakob stares proudly into the sky, his friend's opinion counts for more than many other things in this world, maybe most things, and the things she wrote in the seven letters echo in his head, some in such a way that he wants to write them down and send them to his mother, Margrét, out east in Neskaupstaður, but hasn't had the opportunity to do so, too tired to write letters when he comes home from work. Siggi finishes his cigarette, flicks it away, it soars through the darkness in a high arc. But there's something dangerous about her. Forgive me for saying this, Kobbi, but why are we friends? Well, maybe not dangerous, but some bloody thing you can't put your finger on or understand; are you sure you can trust her? You know how her family is; her mum isn't exactly a lady, of course, and I've heard stories about her paternal aunt, the one who was in Norway, and what girl wants to leave her boyfriend for two months to join a group of gruff men on a herring boat; have you ever heard of such a one? Your life is your own, says Jakob, instinctively interjecting these words that he heard so often from his mother's lips in defence of someone being reproached, who had done something wrong, behaved in such a way that it inspired resentment, even antipathy. Your life is your own, he repeats, calmly, as if to soothe his friend, smiles and suffocates the unexpected rage arising within him, in his belly, it grows, spreads out from there, approaches his heart, perhaps intending to transform it into a fist, because he suddenly sees this so frighteningly clearly, she with that damned Davíð, fucking on the floor while the fish boils over, she is screeching and, for some reason, now with the face of Veiga, her paternal aunt. Your life is your own, he says for a third time, as if saying a prayer, a mantra, a magic spell, gropes for a new cigarette. If you say so, says Siggi, glancing over at Jakob, the sky so heavy with darkness that it's incredible that this calm can hold it up. A black Chevrolet comes speeding up, brakes abruptly a short distance from the friends, and an American steps out, short, stocky, with a buzz cut, Johnny Tillotson at high volume on the cassette player, the song "Without You". The catchy melody fills the night, the bright voice that swings between enthusiasm and depression, you made me happy, you made me swing. Bloody fine song, and catchy, it makes you want to start singing and whistling along with it, even dance, the song tugs at your legs, but, oh, my darling, I love you still (he loves you still), I dream about you, and I always will. The American snaps his fingers, winks at the two friends, goes behind the car, opens the boot, singing along with Johnny, and helps two girls, or young women, clamber out. One of them emerges from the boot like a curse, kicks the man in the shin and hisses, I told you not to drive like a bloody idiot, we were nearly carsick, asshole! Love your fire, baby, shouts the Yank, ignoring the kick, shuts the boot, kills the engine, turns off the cassette player. The officer comes out of his flat and yells into the night, If anyone is a genius, Sid, it's you! Sid, the short man, the solid block, grabs the women by the waist and yells back, happily, because it's a magnificent night, calm, starry, an abundance of beer and wine, music, good friends and two sweet girls, There are women who make life fucking worth living!

What a night this is going to be, says Siggi, after they've polished off two more beers and go in to the music, the tobacco smoke, the fun, leaving the sky outside with its dreams.

About the size of the universe

— BACK IN THE DAY —

The night is bigger than all the days in the world

Weeks pass, many weeks, there's actually nothing wrong with living up here on the heath, in a big house by a lake that's loaded with fry that shoot out from beneath the banks like happy, unexpected thoughts, the teachers stroke your cheeks, say friendly things, they're big and good, there are loads of kids and the days are full of games; nothing to complain about here. This place, this stay. If it weren't for the painful distance, if it weren't for imminent death. And if it weren't for the fact that every day, no matter how bright, saturated with sunlight, making it seem endless, is followed by a night that silences life. Some of the kids cry every night. Cry into their pillows, whisper into them the names of their parents, grandpas and grandmas, siblings, dogs, everyone they miss. Their pillows take it all in but comfort no-one.

Ari lies there with his eyes open, looking out at the dusky night, sees that the moon is almost yellow, sees the door to the dormitory that their teachers shut tightly behind them every night, the doorknob so high that the children can't reach it, can't escape. Some say prayers, recite the Lord's Prayer, recite "Father God, Be My Father", say every prayer they know, even add some from their own hearts, Dear God, let me grow up tonight so that I can be an adult and have children and be good to them.

Ari listens to the prayers ascend, they slip through the roof out into the night, which grabs them like small, frightened birds. He lies awake so long that he hears all the sounds gradually die out, the whimpering, the prayers, and is finally falling asleep when a hand is placed on his shoulder, very gently, so as not to frighten him. It's Einar, his friend, who's been here the longest of all the kids, he and Ari have often concealed themselves in one of the countless hiding places that Einar has in the lava, there's no shadow between the two of them, only trust. Ari opens his eyes, Einar puts his finger to his lips as a signal for silence, then whispers to Ari that he should get dressed, which Ari does, sees that Einar is fully dressed, and then they sneak between the beds, past the sleeping kids, past dreams, nightmares, regret, to the door with the knob so high up. Einar kneels down, signals to Ari to get onto his shoulders, then rises slowly with his friend on his shoulders, so strong that he doesn't need to support himself on the door, rises to full height, almost a head higher than Ari, who just manages to reach the handle with the tips of his fingers and pull it down. The door opens with a soft creak, a long, half-dark corridor appears, so incredibly long, silent, and night waits outside.

Soon, they're sitting together in one of the hiding places, which is entirely different in the night, the lava that conceals it is much darker, almost black, and seems to breathe, but Einar isn't afraid, he stopped being afraid a long time ago, has no reason to be afraid, nothing in this world can threaten someone who's lost everything, which is exactly why he isn't going to run away with Ari, there's nothing out there waiting for him. His dad is dead, he was a carpenter and was working up on the bloody roof of some bloody block of flats when a surprise gust of wind blew him off; that was two years ago. He often lifted Einar up on his shoulders and carried him around when he came home from work, called him his mate, sang or read to him in the evenings. We two are mates, he said, and always will be. His mother wasn't always at home, something

172

in her head made her peculiar sometimes. Then came that surprise gust of wind. One day a stranger came to live with them, whom Einar was supposed to call "Dad". It was then that he started finding his hiding places. Under the bed, in the closet, down in the basement, behind the sofa, the worst thing was that his mother never came to Einar's defence when his stepfather found him, which he always did, eventually, grabbed him and hit him and slapped him, that was the only way he was going to learn to show respect, maybe she was just relieved to be left in peace; he couldn't beat them both at once. Then she began hitting him, too. Gently at first, as if she were stroking him, then harder. Don't, Mummy, he begged, don't hurt me, but then she hit him even harder, grabbed him, held him tight and hit him, seemingly unable to stop; he managed to wriggle out of her grasp, get out onto the balcony, they lived on the third floor, it was snowing and windy, but he managed to climb over to the next balcony. Since then, he's been here. Now Ari has to leave. Something tells them he's the only one who can save his mother; he just has to get to her somehow. Look, you go down this road and then you come to another, bigger one, turn left and keep going until you reach some houses, then you're in Reykjavík. Now get going, we won't ever see each other again, I'm going to go wait by the lake, so that the teachers see me when they wake up and discover that we're gone. I'll tell them that you waded out into the lake and drowned, that I tried to stop you but you hit me, so you've got to hit me now and give me a bruise, hit me here, and hard, he says, pointing at his right cheek. I don't want to hit you, you're my friend. Hit me because I'm your friend, hit me now, you've got to get out of here. Harder than that, says Einar after Ari pats him on the cheek, and Ari hits harder, so hard that Einar totters and says, That was a real hit. Now get going, you'll always be my friend, I'm going to sit down by the lake, totally drenched, so that when the nannies come out they'll think I tried to save you, which will give you more time, I've thought this through, now go.

He doesn't want to say goodbye to Ari. Doesn't even watch him go. Ari looks back five times, and each time, Einar is standing there with his back turned, hanging his head as if he's waiting for a surprise gust of wind.

That's where we're going, then; that's the planet we'll head for

How long is the night? Long enough and patient enough for short legs heading for Reykjavík, heading down from a heath and needing to make it before daybreak, before the teachers wake up and see two empty beds? It's a long way to Reykjavík, a dreadful distance when both legs are little more than five years old. At first, it crosses his mind to sing the songs he learned from his mother, but he soon stops. The singing just calls attention to the fact that he's by himself, alone in the night, and something tells him that the dead gravitate to life like flies to light. Best keep quiet. Best walk as quietly as possible. Which is why he takes off his shoes, in the hope that he'll make less noise, which is indeed what happens, but his socks are quickly torn, the gravel on the road bloodies his feet. How long is the night? Is it possible to measure it, is it feasible, or the distance to Reykjavík, not the one shown on maps published by the Road Administration but rather the distance for five-year-old legs? Bloody hell, the world can be stupid, to think it's enough to have just one unit of measure, that the night is as long in minutes for the lonely as for those in love, that the metric system has the imagination and understanding to measure all the different distances in the world of human beings; as if the distance from the heath to Reykjavík is the same for five-year-old bloody feet as it is for a car with a decent heater, for example. God help us, how far it is down to the main road, where he's supposed to turn left, towards the heart, I'm guessing he'll be seven or eight years old when he finally gets there, he's walked for a long time, such a long time, become dreadfully tired, his feet and legs so sore that he doesn't have the energy to conceal himself by the side of the road when a car comes from the east, on its way to Reykjavík.

The beams of the headlights drag Ari out of the semi-darkness, the car drives by and the lights leave him behind in the night. He watches the rear lights recede, uncertain whether he should run off the road and hide in the lava, when the car stops a fairly good distance away and stands unmoving on the road, the engine purring, as if the driver remembered something so unexpected that he's had to stop the car to think it over. Then it starts to reverse. Approaches Ari. Who has to get away, to hide, but he's just too tired, too frightened in the night, dreading the thought of watching the car disappear, watching its lights fade in the distance and wink out, leaving him alone in the night, which is full of ghosts and dreadful distances. He stands there, unmoving, and waits. The car reverses, the driver slowly rolls down the window, and they look each other in the eye. For a bit too long, Ari feels, until the man says, as if to himself, Well now, a little boy up on a heath at night. Ari nods, as if to confirm the details: a little boy, a heath, night. The engine purrs. The man lights a cigarette, inhales, looks away, then abruptly back at Ari. He takes another drag and says, I was just checking to see whether you would disappear if I took my eyes off you. Ghosts tend to do that, disappear I mean, if you take your eyes off them. Don't ask me how they do it, I've never understood a thing in this bloody world. In any case, you're probably just a little boy up on a heath at night, not a ghost but alive, like me, that is to say, if you want to be generous and charitable enough to call my existence living. The man pauses, he smokes, the engine purrs. The man looks at Ari, who lowers his eyes, still only five years old which is why he has no idea what to say. The man finishes his cigarette, tosses the butt onto the road. It would be easiest, he says, to leave you here; I'm not entirely certain that you exist. But then Ari looks up, afraid of being left behind. Soon he's sitting in the front seat of the car.

The man puts his hand on Ari's thigh, squeezes, nods his head, says, It's good that you're alive, drives off.

It is of course much better to sit in a warm car, rest your exhausted feet and toes that whimper with fatigue, the night has suddenly become soft and friendly, like a big dog that wants to protect you. The car keeps going, approaches Reykjavík, distances itself from the big house, the lake, Einar, who sits alone in the night and fears nothing, because there's nothing left for him in this life. Approaches and recedes. Not quickly though. The man drives slowly, as if taking pains, both hands on the wheel, silent, staring straight ahead and taking his hands off the wheel only to light a cigarette, only to take a drink from a silver bottle he keeps in his jacket pocket. Stops the car once after pulling over, gets out, positions himself in front of the car, as if wanting to be in the headlights, unzips his fly and pees. Ari stretches a bit and sees that the man has a big penis. It must be uncomfortable having something so big hanging from your front. The man settles back into the car, looks over and seems startled to see Ari. Dammit, he says, taking a swig from the bottle as if to compose himself, I'd forgotten you, heath-boy! Where are you going, by the way; did I already ask you that? Maybe you'll evaporate as soon as we get to Reykjavík, or you'll just keep sitting there and make me find some way to get rid of you. I can't keep you, he continues, when Ari says nothing. There's no room for a heath-boy in my life, dammit, there isn't even room for myself. He stares into the headlights that shine in the night and make it darker than it is, and then the moon reappears. The engine purrs, the man stares at the road for a long time, he takes a drink, glances at Ari and appears startled: Oh, yeah, you're still here! Did you answer my question? No, probably not; was I asking you something? Yeah, hey, I'm probably on my way to Hell; where do you want to go? To Mummy, says Ari, his voice suddenly so thin that it sounds as if it's breaking. Bloody hell, says the man. That's where we're going, then – that's the planet we'll head for.

Is it possible to take revenge on death?

Here we are, says the man, we'll make it together, even with the night and most everything else against us, right, huh? He has got out of the car, is humming some meandering tune, they're at the front of a large hospital and see that the roof is as red as despair, so red that it's as if this big house is shouting at God, who says little except with pain and death. The man has to pee again, and Ari is as surprised as before, pretty terrified in fact, by the size of his penis, which reminds him of a monster from the underworld; it must be awful to grow up. Do you know where she is, asks the man, shaking the last drops, then he fishes the bottle from his jacket pocket, takes a drink, hands it to Ari, who shakes his head,

177

both to decline the drink and to answer in the negative, that he doesn't know where she is. The man sighs, says, Well, to hell with it, then leads Ari into the building.

They are met with silence and very long corridors. There are doors half-open into dimly lit rooms where people lie sleeping or dozing, waiting for life or death. The man sighs, is suddenly gone. We don't know where he went, and why so suddenly, whether he said something to Ari, gave an explanation, meant perhaps to ask for information, but either encountered someone who meant so much to him that he forgot everything, even forgot a five-year-old boy in search of his mother, or simply couldn't bear being inside this big hospital, built far up on a heath in the 1920s, for tuberculosis patients, so many people have died there, many of them so young that it's strange the building was never demolished in retaliation. Is it even possible, by the way, to take revenge on death, can anyone answer that, anyone at all, and why, for that matter, did the man disappear so suddenly? Perhaps he felt unwell. The place smells strongly of medication, and the muffled sound of weeping comes from some of the rooms, painful groans; maybe he needed to get out of there quickly, suck in the night's fresh, cool air. I don't know, and won't dwell on it; I mustn't lose track of Ari, who continues to wander the corridors; there, he's disappeared round a corner, I've got to hurry, we mustn't lose him, I'm all he's got. Without me, he'll ramble motherless and lost through the long, dimly lit corridors of eternity.

Eastfjords

— PAST —

Few things thrive in shadow, certainly not people:
Mr Gunnar Gunnarsson receives a letter

Perhaps our lives will be judged by what we didn't do. The world sleeps, Margrét darns trousers.

She has a book open in front of her, reads as she works, making use of time, it isn't long until morning, the semi-dark night will end soon, it's spring. She reads *Skibe paa Himlen* by Gunnar Gunnarsson, who is from the Eastfjords but moved to Denmark when he was seventeen to become a writer and conquer the world.[10] It's not inconceivable to conquer the world using Icelandic as one's weapon, but for the longest time we were too poor to feed writers, there were too few souls to buy books, and after the golden age of the Icelandic sagas, all we had were poets who composed verses while labouring for their daily bread. Composed alongside sheep, haymaking, fishing lines, kettles on the hearth, but Gunnar wanted more, he wanted to become a writer and nothing else, not a farmer and poet, priest and poet, man of lousy luck and poet, just a poet, a writer, and for that reason went abroad, abandoned his homeland and his language, followed his dream. People smiled at him as people smile at idiots, a dreamer whom the world would eventually lock away; poverty tried its best to defeat him, starve him to death, but he transformed adversity into literature and wrote numerous novels in Danish, some of them world-famous. Margrét reads: "*Stenene langs Vejen er vaagne hver*

10 *Skibe paa Himlen* (Danish): *Ships in the Sky* (1925) is the second volume of Gunnar Gunnarsson's (1889–1975) autobiographical novel *Kirken paa Bjerget* (*The Church on the Mountain*, 1923–28).

og en, lige fra Morgenstunden. De er saa forskellige som folk paa Kirkesøndag."[11]

Long ago, Margrét developed a technique for sewing, knitting, darning, without using her eyes; if you have the knack, and the will, your fingers can see for themselves, do their work, allowing your eyes to read in the meantime. She gets up early, cuts sleep short in order to have time to herself. She finishes mending Gunnar Tryggvi's trousers, goes and gets one of Elín's dresses, but stands for a moment at the window, looking out into the silence; soon the morning light will enter the fjord and wake the world. She's half-expecting them today, Oddur and Þórður, it's been six days since she sent Oddur her weekly letter, short like the ones she's already sent, just recounting the main news, news of the village, their lives, and concluding with what the letter is really about, the reason why it's been written and sent: the sea temperatures here in Norðfjörður. A task that Oddur gave Gunnar, and which he undertakes, proudly and responsibly, eight years old, running every morning down to the pier to gauge the temperature, and Margrét has to focus so as not to smile when he returns and tells her the numbers, determined to, wrinkling his forehead to appear older. Last week the temperature climbed to 6 degrees centigrade, which meant that the sea had warmed up so much that the fish could start migrating here in the east – it was safe for Oddur to finish fishing beneath the glacier, sail home and fish from here.

Margrét leans against the window frame, feeling the fatigue in her body, which has aged, it can't take as much as it used to, sometimes she shuts herself in the little bathroom where the mirror is,

11 *Stenene langs Vejen . . .* (Danish): "Each and every stone along the road is awake from early morning. They are as different as the folk in church on Sunday."

undresses and regards her body, which, on some days, seems to belong to another person; where did the body go that she knew so well, with its flat stomach, firm breasts, sturdy thighs, the body that was such fun to dress in beautiful clothes, which was so light to carry, who took it from her and left her with . . . this? She sighs softly, returns to the dress, and her book, making best use of her time, she so rarely gets to be alone with her thoughts. She once met Gunnar Gunnarsson's father. Yes, *met*, admittedly not the right word, an exaggeration, but he wasn't far away, scarcely more than two, three metres between them, and two people. Last summer, in Snædalur, at the festival held there every year, which everyone looks forward to. Speeches are made, songs are sung, all sorts of sports are played, and then there's a dance. Gunnar's father had been visiting relatives, and more than once Margrét went out of her way to stand near him, which was a bit silly, since she had no business with him, didn't know anyone he was talking to particularly well, but so wanted to hear him speak, convinced that there was more to him than to other people, the father of the author who'd worked himself up out of poverty and made a breakthrough, entirely on his own, had to learn a new language and has now written novels read by the world, each book a newsworthy event in many countries. But Gunnar's father spoke just like any other farmer. He seemed no different from the others, was so ordinary that Margrét almost started crying from disappointment. But then she became happy, jubilant, and no-one danced more enthusiastically at that festival than she did.

If the father of Gunnar Gunnarsson, who had achieved all this, didn't have more to him . . . well, if the son of an ordinary man from here in the east could conquer mountains and step onto the world stage, why should the same mountains stop Þórður;

what would prevent her son also rising into the clear blue sky?

Why not?

She wrote Gunnar Gunnarsson a letter.

She, a nobody, writes a world-famous author a letter!

She'd made this decision the previous summer, in Snædalur, where Gunnar's father was just an ordinary man, a farmer among other farmers, and she danced – but needed an entire winter to gather her courage. And it's easier to sit down to write the letter when Oddur isn't around. She knows that in Oddur's dreams, he stands on the slope below the house, an old man, watching his son Þórður set sail as skipper of a new and bigger *Sleipnir*. It's a beautiful dream, sincere, and we have no interest in clouding it, but that dream in no way harmonises with writing Mr Gunnar Gunnarsson a letter and sending it to Copenhagen, just to ask his advice and say clearly, albeit indirectly, My son doesn't belong in his father's dreams. "I think he's too complicated to live like the rest of us, amid fish and the sea, and find any joy in it. There is, as you know, nothing bad or trivial about such a life, but I believe he has talents that point in an entirely different direction. You know better than anyone that a person who doesn't utilise his talents can never be happy, will live in the shadow of what never was, but should have been. Few things thrive in shadow – certainly not people."

At the beginning of the letter, she apologised for herself, of course, as Icelandic folk have done for centuries, forgive me for existing, forgive me, an ordinary woman from Norðfjörður, for disturbing you, a writer . . . how else could she write to a person whose novels speak to all humanity, who creates immensely beautiful, intricate worlds that have a profound influence on hearts across the globe? "Maternal love gives me the strength, or sufficient insolence, to write to you. My son is called Þórður, son of Oddur. His father is a distinguished ship's captain here, a man with few equals. I say this not to boast about my husband, simply to state a fact ... But who is my son? Does he justify a simple woman scribbling a letter to an important author who has plenty to do besides read such a letter?"

I contend that he does, she writes, and encloses three of Þórður's poems. "One of them, simply titled 'Poem', and with a bird in the final verse, was published in *Eastfirthers*, and praised by the editor."

Margrét also describes Þórður: sweet but with infectious enthusiasm; has always been bookish and done so well at school that the headmaster wanted to send him south for more education. She describes his visit a year ago, albeit not in the way that we have done, her hands red and swollen, shamefully roughened, acting as if his visit were a nuisance, that learned man who had looked at her so sternly; she wrote what he had said about Þórður, that it "would be a great shame if his talents were not utilised; it would be such a waste".

Now, you're probably thinking, writes Margrét, why not send the boy to school? If he is so talented, it should be no trouble to find sponsorship, and a successful ship captain is hardly poor ... That's correct, they could pay for his studies, but now we come to what might be called the purpose of the letter; the matter is not so simple: "I hope that you can forgive my forthrightness. You must know that I have never spoken to anyone in this way, except for my brother and dear sister-in-law; my husband and I are engaged in a tug-of-war over our son. I've told you how my husband views our son's future, and you can see that I want something different. He is closer to me than to his father but respects him very much

185

and, what is more, is a diligent fisherman, strong and capable, and would undoubtedly make a good skipper. But wouldn't Þórður's unused talents make him unhappy over time? He has his own desires, and would undoubtedly choose the path that I imagine for him, but he respects us both, me and his father, and is the kind of person who never wants to hurt anyone. Such people sometimes end up hurting themselves so badly that their wounds never heal entirely. Advice from you, even a brief sentence, as to what direction my son should go in, would help me so much. Do you think our son should aim, on the headmaster's advice, for further study down south in Reykjavík, or perhaps venture forth like you, and put his life on the line for his writing? Or live here like the rest of us, amid mountains and fish? God knows I would prefer to have him with me for ever, but everyone must live his own life. Your sincere admirer, Margrét Guðmundsdóttir."

. . . because love is both a sacrifice and a balancing act

To love is harder than we realise.

They're home from Hornafjörður, Oddur and Þórður. Gunnar had waited for three days in a row on the foredune, a short distance from the village, from where it's maybe twenty steep metres down to the shore, with an excellent view out over the fjord, anxious to be the first to spot them, he can easily tell *Sleipnir* from other boats, even at a considerable distance, recognises it from the way it sits in the water, probably a born sailor – saw them coming and sprinted home at once. Shouting, They're coming, they're coming! so eagerly that he nearly hiccupped between words, ran shouting into the house, from there down to Áslaug and then straight down to the pier, with his sister Elín behind him. Margrét set off down to the harbour three times but turned back each time, uncertain whether Þórður would want her waiting at the pier, it might make him look like a child awaited by a fearful mother; a young person's pride and self-image are extremely fragile. Which is why she waited at home. She prepared some food, brushed her hair, put on some decent clothes, like an idiot; for whom was she primping, anyway? Her sister-in-law, Áslaug, felt no hesitation, didn't wallow in doubt; no, she ran straight down to the pier with her three daughters and they all waved energetically as the boat approached, completely un-bridled, like children, and Tryggvi himself, that sea-dog, was transformed into an over-eager boy, jumping onto the pier before *Sleipnir* had moored and nearly drowning in their kisses – is there a more beautiful way to die than to drown in kisses? Finally, father and son came walking up the slope, Þórður with Elín on his shoulders, she clutching his hair, warbling, smiling from ear to ear, and Gunnar skipping around them. They came into the house and – how shall we say it, how is it best to put it, what words can describe it, maybe these: it was as if a knife had stabbed her in the heart. Or: as if a great weight, half a mountain, had dropped onto her shoulders?

Þórður twisted Elín down from his shoulders, went over to his mother and hugged her, kissed her, but didn't he seem a bit remote, as if he didn't give all of himself to the embrace, as if there were some obstacle, something between them that his embrace didn't encompass? She had a lump in her throat; she needed to clear it, and said, somewhat flustered but feeling as if she had to speak in order not to burst into tears in front of them all: God will bring us a good summer. Then she remembered Oddur, there he stood, slim but so strong and full of the invisible power that has always emanated from him and makes him far stronger than his physical appearance might suggest, power that followed her across the vast Atlantic Ocean when she went to Canada, and never let her be, made it impossible for her to settle there, despite having the chance to do so, and young men, at least three, who sought out her company. That invisible force of Oddur's had slipped inside her, quivered in her blood, disrupted the kisses, because she was kissed, and she kissed, and there was a passionate moment in a wood, she pulled a young man down to her, eager to live, to exist, to discover everything, and he will never forget how he touched her, the sun shone so warmly through the trees – even then, she thought of Oddur, remembered that power of his . . . dear God, how she'd loved him. For so long. For so long that it was as if she couldn't get enough of him, was insatiable. But loving is perhaps harder than we realise, and it's only in the beginning, when love's energy level is as high as that of a war, that all difficulties seem to evaporate, dwindle to nothing. Then it slows down. Its warmth can still be there, deep down – enough to heat planets, if we're determined enough to hold on to it. And are prepared to sacrifice ourselves now and then, without losing our independence. Because love is both a sacrifice and a balancing act.

Margrét lies in bed awake. It's probably night. Oddur sleeps soundly by her side, sleeps deeply, having tossed and turned at first, as if making room in his dreams, then she moved over, gave him more room, which can be a beautiful description of marriage, making more room, better room for your spouse. That's the sacrifice.

They had eaten well and Oddur praised the food; enthusiastically, in fact. Elín sat on Þórður's lap the entire time, Gunnar between father and son, looking from one to the other, as if having trouble deciding which of them he should admire more. She, Margrét, she stood, did not sit down, refilled their plates, laughed at Elín's loquacity, asked about the eight weeks, whether the fishing had been good, whether there had been any accidents, and Oddur answered blithely, using plenty of words, Þórður didn't say as much, not to her, but blathered to Elín, teased the older sisters Hulda and Ólöf about boys, his beautiful hands covered with shallow scars from the baiting, they'll heal, but why did he feel like a stranger in the kitchen, and there's a swelling on his face, his left cheekbone, or redness. What happened? asked Margrét when she noticed this, moving instinctively to touch his cheek, gently stroke his reddened skin, to check whether she should apply something to the skin, put out her hand, but he turned away, leaving her fingertips hanging in mid-air, like five sad dwarf faces. It's nothing, he'd said, clumsiness, ran into something. He sniffed Elín's hair, asked Ólöf with a smile whether it was true that she was engaged, and again Margrét felt something we can't describe adequately, a knife in her heart, a mountain's weight on her shoulders, because she sensed, with every cell in her body, that Þórður had, perhaps for the first time, lied to her. That something had happened that father and son had agreed to keep silent about, to keep from her. That was the remoteness she thought she felt in Þórður's hug and kiss, a pact between him and his father not to let her in; that Oddur had managed to draw him in, away from her. She refilled Þórður's plate, despite it being heaped with food already; Mum, there's more than enough on my plate, he said. She just smiled at him, feeling as if she'd aged ten years.

The uncertain spring has finally turned into an Eastfjords summer, and Oddur and Þórður navigate the fjord at dawn, along with all the others, Tryggvi, Jónsi, Ási, whatever else their names are. They sail towards the sea and fish, and sunlight fills the fjords. Margrét wakes up sometimes when it is still night, slips out of bed, makes sure not to step on the creaky floorboards, goes into Þórður and Gunnar's room, stands silently over her older son, hardly daring to breathe for fear of waking him, gazes at his sleeping face in the hope that it will open to her in slumber, that beautiful face which had always been an open book. Even in sleep it is shut now. In the mornings, Þórður and his father leave the house together, stop at Tryggvi's, she watches them disappear into a world closed to her.

You shouldn't worry so much, Áslaug tells her. Worries are like pests; if you feed them, they multiply and become a plague. Joy comes to those who wish to receive it. Let the summer pass. Remember, he's just sixteen, only now discovering that he's a man; he's a bit confused, it will pass, and don't be angry at Oddur, try to understand him, Þórður's always been your child, allow his dad to enjoy having him to himself for one summer. It will pass.

Let father and son have this summer together, because Þórður will come back. Yes, but as whom? As who he was, or as someone else? Because an entire summer passes and Þórður doesn't touch a book, he who was always reading, and has always been as excited as she was when waiting for the bookseller who travels round the country aboard the coastal ships, his trunk full of books, Icelandic, Danish, a few in English, always sends a letter in advance to his regular customers, one came in early May, addressed to the siblings, Margrét and Tryggvi: "Well, it's time for my annual visit. The sailing schedule says that I should be with you on June 24 – with even more books than last year, but considerably less hair on my head!"

Those weren't lies, neither about the books nor about his hair; Tryggvi and Margrét spent half a day with him, but Þórður borrowed Tryggvi's motorboat and went fishing with two acquaintances, as if he'd lost interest in what had always been dearest to him. What became of the boy, the young man who was always reading, who wrote the poem published in *Eastfirthers* and who some in the village had started calling the professor or the poet; what became of the son who wrote her a long, enthusiastic letter from Hornafjörður, in which some of the sentences seemed saturated with both irritation and joy – where did he go?

Summer passes. It starts growing darker.

One morning, the mountaintops are dusted with snow. Autumn arrives with night frosts and stars, and on one occasion, when Margrét awakes from a shallow, restless sleep at just past one in the morning, and goes to get a glass of water, she sees the headmaster walk past the house, on his way up the mountain, carrying a telescope and tripod. He doesn't walk in a straight line, dressed in his English or Scottish garments of warm wool, hatless, wrapped in a wide scarf; no-one here in Norðfjörður, in all the Eastfjords, dresses like that. He walks slowly but looks determined, and eager. It's a beautiful combination, she feels. Before she knows it, she's started to cry. Stands there crying in the kitchen, it's night, no-one can see her, fortunately. Something's not right, she thinks, retreating from the window – but now, a day later, is standing there in the same place.

Woke again, a little after 1.00 a.m. As if the night were calling to her. The headmaster walks past with his telescope. She thinks, That might not be the best way up the slope.

She hears Þórður toss and turn in his bed, goes in, bends over him carefully, kisses his forehead. And then comes outside. Without thinking.

No, that's not quite right. For some reason, she'd thought about this constantly as the day had gone by: the headmaster passing her house, gently but intently, heading for the stars. Mustn't something happen inside a person when they look through a telescope and see the sky open up? Does his life become larger?

She'd thought about this. Had been distracted, overcooked the fish, spouted some gibberish and is now on her way up the mountain.

Wearing thick knee socks, shoes, her nightdress, a warm coat, and the night conceals her.

She tries to walk fast, to get up above the houses as quickly as possible, it's dark, of course, although the stars glimmer faintly, making it possible to distinguish a person walking by, and who it is, just as she'd seen the headmaster, who had, admittedly, passed unusually close to their house, and although she avoided coming as close to the other houses, she still might have been recognised, if anyone had woken up and looked out, seen the headmaster first and then her, walking by at a good clip; who, by the way, ventures out into the night like that for no good reason? The person in question could have put two and two together and got five. Because she's not chasing him, of course – that is, not like a woman chases a man, or vice versa; what rubbish – she's absolutely not chasing a man, but rather, a headmaster. She's chasing knowledge, a telescope and stars. And she wants to talk to him about Þórður. It's not as if she's worried what people might say about her; some people seemed to expect her to do strange things – though this was a bit much, tramping around in the night with a married man. In search of knowledge? Sure, sure; who would believe that? To view the night sky? Sure – and lying on her back, no doubt. Still, she would tolerate such talk, knowing that many people just naturally view others' behaviour in a bad light, not necessarily out of ill will or malice but out of boredom, dissatisfaction with their own lives. She could tolerate it, though it would be worse for the headmaster, respected for his knowledge, diligence, uprightness; a happy man, married to a beautiful woman who is no less known for her diligence and intelligence; happy people. Margrét, of course, shouldn't be running after him like this, because that's what she's doing, running in the darkness, she shouldn't do that to him, risk the stain of gossip falling on such a man, but she can't help it, lifts her nightdress so she can walk faster, she's a short distance above the village, her eyes are adjusting well to the darkness, and she's no longer visible from the houses, people can stare their eyes out for all she cares; she has merged completely with the night's darkness. I've become darkness, she thinks, smiling, suddenly wanting to laugh out loud, seized with unexpected gaiety or exuberance. You're such an idiot, she mutters to herself, and giggles, it's such fun just to exist, a feeling of freedom grows within her, as if she's young again and life is nothing but possibilities – endless possibilities! She runs over the moor, through the soft grass, wide-eyed, smiling, lets go of her nightdress, lifts her arms like wings, there's so much flight inside her, she's so light, light as a feather – she must be able to fly! She giggles, just as well that no-one can see her, if someone did, they would confirm that she's mad! She laughs, the life force flows through her veins, she flaps her arms to fly, to glide among the stars, but she doesn't fly at all – on the contrary: her toes ram into a tussock and she falls flat on her face, lies stretched out between tussocks. Laughs into the cold grass. Tears at it with her teeth. Looks up, grinning ear to ear, with grass between her teeth, and meets the eyes of the headmaster.

There he stands, in his fine clothes, there's the telescope and the tripod. And there she lies, like an old sheep with her mouth full of grass.

One...

It's good to be alone with the night and stars. Something always happens. Perhaps nothing earth-shattering, or even significant enough to share over a cup of coffee, but something that can remain with you for life.

The headmaster is an educated man. A man of our times. With little belief, to say the least, in ghosts, in superstitions, and hasn't been afraid of the dark since he was eight years old. He had looked through the telescope, concentrated deeply, felt so comfortable in the stillness, with the sky, that when he heard strange noises, he glanced over and saw a peculiar, menacing shape approaching at great speed, heard strange panting, and his heart skipped a beat. He would probably have run off like a frightened child, a superstitious, ignorant person, abandoned the telescope and run as fast as he could down to the village if fear hadn't paralysed him and only one thought had come to mind: Dear God, so everything they say is true!

Everything: legends about spirits, frightening beings, phenomena unexplained by the physical laws that logic could never grasp. And that his final hour had come.

194

Then Margrét falls flat at his feet.

Laughs into the grass.

Looks up with a smile, grass between her teeth, her brown hair tumbling over her clear eyes. Who needs the stars?

two . . .

I hope the headmaster will forgive me for running up the hill like this in the dark, like some kind of nutter! I can be a bit strange sometimes; you may have heard. I don't know what came over me . . . running like an idiot, I'm going to get up off the ground and take my old, foolish body home and promise to leave you in peace with the stars.

Please call me Þorkell, Margrét, he says. And bends over to help her to her feet.

three

He adjusts the telescope for her, explaining softly what she will see, mentions distances and says that light travels through the universe at a speed of three hundred thousand kilometres per second. He speaks so softly that she has to move closer to hear him. Then she puts her eye to the telescope, she sees stars, she feels the warmth of his skin on the eyepiece.

Keflavík

Have Ian Rush and Ingemar Stenmark made it to the stars?

Deckhand urgently needed on a 208-ton commercial fishing boat – it's winter, and there is continued unrest in Poland. Ari and I work six days a week, and most nights as well. We drive over Miðnesheiði, back and forth, Ari falls asleep just before midnight, sometimes later, comes home tired, smelling of saltfish, too tired to read, but puts a record on the turntable, headphones on his ears, falls asleep with the music on, Dire Straits: "Juliet, when we made love you used to cry / You said, I love you like the stars above . . . Juliet, I'd do the stars with you, anytime."

To make love – is that making it to the stars?

Merging with the universe?

God help us, how good it must feel to be with a girl; isn't life divided into before and after? So there we are in the Saab: me, Ari, Svavar (nearly twenty), Árni (two years older), Svavar the only one who has gone all the way, made it to the stars, dated a girl for three months, just before we met, but then she started seeing a deckhand on a fishing boat, four years older than us, with self-confidence in his broad shoulders. Svavar had those three months, and experienced something extraordinary. Did you make it to the stars with her? How was it, did you make it all the way to the stars? asks Ari, and Svavar sighs, gazes out over the landscape, the lava disappearing into the darkening afternoon, we drive back to the church, get out of the car, think about Hallgrímur and the little girl, walk round the churchyard, read the inscriptions on crosses and tombstones, names that tell us nothing and some remembered by none, no longer have anything to say to anyone but once stood for everything that mattered. We lie on top of the church-yard's broad wall, watch the sky grow dark and slowly fill with stars. Ari forms a telescope with his palm, raises it to his eye, looks, and we do the same, lie there together and look.

"Juliet, I'd do the stars with you, anytime."

Ari often falls asleep to this song, it is winter, we smell of salt-fish, yawn while reading *Morgunblaðið*, Ian Rush scored two goals last weekend, Ingemar Stenmark is world champion in the slalom and giant slalom – have those two made it to the stars?

It's Saturday, no processing today, we get to go home early, so early that Ari and I make it, just barely, to Hljómalind before clos-ing, for the first time in many weeks. No time for a shower; smell-ing of saltfish, we rush down to the record shop on the corner of Tjarnargata and Hafnargata. The owner, formerly a singer in Hljó-mar, is about to close when we come splashing through the slush, it's 4.00 p.m., Saturday night ahead, a dance at Stapi or somewhere else, the vodka bottles are waiting, how bloody nice it feels to be drunk and shoot up out of this sluggish mundanity, out of the fish guts, sleep deprivation, nappy washing, frustration, crappy T.V. programmes, shoot yourself free, scream into the night, dance and sweat at Stapi, or somewhere in Hell – but Ari and I think only of making it to Hljómalind before it closes. It's as close as close can be: the old singer is about to lock up when he sees us come splash-ing through the slush, the grey light, and he smiles, as if he's happy to see us, although his wife, who works at the shop on Saturdays, developing rolls of film, doing the bookkeeping, there could in fact be better music there, brighter notes, is impatient, they're giving a dinner party, need to get everything ready. I know, my beloved, the singer says, tilts his head, smiles, then announces that he's been saving something for us, steps behind the counter and pulls out a record. Mozart's *Requiem*. He strokes the sleeve affectionately. Composed for God, he says, before adding, Here, beauty eases sorrow.

Mozart won't cook the lamb, says his wife, hurrying around the shop to finish up before closing, and I reach into my pocket for my wallet, we were actually planning to buy something completely different, preferably a rock album, something we hadn't heard before, something to play in the Saab tomorrow, with guitar solos as long as Miðnesheiði, songs about unhappiness, sex, love – and we end up with Mozart. When I hand the old singer a five-thousand-krónur bill, he takes a step back, holds up his hands, palms towards us, shakes his head, No, no, you don't sell such a thing, that would be wrong, it's not allowed! The accounts have a different opinion, says his wife as she turns out the lights; they don't see beauty the same way you do. I love you, woman, says the singer, looking over at her, and I don't care what the accounts say; you're the melody that's always in my heart! Just listen to yourself, she says, at your age, and disappears into a back room, while we stand there embarrassed, sweating. Ari stares at the floor, as if he's spotted something very interesting there, while I, flustered, grab a couple of records, not only because I have no idea what to do with myself but so that we pay for something, nothing else would be fair, and the accounts needed soothing, as well – to be fed with something they understand. We have money to burn; we work six days a week and most nights, are handed a fat wage packet every Friday, I grab two records at random, say, We'll have these too; the singer smiles as he takes them to the till. Well, well, well, well, nothing less than *America's Greatest Hits*, "A Horse with No Name"; I've had this one a long time. And what do we have here? Yes! Now we're talking, you've gone right back to the basics: *Golden Hits of*

Rock 'n' Roll! What are the songs again . . . he holds the sleeve out to see better, it happens to most of us, our sight worsens with age, as if the world starts shutting off the lights. Yes, he says, and smiles heartily, here we have Johnny himself, my old friend, remember this, my dove, he calls out to his wife, tilts his head and sings softly, yet his velvety voice seems to fill the shop: "You made me happy, you made me swing, but now without you, I've lost everything." It's as if his entire body, with its soft flesh, feminine hips, childlike smile, is singing. Stop it, she calls from the back room, or I'll fall for you all over again, and then who'll cook the lamb?! Yes, lads, he says, then winks at us, puts the three records in a white carrier bag, those were real songs they wrote back then, those were melodies that won hearts, but Mozart, ah yes, he didn't write songs! What did he write, then? I ask reflexively. That's that, says the singer, opening the door for us out into the slush, the grey day losing its light, the night on its way with hopeless T.V. shows, a vodka bottle and a dance. That's that, he repeats, looking outside with a dreamy expression on his face, no-one's managed to find the words for what he wrote, not in any language. I believe it's because the words don't exist anywhere except perhaps in Heaven, where Mozart is played every night in the beautiful cafés with views out over happiness and eternity – I hope we live beautifully enough to earn a cup of coffee there!

Darling, darling, darling, and then Carl Sagan appears

Afternoon turned into evening with an American film on T.V., a vodka bottle and a dance at Stapi or somewhere, but we listen to Mozart's *Requiem* and think, Music is the place where beauty eases pain. We listened over and over to the "Rex tremendae" and "Lacrymosa" –

Ari only got to sleep in the middle of the night. He just lay there and stared; didn't understand a thing.

Is distracted for the next few days, forgets to prepare his lunch on Monday morning, Árni gives him more than half of his, sits reading *Morgunblaðið* and eating his porridge on Tuesday morning, still disorientated from sleep, Jakob went to work unusually early, he has to pour a big floor and wants to be home early, it's bridge night, the Suðurnes tournament, two nights in a row, he hasn't competed for many years and is nervous and excited, cracks an unusual number of jokes, even manages to get Ari to laugh when he comes into the kitchen that morning, but has now driven off in the Lada. Ari yawns over his porridge, yawns over *Morgunblaðið*, reads the T.V. schedule distractedly: news, weather, "The Moomins" at 8.35 but at 8.45: "Cosmos – One Voice in the Cosmic Fugue".

He drops his spoon into his bowl.

The handle hits the rim, his stepmother is so startled that her coffee goes down the wrong way, she spills something. What the blazes, she mutters, gets a dishrag, and something resembling a smile appears at the corner of her mouth. They'd awakened early, before 6.00 a.m., because of the bridge tournament, both of them excited, restless, Jakob tossed and turned, then whispered, Are you asleep? No, she whispered back, and he moved closer, hesitantly, and now she fetches a dishrag; life has many sides. Ari reads to himself: "'One Voice in the Cosmic Fugue', an American show about astronomy and space science, hosted by Carl Sagan, an astronomer at Cornell University in the United States."

Are you going to read a hole into the T.V. schedule? asks his stepmother. Ari slowly looks up and around the kitchen. So that's how the world is; it's still in its place, there's the kitchen clock, it's 7.40 a.m., oops, Ari's late, he has to pick up five people from four places in Keflavík and be in Sandgerði before 8.00, it's not going to happen, not in this life, but light, says the description of the show, travels at three hundred thousand kilometres per second. Ari has to drive approximately 30 kilometres, he'd make quick work of it at the speed of light, but it's questionable whether light would make the turn up on Miðnesheiði at such a fantastic speed without rolling over and maybe getting injured, like Gummi last year. A fugue in the voice of the universe. Ari reads this out loud from the T.V. schedule, can't resist, has to let the sentence resound in the kitchen, over the porridge. You're running late, says his step-mother, reaching for the coffeepot. Máni won't be pleased . . . what's a fugue, she asks unexpectedly, as Ari stands up reluctantly, as if he can't tear himself away from this sentence in the T.V. schedule. One voice in the cosmic fugue. I don't know, I'll have to check, all I know is that it's something very beautiful. He quickly rinses his bowl, discovers that he's barely touched his porridge, forgotten his lunch again. His stepmother turns the newspaper around, A show about astronomy, she reads. Hopefully you won't have to do any processing tonight, she says, and adds, Hurry up, boy! Which he does, he hurries, grabs his coat, puts on his boots, runs outside, there's a light wind, a slight frost, considerable snow coming down. Ari starts the car as I sweep the snow off it, scrape the frost from the windows and lights, Ari says nothing, can't, he has a lump in his throat. A voice in the cosmic fugue: is it a show about astronomy or Mozart's *Requiem*?

Árni thinks that a fugue has something to do with music, perhaps it's an instrument. If the cosmos is an instrument, it must be called a fugue, says Ari. The question is, will there be any processing tonight; in other words, when's the boat coming in, with how big a catch, because if it doesn't come until this afternoon and with a decent catch, we'll have to work until 10.00 or 10.30 tonight. Ari asks Máni, Máni taps his tin of chewing tobacco, Bjöggi, the skipper's son, steps on the pedal of the diesel forklift, turns it round on the spot, fetches a new tub packed with saltfish to be tidied and then salted in stacks. Máni hasn't heard from them – it's up to the fish. It may well be that light rushes along at three hundred thousand kilometres per second, taking turns at dizzying speeds, and it may well be that the cosmos is gigantic and *fugue* is the word you use when someone has changed this same cosmos into an instrument – it's all up to the fish. When everything is turned over and inspected, it's as simple as that.

Ari's stepmother has made fish cakes in tomato sauce for lunch; she laughs when Ari tells her what Máni said when asked whether they would have to work tonight, that it was up to the fish. That sounds just like him, she says, and Ari inadvertently shoves a whole fish cake in his mouth, there's a hint of bass in his stepmother's laughter, and suddenly he sees something girlish in her, as if, for a split second, he catches a glimpse of her youth. The fish make their decision, *Drangey* comes in just after 4.00 p.m., not a giant catch but two trips in the lorry, full stalls, they can't start processing until around 5.00, which means they'll be working tonight. Ari and I are in low spirits as we drive over the heath for supper, the snow has stopped but it's cloudy, there are no stars, it's up to the fish. I thought so, says Ari's stepmother, which is why she went to her brother's that afternoon, when she had finished work, he lives in upper Keflavík and has a V.C.R., which the stepmother borrowed along with two tapes, one with the two last New Year's comedy shows to watch, the other to record the show about the universe. The weather forecast for the coming days was bad, little chance they'll have to work tomorrow night, Ari could watch the show then. You've got to help me connect it and set it up for recording, I have no idea how to work this bloody thing. Ari hurries, his heart pounding with joy, surprise, shyness, and the universe comes in through the window to help him.

Wednesday passes slowly. It's snowing, cars get stuck in all the neighbourhoods, snowmen pop up, some of them looking like friendly aliens, but it passes, night draws in, and Ari has turned on the V.C.R., its wheels spin with the vastness of the universe and Carl Sagan, he appears on the screen, an American scientist, dark-haired, slim, with radiant eyes – and he transforms Ari's existence. Carl Sagan begins to speak. He speaks and moves his hands as if he's conducting a symphony. He speaks, and reality becomes glittering stars. How incredibly charming that man is, says the step-mother, and Ari is startled, so deeply immersed, so lost in space because of what Carl Sagan is saying, that he was unaware of his stepmother's presence, thought he was alone in the T.V. room, she'd come in without him noticing, leaned against the clothes cupboard where Jakob sometimes hides a bottle of vodka or rum, goes to get it when no-one can see him, has a swig, and the two of them pretend to know nothing about it. Jakob, of course, isn't at home, it's his second bridge night, things had gone well last night, he'd been very enthusiastic today, excited, glad, talked to Ari about English football, Kenny Dalglish is his man, whistled a catchy tune that Ari thought he recognised but couldn't put his finger on until he went to his room and read *A Farewell to Arms* by Ernest Hemingway while Jakob watched the news and weather forecast.

Hemingway is a great writer, and a lion hunter as well, it says in the afterword, noting that he's a lion hunter as if it's an honour he's won for shooting a lion from a safe distance with a powerful rifle, but Ari and I admire the book. Really admire it. We talk about it over saltfish and stockfish at Drangey, to the great joy of old Kristján, the old man is uplifted, almost as if he's floating. Hemingway, now there was a real man, he says, every sentence he wrote reflects that. But then he shot himself, he added, as if deep in thought, and the rest of us, Ari, Árni and I – Svavar had gone with Máni to Keflavík to fetch some footropes – were uncertain whether that was also a sign of manhood, to shoot yourself. Maybe there weren't any more lions in Hemingway's life, and that's why he shot himself. Ari and I had checked the book out of the library. What's this godforsaken interest you have in books? growled Halldór the librarian, checking out *A Farewell to Arms* and *The World of Yesterday* by Stefan Zweig for us, we grabbed that book after seeing Halldór thumbing through its pages. Don't you have anything better to do with your time? he asked, as if scolding us, utterly opposed to letting us go home with those books, but there was also a gleam in his eye, almost as if that feisty old dog was glad. Ari read *A Farewell to Arms* while waiting for the news to finish, along with the weather forecast, which his father hates to miss. Ari read: "'Oh, darling, darling, darling,' I said. 'You see,' she said. 'I do anything you want.'"

I do anything, "endless love", I love you so much I could die, shoot a lion, shoot myself, darling, darling, darling. Jakob whistled "Young Love", Ari remembered what song it was when he read "darling, darling, darling", put it on the gramophone, song number 3, the B-side of *Golden Hits of Rock 'n' Roll*, "they say for every boy and girl, there's just one love," but if that doesn't turn out to be true and you love two men, two women, unable to help yourself, you can tell your dog to sit, not your heart, if you suddenly love two women, two men, because something happened that was beyond your control, a meteorite hit the earth, hit our lives, so big that it didn't burn up in the atmosphere and change into a beautiful shooting star, a flash of light over your life, too big to burn up, and it hit you, threw everything out of whack, and nothing was as before, what do you do then, do you compose a requiem, run away from home but leave the telephone behind with dangerous texts on it, make a T.V. show about the cosmos? Young love, darling darling darling; Ari doesn't know any of this yet, he's just eighteen, young love, except that he loves no-one, not anymore, there was someone who got into a car with someone else, he pulled off her jeans, said, Darling, it will be alright, and raped her, darling darling darling, I do anything I want. Since then, he hasn't loved anyone, and is convinced that no-one will ever love him, for what is there to love, look at him, look at me, two boring nobodies who stutter out of shyness, flawed copies, easily forgotten. But then, Ari played the tape, Carl Sagan entered our lives. Open your arms, he said, because I'm bringing you the cosmos.

How incredibly charming that man is, says the stepmother, leaning against the clothes cupboard. Ari is embarrassed to hear her say such a thing, to discover that she thinks that way, and silently curses her presence, it's distracting, as if she's invading his space, watching something that was meant only for him, hopefully she'll go away. A charming man, she says, doesn't leave, continues to watch without sitting down on the sofa next to Ari, perhaps not feeling up to it, or showing him some small consideration. Carl Sagan continues speaking, he dives with them into the universe, and Ari forgets his stepmother's presence, or she no longer distracts him, the world is getting bigger, becoming better. The show is over.

Ari remains sitting there. The announcer appears on the screen, introduces the next show, now we get to see the detective and radio presenter Eddie Shoestring, translated by Dóra Hafsteins- dóttir. But the British detective show barely began, because the stepmother had abruptly switched off the recorder, the screen fills with snow, and then a new image appears, someone slips on the ice, repeatedly, he is obviously meant to be very drunk, it's obvi- ously meant to be very funny, is obviously from the New Year's comedy show aired two years ago. Ari remembers the scene, Laddi slipping and falling on the ice, Jakob had laughed so hard that he'd had to go down on all fours to catch his breath. The stepmother curses. Realises that she recorded onto the wrong tape, the one with the New Year's comedy show, the other one had some movie that would've been fine to tape over, her brother won't be happy, the cosmos for the annual comedy show. The stepmother curses. Had thought she would have a cosy night in with Jakob that Friday if the bridge tournament went well, could watch the New Year's comedy show with him, she remembered how much Jakob had laughed when Laddi slipped and fell. At the time, she'd been angry with him, he was drunk, she was stand-offish, everything was difficult, but not now, now they could laugh together, but her brother won't be happy. Ari gets up, ejects the tape, turns off the V.C.R., and silence returns, suddenly pouring in through the window with such force that the very panes seem to bend. The stepmother has sat down on the sofa, stares into space. Ari decides to go to his room; he wants to be alone, to think about the cosmos and continue reading, darling, darling, darling, I'll shoot a lion for you, why do you want to shoot a lion for me, do you want to show your love for me through death? To this, Hemingway had no answer – and so he shot himself.

Surprise

You can only see the stars when it's dark. Mum said that this was meant to remind us that the darkness can never turn off all the lights. The stars shine brightest during the heaviest winter months. She said that sometimes. My mother.

Ari stops in the doorway, tenses, his stepmother has never spoken of her mother like that – she'd never spoken to him like that. I didn't know, says Ari, not turning round, his back to his stepmother, that your mother was interested in stars.

There are a lot of things we don't know, whispers his stepmother, as if she hadn't meant to, hadn't dared to say it. Such innocent words. Ari bites his lower lip.

His stepmother: She looked at them a lot while she could, while she had decent eyesight, I mean. Now she can barely see her own fingers, the poor thing.

Ari has no idea what to say, whether he *should* say something, whether he wants to, or dares to, so says nothing, turns round, leans against the doorframe. There sits his stepmother, on the edge of the sofa, as if to say, I won't be sitting here for long. She stares into space, contemplatively, not dreamily, but her expression is open, wide open, her expression is beautiful.

Someone goes out into the cold with a woollen blanket

It can be so starry in the north, in the fjord that opens into Húnaflói Bay, in the far north of the world, such a crowd of stars on still winter nights that there seems little room for the darkness between them – yet it's the darkness that creates them.

The stars form countless constellations whose names have their roots in humankind's ancient cultures, in old stories, and for those who know these stories, the night sky is transformed into a giant book. This was why the stepmother's mother looked at the stars so much while she still had the eyes for it, while she saw considerably more of the world than her own fingers. Hallný, her name is Hallný, had, when she was young, around twenty, read a book about astronomy that she found in the district reading-society collection. It covered the main constellations, told where they could be seen in the sky and the stories behind their names. By the time she put the book down, the night sky had been trans-formed into an open book shimmering with ancient tales. Apart from all the unwritten ones that twinkle in nameless stars. The stepmother's mother has always suffered from poor health, though she never lacked for diligence, maintained a decent home, kept busy, both inside and outside the house, worked the seal pups as well as any man, was lightning fast at skinning them and stretch-ing the skins to dry, was so precise in her work that her skins were always first-rate. Yet she was in the habit of gazing at the stars. Not like other people who glanced up at them now and then – the starry sky called differently to Hallný than to other people. In the evening she often went to the door to have a look, leaned against the doorjamb, crossed her bony arms and just looked. Became lost in thought. Let the cold in, through her and into the house.

Returned to herself only when someone nudged her, then shut the door reluctantly and resumed her chores, of which there were many; the stars are certainly vast in number and captivating, we can certainly say a lot about them and draw lessons from them, but they've never done our chores for us. This Hallný knew, but sometimes she was so captivated, so absorbed, that she, well, shut the door behind her as she stepped outside, crossed the yard to the cowshed, or went further, down the hill, sat down there or leaned against a hay waggon, continued to look, to read the sky. Forgot that it was cold, that the cold arctic breeze breathed through her, no coat, nothing on her head, so skinny that it didn't take long for the cold to bite her. Mum is outside, someone would say when her absence was noticed, when an undone, unfinished chore drew attention to her absence, and her husband, the stepmother's father, the block, the taciturn one, muttered something that sounded like, More goddamned nonsense, grabbed a woollen blanket, a cap, went out to look for her, found her in the dark, beneath the stars, draped the blanket over her thin shoulders, stroked her head quickly, so quickly that you'd have thought your eyes were deceiving you, before he slipped the cap on. Stood with her for a while, looked as well. Then returned to the house.

One . . .

I've always found this beautiful, says Ari's stepmother, still perching at the edge of the sofa. What? asks Ari reflexively from the doorway, having been sucked so deeply into her tale, her reminiscence of times long gone, that he forgets himself, and for a moment it's as if there'd never been any silence between them. That my father went out with the woollen blanket, she says, and the cap, and stood with her . . . stroked her hair, unless my eyes fooled me; I was standing in the yard and it was dark . . . that he brought her a woollen blanket and didn't tell her to come inside, he who always found it kind of silly to gaze at the stars, let alone so poorly dressed and sensitive to cold as Mum was . . . she looks at Ari, stares at him, for more than a few moments, smiles faintly, and says unexpectedly, Do you know that you have your mother's eyes?

Ari runs his hand through his hair, pulls at it.

He's certainly charming, that man, the scientist, she says.

Carl Sagan, Ari says quickly, grabbing at his name. Yes, says his stepmother. That show was seriously enjoyable. I truly didn't know that the world was so big. I've got to tell Mum about him, that man. She would definitely have a crush on him! It's too bad I taped over the New Year's comedy show. My brother won't be happy.

two . . .

So love isn't, after all, I love you so much that I could die, you'll always be my endless love – but when someone goes out into the frosty night with a woollen blanket and a cap so that another person can keep gazing at the stars . . .

three

. . . which is why the stepmother's mother, Hallný, wept at her husband's funeral, that man who was taciturn, stocky and hard as stone, because who was going to drape a woollen blanket over her shoulders now?

Keflavík

"The cello drags a heavy sorrow ashore"

Pablo Casals plays "Nana" by Manual de Falla. He bows his cello, his "knee violin". Where do these notes come from – from within our pain, or do they arise out of deep longing? Ari had poured himself a glass of whisky, then doesn't touch it, he listens to Pablo and the memories come streaming, as if the cello doesn't drag a heavy sorrow ashore, as if all of life, death, drags Þóra ashore, his wife for more than twenty years, how she smiles, how she walks, softly, a bit like rain in a mild breeze. Also drags Katrín, whom he kissed, betraying Þóra with each kiss, yet still kissed because it was as if he had longed for her lips, her breath, her dark, melancholy eyes, for as long as he had lived. The cello drags his cloven heart ashore, his three children, triple responsibility, drags Árni, Svavar and Ásmundur as he handed us box cutters early that Saturday morning when we leapt onto the Yank lorries, it drags Jakob ashore, whistling "Young Love", and then Ari finally notices that his father has a beautiful smile, he sees it, and then the blow comes, Jakob's hard palm slams into Ari's cheekbone. He totters, he grabs for me but then is alone up on a heath, in that big hospital, walking down endless corridors in search of his mother. Maybe she is Pablo's cello, the cello that drags Sigga ashore, the wildcat, the wild flame, except that it's the stepmother, of course, who wades into the icy ocean, swims after Sigga, who intends to drown herself, turn off life, cut the cords, change into a silent instrument, Sigga, who punches and kicks at the stepmother, calls her a fucking cunt, but the stepmother swims back to shore with her, drags her out of the sea, lets her hit her, call her black names, and then they stand

217

there in the frost, drenched and chilled to the bone, shivering from the cold, the stepmother holds Sigga in her arms and they both cry at being alive; the cello drags all this ashore. Then the song ends.

"Nana". By De Falla.

Ari reaches for his stepmother's letter. It had been delivered in Copenhagen a few weeks ago, dated October 2, it was quite long, Sigga's article had been enclosed with the letter, "The Male World", with the subtitle "Those Who Have the Power Can Take". Take women. A woman is raped every twenty-two minutes in India. Kári took Sigrún to his car, yanked down her jeans, pushed her young legs apart and thrust his cudgel into her. Darling darling darling. Ari puts Pablo and De Falla back on. The cello drags a heavy sorrow ashore. And his stepmother's letter.

Sandgerði

OCTOBER 2

"I guess you shouldn't write letters unless it's to the director of the Co-op on behalf of your dad because they pay too little for sealskin."

Sandgerði, October 2

Now you're surprised; the old lady, writing a letter! Nor do I know how to do it correctly. It's been a long time since I last wrote a letter. It was back home in Oddi, sixty years ago. Sixty years! How ridiculous! It was when I wrote a letter to the Co-op manager for my dad, because Dad said that they priced the sealskins too low. Remembering it makes me want to eat seal meat and half-dried fish, so not another word about that. Sixty years is a long time between letters, so it's hardly strange that I don't know how to do it without embarrassing myself, and on top of that, I've never been confident about my blessed spelling. You'll have to be patient with me, just like I was patient with you when you were so clumsy, I'd never known anyone with so many thumbs as you, goodness me. Didn't I have to be patient with you sometimes? Have you heard from your dad? I hardly ever heard from him, as you know, and never after I started seeing Máni. I never hear from you either, or seldom, you're probably busy, I read about you in the papers sometimes, though I find that worse. Everyone seems to be in such a hurry nowadays, though I've no idea where everyone is going. When people were in a hurry up north, it was because they were late for a meeting, or something had to be brought in from a storm, those kinds of things. Getting old is strange. I've heard this and that about your father – and plenty of cause for concern. I guess it's no use talking to him, and definitely no use seeing him. Last time I went, he threatened to shoot me. He was drunk, though. Anyway, he doesn't have a gun. The three of us lived together for fifteen years, starting when you were just a child. Fifteen years is a long time, sometimes, and your dad threatens to shoot me. What would he threaten to do if we'd spent thirty years together rather than fifteen? Would he maybe get a gun then? Oh, I guess I'd have done something to deserve it by then! I made mistakes, probably said a lot of things that were ugly and hard to forgive. Jakob complained that I was too quiet, that my silence was poisonous. It's extremely difficult to know how you're supposed to be. My dad drank very little, mainly when he was angry about some injustice, or was depressed, as I guess we all become sometimes, or just because someone came for a visit and brought alcohol. He had a habit of getting drunk with a friend of his, Reverend Björn, and sometimes they would argue. Reverend Björn was as big as a polar bear. Mum would always banish them to the sheep shed when they were about to have a row; there they could break things but not in the house. The day after, Dad had always got over his anger, or sadness, or whatever it was that made him get drunk, except that he'd have a headache from the alcohol, of course, and was maybe swollen and bruised from fighting Reverend Björn. That man truly had giant hands. I was terrified of Reverend Björn as a child, convinced that he was either God or Death; I have no idea how that nonsense got into my head. For a time, I'd crawl under the bed when he came to visit, and hide there. Mum once pulled me out from under there and asked, "What's the meaning of this?" I told her how I felt, that I thought the Reverend was either God or Death. Reverend Björn laughed so hard that I could see every ruined tooth in his mouth, and of course I became even more frightened of him because of that. Mum spanked me, though not that hard; she wasn't very strong, poor thing, and did it mainly to show the priest that that nonsense didn't originate with her. She never really liked Reverend Björn, you see.

What's this rubbish I'm spouting? I really didn't mean to tell you all this; I'm astounded at myself. That's how it is when you start trying to do something you haven't a clue about; everything goes to pot. Now, where was I? Right, I wanted to say that perhaps I wasn't the best person for you and your dad, probably far from it. I also came into your life rather quickly. Far too quickly, I've sometimes thought. Your mum had just passed away, and I remember hearing you crying in your room at night sometimes, before you fell asleep. I should of course have gone to you but knew all too well that it wasn't me you were calling for; far from it – you were calling for your mother. I was little more than a kid myself and had no idea how to raise a child, let alone a nearly six-year-old motherless one. I didn't know what to say or to do, what clothes to buy, what food to cook. I remember that you never really liked seal meat and half-dried fish. I found that hard to understand, but I was certain you'd change over time and therefore decided to ignore your protests. It isn't always easy to look back at your life; the mistakes stare you in the face, big and small. I knew my way around lambs and knew how to get a sheep to adopt a poor little orphaned one, but those methods didn't help in getting children used to new mothers. Your father said you'd recover, get used to the changes. And you did, in your own way. I find it terribly sad that you and Þóra divorced. To tell the truth, I was astounded to hear it; you always seemed the perfect couple. I've sometimes thought it was my fault; I'm so stupid, of course, which is why I come up with strange ideas. That's why I heard you crying in the evening but didn't go to you. I don't know why I'm saying this. I guess you shouldn't write letters unless it's to the director of the

223

Co-op on behalf of your dad because they pay too little for seal-skins. Letters like the one I'm struggling to write now almost make you a different person. You have to look in the mirror to make sure you're still the same. Yes, I look in the mirror and see the same old wrinkled face! I can't write anymore. The fingers of my right hand have started to stiffen and the arthritis in my shoulder is acting up. I'll continue tomorrow, if I haven't tossed this rubbish out by then.

October 3
This is even worse than I thought. I'm deeply ashamed of myself for writing these things – my ugly old head must be cracked! So this is how old age treats you! But instead of tossing this letter in the bin, I'll keep going!

After I stopped writing yesterday, I looked through the photographs I have from these fifteen years of ours. There aren't many, maybe thirty, and I don't know what to say about them. These days you don't open a newspaper, turn on the T.V. or the radio without somebody going on about happiness, about love and feelings, as if everyone should know about them, as if they were everyone's business. If they're not blathering about their feelings, they're kissing their children or spouses, even in the corner shop, just to make sure that everyone will see them. I never saw my mum and dad kiss. It's as if everyone's supposed to be happy every single day, cheerful and energetic, and love their spouses more than can be expressed in words, or else your life is a failure. At least that's what it seems they're saying and thinking; it's hard to understand all this talk about feelings any differently. I read the other day that those who never talk about their feelings gradually become rigid, closed shells, and make things worse both for themselves and for those close to them. It isn't easy being so old and having it shoved in your face that your life is a failure.

You start thinking so many strange things when you get older. Worst is that I don't know if it's a sign of maturity or dementia. I was happy to meet your dad when I did; he was quite cute and lively, and I had the feeling that he was a diligent, tireless worker. He could be hysterically funny, too. I'd just come from the north and was extremely flattered that such a handsome man, a man with a good job and who even spoke English, was interested in me. He seemed to be from a good family out east. He used to tell me stories about his father, about his accomplishments and awards. Yes, I was a terrible nitwit, I must admit. I knew nothing of your mother's illness, not at first; didn't even know you two existed, neither you nor she. One night he told me about you, that he was married, that he had you and that his wife was dying, had been dying for two years or so. Then he started to cry. I've often thought about that, about him crying. About him bawling like a child. I've thought about what tears do, especially if people you think are strong start crying. I've sometimes felt as if I'd been conquered by tears. Yes, yes, goodness me, I had a massive crush on him, I found him so exciting, but it wasn't nice of him to hide the fact that he was married, that he had a young son and that his wife was dying. I wasn't sure I could forgive him for that. I remember that I intended to get up and leave; I didn't want anything to do with that sort of thing. But then he started crying, and I was won over. I saw your mother just once, a little more than a month before she passed away. You were at Silungapollur, which, at the time, was a home for children from broken and troubled homes. I went to see her at Vífilsstaðir without telling anyone, stalked like a thief through the corridors, avoided answering any questions, too much of a coward

225

to lie, so I just kept quiet. I couldn't tell the truth, that I was the mistress of the husband of this woman who lay there waiting for death, and that I was curious to see her before it was too late. I finally found her room; she was asleep. I stood over her for several minutes, spoke to her, but I don't know how much she heard; she was on a strong dose of morphine, I suspect. She was terribly skinny, the poor thing, and I spoke to her and spoke to her and she slumbered on morphine, if you can say that, which was probably why it was so easy to speak to her, to tell her whatever came into my mind. I may never have spoken so much as during those minutes. Suddenly she opened her eyes. They were big and so incredibly blue. She looked directly at me and I started thinking, without being able to help it, about the lake on the heath up north, and how enjoyable it can be to fish for trout there on summer nights. I don't know why I started thinking about that. You have her eyes, by the way. I think that that bothered me sometimes, and that's because I felt like I'd done you wrong. Could it have been the reason why I didn't go to your room when I heard you crying at night, when you were supposed to be sleeping? Because I'd done wrong, and it would have been dishonest, even fraudulent, to go to you like a comforting mother. I asked your mother to forgive me. I said, Can you forgive me for being with your husband? I simply can't control myself, but I mean no harm. I'm so sorry.

I don't know how much she took in, the blessed sweetheart, not yet thirty, hardly more than a baby, and that horrible disease had been eating her up for the past two or three years and there was nothing left of her but those big blue eyes. I'm not even certain she knew I was there. She looked at me with those eyes that seemed to see everything, understand everything. I stood there feeling like

I was being X-rayed. I moved in with you too soon. It was just a fortnight after the funeral. Your dad wanted me to come in the night, it would be better, after you'd fallen asleep. He said something along these lines, that then you would wake up into a new world, and would be quicker getting over the loss. I was making porridge when you came into the kitchen. You stopped in your tracks when you saw me. Your dad said that I was your new mummy. You weren't even six and I saw in your eyes that you would never forgive him. Or me. I remember that the light was very beautiful that morning. You may remember that the kitchen at Safamýri faces east, and the light was beautiful that morning, not strong – it was winter, of course – but beautiful. We'd got up late, which is why the sun was shining. That winter light brightened your eyes, so much like the eyes that had looked at me at Vífilsstaðir, and I felt them telling me that you would never forgive us. I just wanted to run away and not slow down until I was back in the north, at home. But I also thought, Stop this nonsense, he's just a kid. Anyway, it was out of the question for me to run away, I'd found in your dad something that I didn't want to let go of, just as he'd found something in me. You said nothing, just stared at me, but I saw you clench your fists, and for some reason I recalled the sheep back home, how they bleated in the autumn for a few days after their lambs were taken from them. You said nothing, just ate your porridge, like your dad, I stood there leaning against the kitchen cabinet. I've always appreciated silence, but I remember that that particular silence was quite hard. Your father sprinkled sugar over his porridge; I'd never seen anyone do that before. Then he left, late for work, and it was just the two of us. You were struggling with your porridge, which was way too thick for you; I didn't know that then, didn't realise until many mornings later. You sat there staring down at your porridge; we said nothing and I just felt like crying.

Well, my fingers are getting stiff again, and the arthritis in my shoulder is saying, Good morning, you old crone! I guess I'm writing to ask for your forgiveness, on behalf of both of us, Jakob and myself, I don't expect that he'd ever do anything of the sort, you know how he is. To ask you to forgive us for how we conducted ourselves after your mother's passing; for how I didn't come to you when I heard you crying, and for not trying harder to make up for your loss. I ask you to forgive me for making your porridge too thick for so long. Forgive me and Jakob for being the flawed things we are, and for doing so many things wrong. Hopefully you know that it was due to immaturity, not malice; far from it. I often tried to do things better but not enough came of it. You've always been stubborn. Sometimes it was as if you'd decided not to accept whatever came next. Coping always seems so hard.

I'll stop now. I already feel better for having written this. You mustn't think that I feel bad, because I'm fine. Máni and I even went to Spain last summer. Imagine that! And I've considered starting smoking again. Well, it's best to stop before I make even more of a fool of myself.

Second part

Keflavík

— PRESENT —

Go giggling down the slide with the ones we love

Things are lively on Hafnargata, people are hurrying hither and thither, frost and stillness hold up the sky and there's a pub quiz on Christmas at the January 1976 bar across from the New Cinema: which is the third Yule Lad to come down from the mountains; which shop gives a 50 per cent discount on everything tomorrow between 2.00 and 3.00 p.m.; what is St. Stephen's Day?

I see all this as I walk up Hafnargata. The questions, how the sky is being held up, who offers the biggest discount. Bylgjan radio is broadcasting live from Keflavík tonight, under the title "Keflavík Is Where It's At", and the radio personalities, that famous couple Sigmar and Kolla, stroll around town like pop stars. At 10.00 they'll announce the winners of "Love of Keflavík", people are being asked to phone in suggestions or leave comments on Bylgjan's Facebook page, to nominate the couple most in love in Keflavík. A fabulous prize will be awarded, and Björgvin Hall-dórsson, Bó himself, will sing to the winners in a live broadcast from the January 1976 bar. Bó himself is coming to Keflavík! We're going to reward love, shouts Sigmar, excited by the attention he receives here behind the world, and by the beer at the January 1976 bar. Love is what it's all supposed to be about, we should always be talking about love, and rewarding it, treasuring it; I love you, he shouts, I love Keflavík! Bylgjan's switchboard lights up, suggestions for the greatest love flow in, I can't help but hear it, Bylgjan resounds over Hafnargata, the lines are open, call in about love, I love you so much I could die – Helga and Siggi at Heiðar-bóli 12 have sixty-nine votes, Mayor Sigurjón and his wife have forty-six, others considerably fewer, but Svavar's tourist shop is open, he's standing in the doorway, holding a beer can, chatting with two brightly smiling women. Svavar is fun, the world is always a little bit better around Svavar. They laugh at something he says. Oh you, moans one of them between spouts of laughter. He smiles, sips his beer, has his phone in his pocket. He's hoping to hear from Snæfríður, who went on a date with a man she met on some chat site. Svavar encouraged her to go, she'd rung him, unsure whether to wear her purple dress or just jeans and a nice blouse. Wear the dress, he said, and swallowed his fear, scared to death that the man she was going to meet would fall head-over-heels for her, which he would do, of course. Svavar had sent her a text: "Call or text if you're bored, and I'll pick you up and we'll get drunk together!" But his phone is silent; silence can be so heavy that life can barely stop spinning its wheels.

I walk past just as Anna, Jakob's girlfriend, phones in to Bylgjan and tries to ruin everything by asking, How do we measure love, with a tape measure or life? Kolla bursts out laughing, shouts, You've got some nerve, granny, and switches to another listener.

That girl's as smart as a tyre, says Anna, putting her phone down; Jakob looks at her. You've always been so beautiful, he says. Even when I was lying under the Yank? she asks. Why didn't we get to be happy? he asks, and she says, Maybe I should have suggested us. I haven't loved enough, says Jakob, his voice trembling; there isn't much left of him, the cancer has spread like darkness, he's sitting on the sofa with a photograph album open on his lap, a stack of four albums on the table, looking at a photo of himself, the stepmother and his sister Elín, they're playing bridge at the dining-room table at Kirkjuteigur, the picture was taken by the skipper, Elín's husband, which is why he's not in it; he's the empty chair. They smile, but Jakob focuses on his cards; he's immersed in the game. She was quite beautiful, your second wife, the girl from Strandir, says Anna, I remember her well from when she was working at the Base, one of the few people who spoke to me like I was a human being. Maybe she's still beautiful, says Jakob, softly, as if he's surprised, or thoughtful. Is she happy with him in Sandgerði, the quota man? Happy, fuck that, what's happiness? asks Jakob, and his head trembles a bit.

What's happiness, Bó? shouts the radio presenter as I cross Hafnargata with the January 1976 bar on my right; Bó is on the phone, in a car on his way to Keflavík, and he replies immediately. Singing about love, Simmi, that's true happiness. You are beauty incarnate, screams the radio presenter. Beauty is finally coming to Keflavík, how will that go, I mutter as I enter the Flight Hotel, escaping the radio station that has occupied Hafnargata and the frost. Ari is waiting at the bar, has chosen a table by the window, just received a text from Helena, the woman who sat next to him on the flight from Copenhagen, and her fiancé, the huge, silent but happy Adam. They're having a good time. Went to three swimming pools today, tried out all the slides, tomorrow it's Eyjafjallajökull, where they're going to make love in a small tent while the guides wait in the big jeep at an appropriate distance. "God in Heaven, it's such fun to be alive," she writes, "but where did your happiness go, Icelander? Can't you find it again in your tears? By looking at the sky, or by giggling down the water slide with the one you love?"

That's not such a bad idea, I say, to go down a water slide with the one you love; whom would you take with you?

235

Ari doesn't answer, just looks at me, and in his eyes is the sadness that always makes me think of an abandoned puppy. Why do you have to have such eyes? asked Sjöfn, the hotel manager from Hólmavík, when she visited Ari in Copenhagen over a long weekend. They had met when Ari checked into her hotel in Hólmavík – after sweeping everything off the breakfast table and running away from Þóra, from his life.

I promise not to make a pass at you, wrote Sjöfn, adding a smiley face, when she asked if she could stay with him, but then whispered, Can you forgive me? after they were together, made love; that wasn't supposed to happen. They'd gone out to eat and were back in his flat, drank some whisky, he put an Asaf Avidan album on the C.D. player, smiled when she asked him to dance, with "Devil's Dance" on repeat. Some songs are impossible to dance to except when seeking comfort. Why do you have to have such eyes? Sjöfn had asked. You know, I don't know anyone whose embrace is as warm as yours, is it regret that makes it so warm? Then she asked, May I cry? and he replied by placing his hand softly on the nape of her neck, pressing her head to his shoulder. She cried and Asaf sang, "dance, little devil, dance". I'm soaking your nice pullover, she whispered, and the painful string in his chest quivered, the one that goes straight through his heart, cleaves it. Kiss me, she said, kiss me. We can't always be alone together, it's so difficult, it's so unfair, kiss me, and he did, kissed that beautiful, lonely woman, and then, as they lay there together, their rapid heartbeats slowing, she said, I'm sorry. He kissed her shoulder and said, Thanks for being so kind. Then she said, Do you know now which one of us you love more?

*

Which one of us you love more? I exclaimed. Ari rotates his beer glass, people trickle out of the bar. The giant bartender refuses to tune the radio to Bylgjan's live broadcast from Keflavík. This is supposed to be a sanctuary, he says when someone asks him to put on Bylgjan; Keflavík is where it's at. Keflavík, which has never been where it's at in Iceland's entire history. Instead, he turns up Gullbylgjan, where one classic follows another, almost all of them about love. Do you know now which one of us you love more? Ari rotates his beer glass.

God how I wish you would ignore this request of mine

At one point, he'd kissed Katrín with an eagerness bordering on desperation. Things didn't go any further on that occasion; her husband rang, and they broke off the kiss. It took him a long time to fall asleep that night, and it was difficult to wake up the next day, recalling Katrín's lips, her breath, hearing Þóra doing this and that, then teasing him for being so hungover, so spaced out. Most difficult was having betrayed the person who mattered most to you but not to feel guilty. Two mornings later, happiness coursed through his veins when he read a text from Katrín: "I awoke and missed your lips."

He read this, happiness coursed through his veins, the coffee brewed, Þóra read *Fréttablaðið*. Missed your lips.

A few weeks later, several dozen texts and dozens of emails later, Ari swept everything off the kitchen table and fled to Hólmavík but forgot his mobile, or left it behind, with all those texts on it. Fled from Þóra, from Katrín, everything else, the heavy baggage of blood. Fled because Oddur had hit Þórður at the same time as Jakob swept the curtains away from the window, hit Ari, shouted, hit his mother, knocking her into the refrigerator. Fled from all the blood, fled because suddenly he didn't know who he was, who he was supposed to be.

> You know better than anyone that a person who doesn't utilise his talents can never be happy, but will live in the shadow of what never was, but should have been.

It was as if Katrín's kisses had awakened him. Which made no sense; he'd been happy with Þóra, loved her so much that sometimes it hurt, had three children with her, triple responsibility, triple joy. That can't be called sleep; that's life. Yet it was as though her kisses had awakened him. For two days and nights he lay in Sjöfn's hotel in Hólmavík, which she sometimes called Heartbreak Hotel, and understood nothing. Weeks passed, and sometimes he put his head under a stream of ice-cold water, held it there, as if that would release him from the paralysing fact that he loved two women.

If he could love two, couldn't he just as well love three, or four, or maybe five?

And wasn't it pure chance that he'd had a life with Þóra and not someone else? Sturla, Gréta and Hekla – chance as well?

He who had believed that destiny had brought him and Þóra together. His entire existence had probably rested on that conviction: it was the foundation of his life.

Pure chance that he'd had a life with Þóra?

And therefore, a coincidence that they all became the people they are now, because we all must be shaped by the people with whom we share our lives.

*

Ari finishes his beer. Every table in the hotel bar is occupied. There's the American couple from last night; she's holding her tablet up to her eyes, laughing as he makes faces. Mayor Sigurjón comes in, greets people left and right, a young woman jumps up and buys him a beer. He attracts attention; power is sexy.

Ari looks at me apologetically. He and Katrín were together four times before he moved to Copenhagen, and it was beautiful. They were so ardent, couldn't help themselves, he was scared to death that the neighbours would complain, pound a broomstick on the floor. He fled overseas, had to get away, to catch his breath, get his bearings, torn between Þóra and Katrín, with whom he continued to exchange messages, and one time she came to be with him, was at a convention in Gothenburg, concocted a reason to go to Copenhagen. It was their best time, four days, they cooked together, went out to eat, lay in bed, made love, joked around, talked, were silent, gazed at each other, stroked each other. "It scares me how much I love you," she wrote after returning home, in an email, their record was fifty-four emails in one day. Full of love, passion, they discussed politics, books, their children, films, the best pizza toppings, and wept over not being able to show the world their love. But then she couldn't cope anymore; her last email:

"I want you to write to me; I need you to write to me. I love you so painfully much and can barely think about anything but you. I long to see your name appear in my inbox, practically jump every time it comes up, am filled with joy, excited as a girl. I gaze constantly at your pictures, shut my eyes and you start kissing me, you start biting me softly here, harder there. My God, how much I love you, beautiful beautiful man. But I must ask you to stop writing to me. I beg you not to reply if I'm not strong enough, give in and send you a message. I ask you to delete it, unread. I can't do this anymore. I can't love two men. It's killing me. I'm shrivelling up, sleep badly, can't concentrate, respond to people with nonsense. My dear, darling husband is worried, I can see it in the way he looks at me, sense it in how considerate he is towards me. My God, if he knew . . . it would destroy him, for which I could never, ever, ever forgive myself. My love, darling, if you love me, don't write to me again, and don't reply if I'm not strong enough to restrain myself. God how I wish that you would ignore this request of mine!"

Reykjavík

— THE 1960S —

Love throws us to the lions

I'm sorry I bit your shoulder before, she says.

She has come home from the herring, Ari's mother, so passionate that she bit Jakob's shoulder when he was inside her. So hard that he yelled involuntarily, which frightened her; she kissed his shoulder, said, Sorry, my love, sometimes I just want to devour you.

He forgives her completely, despite feeling the bite at work the next day, when he raises his arm, feels her teeth, the excited life. Happy that she's back, to know she's at home on Skaftahlíð, resting after the herring and seafaring, he tucks the bedcover around her before going out into the autumn morning, because autumn is coming, tucks her in and tells her to go back to sleep, she's exhausted, of course, it isn't natural for women to be at sea, in the fish guts, the pitching and rolling, he strokes her hair, kisses her forehead. You're so good, she mutters, far too good for me, I'm so flawed. Don't say that, you're the best thing I know, he says, and kisses and kisses her and grabs his coffee and lunch and goes out into the morning, steps out into the darkness, "young love, first love, filled with true devotion". Jakob walks briskly to work, swings his arms, both strong and soft, it's hard work, it toughens and strengthens your muscles to lift bags of cement, plaster walls, shovel material into a concrete mixer. He smiles. What luck to be young and in love, nothing ahead but possibilities, endless life. He whistles, strides across Klambratún Park, whatever the weather, looks forward to going to work, looks forward to life, but she shoves the bedcover aside, jumps out of bed, hurriedly puts on a pot of coffee, goes into the little storage room, grabs the stack of papers that she hides under some cleaning rags, sits down at the kitchen table, lights a cigarette and continues writing the short story where she left off yesterday. Enthusiastic, happy, excited, but it also feels as if she's betraying Jakob. Tired out from being at sea? No, quite the opposite, trembling with incomprehensible energy, sits there writing for three, four hours a day, for two weeks, writes four short stories, forty-six pages in all, she writes and it's as if she goes deeper into herself with every word. These are strange stories, she doesn't know where they come from. Two wonderful weeks. Can hardly wait to hear Jakob shut the door behind him, then jumps out of bed, watches him disappear down the street and continues writing these strange stories. It's not nice to lie, it's the worst to lie to the one you love, but she can't control herself, keeps lying, lying to Jakob, she'll probably burn in Hell for this.

Enough of your nonsense, says Veiga, her paternal aunt, the sister of Lilla, about whom we told you, the only poem Lilla wrote in her long life was when death came and took her eight-year-old daughter, then she wrote a poem, as if the poetry was supposed to stop death. Veiga is the oldest of four siblings, has published a book of poetry and is working on her first novel, she also paints, plays Chopin and Erik Satie on her piano. They occasionally meet at Lilla's house, Veiga lends her books, Virginia Woolf, Jean Rhys, and says, Enough of your nonsense, don't be such a bloody witch. For too long, many thousands of years, we've had to keep our talents under wraps, our passions, desires, have had to take care of the children, do the cooking, do the laundry, while the men have been able to do whatever they wanted. We're the leftovers, we're meant to be mothers, housewives, prostitutes, and it's never been accepted when we tried to step out of those roles. That's why we've got to be like a resistance movement and follow hidden paths, develop and gain strength before we come up to the surface. Otherwise they suffocate you at birth. Not out of malice, simply out of the *naïveté* of supremacy.

Don't ruin the girl, says Lilla as she makes cocoa, she isn't you, allow her to be happy, and Jakob is a lovely boy. Veiga, smiling, looks at Ari's mother, smiles beautifully and says, The girl is happy because she is young.

Jakob comes home from work, kisses her, it's "young love, filled with true devotion", she hides her stories and her guilty conscience under the cleaning rags, says she visited Lilla but says nothing about Veiga, they don't see eye-to-eye, Veiga and Jakob. It's as if she hates men, he said once, before adding involuntarily, unable to restrain himself, hates them as much as she's gone after them. Then they had a row, both said dreadful things, she rushed into the bedroom, slammed the door behind her, he threw himself onto the sofa, let off steam by shouting into a pillow, fell asleep but woke up half an hour later to her kisses. My love, she muttered, forgive me, I don't understand how I could say all those ugly things to you, maybe it's best that we don't speak about Veiga. Yes, he mumbled through her kisses, you're right. My love, she whispered.

Love, says Veiga to Ari's mother, equals defencelessness; it throws us to the lions.

She smokes. Squints through the fug, laughs quietly, as if to soften her words. Lilla brings cocoa and crullers. Oh, says Veiga, I always feel safe with you, sister, and she shakes her beautiful blonde hair. It grew back. She lost it in Norway. Lived there for twenty years. Went there at eighteen to work, met a Norwegian man, it was love, a grand passion, then came three children, then came days of unemployment, struggle, then came the war, the Germans came, and one of them had big brown eyes. She'd slipped on some ice and fallen, hit the ground hard, felt a pain in her hip, someone bent over and proffered a hand to help her to her feet. She looked up, straight into those big brown eyes. Didn't see the uniform, the nationality, the world war, just saw the depths of those eyes, and then a hint of sorrow in his beautiful face. It was the winter of 1942. Now I'm a German whore, she thought the first time they kissed, knew that it was wrong, every bit of it, but couldn't stop herself. Love has never taken circumstances, class, enemy lines, distances or age into consideration. He could be so beautiful and fiery when he entered her that it was as if she was alive for the first time. Nothing could hold her back. Not threats, prayers, tears, her husband's fists or the growing contempt and open hostility of her neighbours. Love is blind, unbridled, it throws us to the lions. When the war ended, everything was turned upside down in a single day. The Germans, who had been in control of everything, who had ruled with terror and weapons, were suddenly defenceless prisoners. Now you'll reap what you sowed, her husband said calmly, as if talking about the weather; they stood at the living-room window and watched people gather in the street to celebrate. Veiga looked at her husband; he was beautiful in the light coming in through the window. I've never stopped loving you, she said, just so you know that, and I completely understand that you hate me. Grabbing her coat, she went out, pushed her way through the celebrating crowd, cast off the remaining shreds of social standing to try to speak to him, but was left with nothing. He was gone, and no-one could, or would, say where. A few days later, she got to see his belongings, his books, records, clothes, before they were sent home to Germany. She got to see his bloody clothes, they asked if she wanted to wash them, his tattered trousers, his shirt, jumper, jacket. He was one of five hundred Germans who were made to clean up the landmines that they themselves had laid in northern Norway. They crawled around, dug them up, defused them, hardly daring to breathe, but didn't find them all and were therefore ordered to walk over the area, in a line, shoulder to shoulder, to ensure that no mines were left in the ground, which was a good thing because they'd over-looked quite a few: 184 were killed, 225 were wounded. He was in the first group. The explosion was so powerful that his genitals were blown off. She was informed of this; it was specified. She was allowed to take his bloody clothes home to wash them, on the condition that she return them in two days. Then they would be sent, along with the rest of his belongings, to Germany, home to his wife and two children. She knew that he was married, of course?

Two young men waited outside for Veiga. They escorted her downtown, brought her to a pleasant back garden where six women whose heads had been shaved stood ready in a cattle waggon, holding on to its grating like abandoned children, watching dully as Veiga was made to sit on a chair, her head was shaved with shearing clippers, then she was made to climb into the filthy waggon decorated with two big banners: GERMAN WHORES! TRAITORS!

Then they were driven around the town centre. It was quite a show.

What is love – to love so much that you are willing to betray your country, betray your spouse, sacrifice everything, be thrown to the lions? Veiga smokes. Don't ruin the girl, says Lilla, and Veiga smiles; awaiting her at home is husband number three, a writer like herself, alcoholic, bitter, a disease endemic to that line of work, but sometimes lovely, a companion, holds her in the night, you couldn't ask for more, life probably doesn't have enough happiness for everyone.

He reads the cognac, drinks the story – night

Ari's mother came home from the herring with fistfuls of money; she had a wad of bills in her purse, what a catch, a shock for Jakob when she took it out laughing, he stared at the bills and for a second he seemed to have shrunk, but then she laughed so heartily at the look on his face that it was impossible not to smile. Later that autumn, on the verge of winter, they buy a flat in a block in Safamýri, despite being so young, her wad of bills is enough for the down payment. She's so proud and excited that she has a hard time sitting still as Jakob signs the papers, and then chats with the estate agent, who offers him a cigar, they talk about the country's prospects, they talk about politics. Bloody leftists, says the agent, and Jakob has so much respect for older people and the big desk that he feels he can't object; bloody leftists will bankrupt us as soon as their turn comes, and then we'll have to clean up after them. But there's always hope as long as young men like him know how to make good lives for themselves, plan ahead and are thrifty. Even better if they have such radiantly beautiful wives, he says, enjoying watching her fidget in her seat. Old bastard, she thinks, but accepts the chocolates he offers her.

That evening, they go out to dinner. They need to celebrate; her father and Norwegian stepmother invited them to dinner, but

Jakob wanted to make it a grand occasion and takes her to Naustið. That it doesn't get any more elegant in this city is clear from the fact that they're the youngest patrons in the place, a bit shy with the courteous, cosmopolitan waiter, they order a whole rib roast served with béarnaise sauce, *pommes frites*, *pommes au four* and French peas. She nearly chokes with laughter as Jacob pronounces these incomprehensible, ridiculously exotic words: *pommes frites*, *pommes au four*. The waiter, a middle-aged man with greying hair, addresses them both respectfully, as if they belong nowhere else. The red wine arrives. Jakob and the waiter look so serious as the latter pours some wine into Jakob's glass, Jakob tastes it, nods and says, Absolutely first-rate, that she can't take any more, it's simply too much, stands up, whispers, I'm sorry, excuse me, hurries to the loo, has to cross the dining room, pass numerous tables, people look at her, middle-aged Icelanders and a few foreigners, embassy staff, this remote capital city has only two acceptable restaurants with decent food but, sadly, rather lacklustre wine, and of course no beer. They watch the young Icelandic woman hurry across the room, past the tables, half-running as if she really needs to get to the loo or feels ill, because she's holding her mouth, has probably drunk too much too quickly, most Icelanders can't hold their liquor, are so primitive, but at least this young woman looks almost elegant with her hair swept up, wearing a beautiful green dress that looks lovely on her, fits her like a breath, both reveals and conceals her small but firm breasts. She would be stunning if she only knew how to present herself, mutters a French embassy employee. It's sophistication that makes a woman beautiful, chimes his colleague, but they are splendid breasts, perfectly suited for export. The other man agrees – she barely reaches the loo, manages to shut the door, before the laughter gushes out of her.

They aren't used to red wine, aren't used to drinks that are 14 per cent alcohol and taste rather nice; after three glasses she stops trying to smother her giggles and becomes so unrestrained that she gets the waiter to teach her how to pronounce the name of the dish, *pommes au four*. The waiter, smiling, watches her lips, the lower one is plumper, making her look voluptuous. The waiter stares, Jakob notices and empties his glass. She laughs so contagiously that the waiter laughs with her and says bravo when she manages to pronounce it correctly for the third time. *Bravo* is yelled from a table not far from them, where two men, probably just over thirty, applaud, making her look down, suddenly shy again, but so beautiful that Jakob's heart pounds. Shortly afterwards, another bottle of red wine arrives at the table. From the French gentlemen over there, says the waiter, smiling, nodding at the two Frenchmen, who smile and bow in return, one lifts his glass and says something in French that no-one understands, not the waiter, not Jakob, not her, not us, none of us knows a single word in French, which is no good of course, which is a deficiency of course, a sign of poverty, the Frenchman repeats what he said in broken English: For the beauty!

For the beauty. All for her. Here's to her! The evening passes. They order dessert and she suddenly seems shy to Jakob, reaches into her handbag and takes out a magazine that she'd somehow managed to stuff into it, smooths it out, he recognises it, a literary magazine that his mother had a subscription to as far back as he could remember. Look, Kobbi, she says, and her slim fingers tremble as she opens the magazine and points at her name in the table of contents: Imagine that, Kobbi, my name! A story by me!

Yes, imagine that.

He looks at the magazine. It's as if he can't see straight, the heavy food, the exotic environment, the red wine, the people around them speaking foreign languages. He looks. There's her name. She has a short story in the magazine. Which Margrét will read back east in Norðfjörður, as will Áslaug and Tryggvi at Vatnsleysuströnd, and then they will write to him, proud, excited, about her, about him for having her for a fiancée. They've always been so . . . excited about such things, literature. Margrét tried to provide him with all sorts of books but gradually stopped, said nothing about it, although Jakob could sense her disappointment. Could sense . . . She's saying something, she's talking about the story in the magazine . . . no, that she'd written a lot of stories, or tried to write . . . he doesn't catch it all, his mind is a jumble . . . the red wine, the pudding, foreigners, the Frenchman toasting her . . . the dress that suits her so well, tight yet so light on her. She'd had it adjusted without telling him; came home today with a long, slender box, went into the bathroom, came out in the dress, so breathtakingly beautiful that he was almost struck dumb, and thought, Dear God, how beautiful she is! But also thought, That must have cost a pretty penny! Which it did, she showed him the receipt, paid for it with her herring money. That's her money, not his, he thinks, the magazine in his hands. Apparently she's written a lot of stories. When did she do that, he had no idea that she was writing stories, shouldn't he have known about it, does that mean he doesn't know who she is – doesn't she give herself entirely to him?

Every man needs his freedom, Kobbi, Siggi had said to him that night up at the Base, as they stood beneath the sky above Miðnesheiði, the Yank had gone into the flat with the women, the two girls, he'd grabbed their bottoms playfully and pushed them along, and now they hear the sound of laughter and rock music. Every man needs his freedom, repeated Siggi, this time to himself, thoughtfully, as if reminding himself of something important. Freedom, said Jakob, is found at sea, freedom means to sail, I can't tell you the number of times I've heard my dad say something along those lines. Siggi glanced over at his friend, swallowed the last of his beer, squashed the can between his strong fingers, tossed it into the darkness. You've never been to sea, have you? No, and I guess I've never been free, said Jakob with an abrupt laugh, before accepting another beer that Siggi pulled out of his pocket. The sky was silent above them. Strange that something so vast can be so silent. Freedom, said Siggi, is for those who dare; what a night this is going to be!

Why has that night at the Base come back to haunt him? He would rather erase it from his memory. Jakob pours some wine into his glass and begins to read her story:

> It's pouring with rain. It streams down the window and forms puddles on the roads and pavements. I feel I must describe these events, even if no-one will believe me. Or wants to believe me. It's raining so hard; I'll smoke a ciga-rette, and tell you of things as true as the word of God.

No, don't read it now, not here, Kobbi, she says, I'll be embarrassed!

I didn't know you were writing, he says as he stops reading, let alone that you'd been published in this magazine; Mum will be happy, that's for sure!

She is so happy that her eyes shine. I'm so happy, she says, let's drink a toast! Which they do, toast their happiness, the flat, the story, the life that awaits them, stretching as far as the eye can see, with children, travel. And maybe books by me, she says with a laugh, and he laughs as well, and the evening passes and the waiter delivers a message from the two Frenchmen, would they like to come and sit with them? Jakob is about to say no thank you, has no interest in bloody Frenchmen, but she has stood up, says, Oh, let's go over, Kobbi, it's not every day that you get to talk to foreigners, and then she's halfway over to the table, making it a bit late to protest. They order cognac for Jakob, sherry for her, and she's not shy about speaking to them in English, doesn't hesitate, while he can barely utter a word, despite his English being much better than hers and the two Frenchmen's combined, he was often complimented for it, the year he worked at the Base. One of the Frenchmen recites a poem to her in French. By Paul Éluard. One should only speak to women in poetry, and only Éluard can describe how beautiful you are. Young man, he says to Jakob, placing a hand on his shoulder, let me know if you die, for I shall then treasure this jewel of yours all my life!

Cognac is a heavy drink, Jakob's heart is thudding, the three of them talk, laugh, he reads the story she wrote without his having had any idea of her doing so. What else is she hiding from him? Didn't she say that her aunt Veiga had encouraged her to submit the story, that fucking old crone! She laughs . . . and looks at the man who recited the poem to her in French. The poem – probably little more than goddamned smut, these bastards are nothing more than their dicks, look at my poem, they say, and pull down their trousers.

He reads the cognac, he drinks the story . . . which is about a young woman. She is completing a mathematics degree at university, is having an affair with one of her professors, he's married, twenty years older, but says that he loves her and that they share so many beautiful things. Then he starts to feel strangely uncomfortable when he is inside her, almost as if his penis is shrinking. The feeling worsens. One night he "pulls out in a panic, rummages in his desk, takes out a ruler: his penis is only twelve centimetres long. It has shrunk by five centimetres!" She tries to calm him, knowing that most men are both preoccupied with and sensitive about the size of their penises. It's just a coincidence, she says, then adds that his penis was never more than fifteen centimetres, is about to say that that's more than enough, is just right for her, but then he hits her, fist clenched, she's knocked against the wall, falls to the floor unconscious. He's gone when she comes round, just a little message, that she's a witch, and he's going to make sure that the whole world knows it. Which is exactly what happens, it's as if everything turns against her. Weeks later she's roaming the streets, homeless, in bad shape, when a middle-aged man takes pity on her, gives her some food, speaks to her nicely, starts stroking her hair, tries to kiss her, she asks him to stop, he becomes angry, pushes her down and rapes her. He hasn't been inside her for long when he screams in pain, leaps to his feet – his penis has shrunk so drastically that it's little more than a shred of skin . . . The story ends with her on the run from a large group of men, young, middle-aged, old, they're just about to catch her, she's exhausted, about to give up and allow the men to overtake her, but suddenly decides to cut off both her breasts and throw them to them – and their interest in her seems to vanish. What's more, she can suddenly run much faster, disappears among the mountains, the rocks on the mountainside shiver as she runs past, the stars sparkle above her, and it's a shorter distance to them than between her and the men.

It's night, it's so much night that Jakob feels completely lost. As if life is happening in the distance. As if there's a cocoon around him, preventing him from getting close to anyone, from anyone getting close to him – except they did leave Naustið with the Frenchmen. Who invited them home, to a fancy flat in the western part of town. Jakob has another cognac in his hand, the Frenchmen have put on some music, wild jazz, bloody barbarian. They dance like madmen and she dances too, not madly, moving slowly, like a flower in a sluggish stream . . . strange, that's how Anna had danced as well, at the Base, tonight a star, because her name is Anna, the silent one, the shy one.

My name is Anna, she told Jakob, I didn't expect any Icelanders to be here, Emma said there would just be Yanks, and only officers. We were playing bridge on the Base, said Jakob apologetically. That's O.K., my English is really bad anyway, she said. Cheers, he said. Cheers, she said, and they drank and smiled at each other. She's cute, he thought, has cute dimples. You know what, she said, but then a Yank pulled her away to dance to the wild jazz that had taken over from the rock 'n' roll, and the night was a night and everyone was dancing and drinking and yelling, and Jakob was no longer sure whether he was dancing at the Base or here in west Reykjavík, not sure what night it was in the world. He'd wanted to touch Anna so very much, and he did, stroked her back, her waist, but then one of the Yanks had pushed Jakob, thrown his arms round Anna and kissed her neck and she'd screamed, they were so deep into the night that there was probably no way back. Cheers, yelled Jakob, but no-one paid attention because there was just the jazz, someone blew like a devil on a trumpet and one Yank threw up in a flower pot, another had squeezed himself behind the T.V. and fallen asleep there, two carried a giggling Emma into the bedroom, she was half-naked, her big breasts loomed at Jakob as if they were calling to him, he had never seen such big breasts and instinctively followed them, watched the three fall giggling onto the big bed, and then one of them was inside her, pounding her from behind and Jakob saw her breasts jerk and swing, while Siggi and Sid, who'd brought the girls, were kissing Anna, appearing for a time to hold her up, she muttered something and then they laid her on the sofa and Jakob staggered over to the gramophone, the jazz record was finished and the silence wasn't good, the records lay in a pile on the floor, few of them in their sleeves, he saw the name Elvis Presley, put him on: "Wise men say, only fools rush in." Siggi had pulled down his trousers. He's got a bigger dick than me, thought Jakob, and felt somehow sad when he saw his friend's erect, hard and quivering penis. Siggi parted her knees and entered her, had to push, shove, use force to get in, but he managed it, and then gasped, shut his eyes, "Shall I stay, would it be a sin," Sid took off his trousers without taking his eyes off them and Jakob felt almost grateful when he saw that Sid's penis was smaller than Siggi's, who opened his eyes wide, groaned deeply as he pulled his penis out and his semen gushed over her skirt, onto the sofa, "Like a river flows surely to the sea," someone yelled and moaned in the bedroom, Jakob swallowed, but Sid impatiently pushed Siggi aside. Move, man, you aren't the only one with a dick, you know. Shut the fuck up, you goddamned moron, growled Siggi, pulling up his trousers. Sid pushed him again, impatient for his turn, but then Siggi turned and punched him, hit him two, three, four times in the face, heavy blows, heavy fists. Anna staggered to her feet,

grabbed at air, Jakob caught her just as she fell and helped her out
into the night where the stars were on the verge of dropping the
sky, dropping that heavy darkness over the earth, and Siggi came
running out with a six-pack of beer. Let's get out of here, he said,
and grabbed Anna, and they ambled off towards the Officers'
Club where they'd parked the car. Anna slipped out from under
Siggi's arm and the three of them walked off with the darkness
between them . . .

. . . just like Jakob and Ari's mother as they walked away from the
Frenchmen's flat somewhere in the western part of the Milky Way.
They pass Landakot church, which is so shrouded in darkness that
God probably doesn't exist. She turns onto Suðurgata and Jakob
follows, past the old churchyard, it had been such fun to dance,
cosily drunk, nice to flex her body dreamily in the dance. If only
I could dance like this for a thousand years, she thought, but
then one of the Frenchmen had taken off his shirt, the one who'd
recited the poem, he'd been so polite and fun and she'd never met
a man with such a genuine interest in poems, and he seemed to
know so much, but then he'd taken his shirt off and was no longer
interested in poems, just his abs, his biceps, he's beautiful, for sure,
it's not that, but how he started to touch her, dance uncomfortably
close to her, force himself on her, make her feel his hard penis,
perhaps convinced that she would be as impressed by that as by
the poems, which was so sad that she couldn't even get angry, just
closed her eyes, kept on dancing, escaped into movement, but
then he moved even closer, she pushed away his right hand only
to find the left one somewhere else, and it was then that Jakob
shouted something and kicked the Frenchman hard in the knee,
then in the stomach, and they were out on the street and seemed

somehow to be holding the darkness up between them, yet that day had started so wonderfully. She, excitedly looking forward to signing the papers, to putting on her dress, looking forward to showing him the magazine, looking forward to seeing his face, telling him what the editor, a well-known media personality, a well-known writer, had said, that her story was "unusual and daring". She'd bought an extra copy of the magazine and posted it to her sister, who is studying theatre in Vienna, they write long letters to each other, and she'd looked forward to the reaction of Margrét, Jakob's mother, whom she'd only met once, an older woman, her movements a bit heavy, stiff, with a low voice, but her eyes sparkled, and Margrét whispered, My child, when they embraced before parting.

They cross Þingholt and suddenly she realises that Jakob has barely said a thing since they moved to the Frenchmen's table. Did she pay too much attention to the Frenchmen, did she seem so interested that they misunderstood and thought she was . . . up for it? If so, Veiga was right: it's impossible for a woman to show interest in a man without him getting an erection – makes no difference whether he's an educated man with a passion for poetry or a rustic sailor on a herring boat – does poetry do nothing to make their feelings more profound?

Jakob still has the rolled-up magazine in his left hand, hasn't said a word about the story, even though he has definitely read it, she saw him do it. Is he angry at her, then? She hadn't really thought about whether the subject might affect him badly, Veiga had asked if Jakob had read the story, and said that it was unlikely to make him happy.

He's holding the magazine like a club.

Are you angry at me? she asks at Klambratún, startling Jakob, they haven't said a word since leaving – or rather, fleeing – the Frenchmen's flat. Are you angry? she asks again, when he says nothing; do you think my story is ugly? The editor praised it, you know who he is, and Veiga said that . . .

Veiga!

They're both startled when he shouts her aunt's name, startled that he should shout in the stillness of the night. Jakob clears his throat, feels anger course through him. I should have known, he says, that she was involved in all . . . of this . . . and when did you write this story, might I ask, why couldn't I know anything about it, or am I maybe so stupid that you didn't feel like telling me, let alone ask my opinion about it? Is there maybe more that I don't know about you, more that you're hiding from me . . . and how on earth did you get the idea to write . . . this?! Is this what you think, then? What do you think people will say, what do you think my friends will say, if they read this? They'll probably think you're half nuts, like that drunkard, your mother, and that . . . crazy aunt of yours, and what will they say about me, huh? Maybe they'll think it's about us, huh? Maybe they'll call me Dickless Kobbi from now on?

Can you offer me a better life?

They walk up Skaftahlíð, she and Dickless Kobbi. Say nothing. His shout still seems to echo in the night. The commotion has reached the stars. A car drives slowly down Miklabraut.

They'd driven through the night to Reykjavík, Siggi and Dickless Kobbi, but not Anna, she went back, didn't want to leave her girlfriend behind. Enough of your nonsense, said Siggi, don't be so bloody stupid. Why go back there! You know what they want from you, those losers? Yes, she replied, the same thing as all of you, except with them I've got a chance at a better life, a chance to go to America and get away from this shitty island, this fucking wet old rock! You think you can offer me a better life, can you offer me anything besides your cock, are you interested in offering me anything else? She started walking back. Go to hell then, damned Yankee whore, yelled Siggi after her, and they drove off, the cop at the main gate so sleepy that he couldn't be bothered to come out, just waved them through, Siggi smiled and waved back, grabbed another beer, took a big gulp, passed it to Jakob, who drank, the car cleaved the darkness. Why didn't you do anything in there? asked Siggi. What was I supposed to do? Don't be such an idiot, you know what I mean; are you asexual? I didn't make it to Anna because of you, so I went to the bedroom, where Emma was, you should've seen her fucking breasts!

Siggi looked at him.

Everything is clear. Everything

They're in the basement flat. She takes off her shoes. He pours some vodka into a tall glass. Asexual Kobbi. Dickless Kobbi. He'd put the magazine on the kitchen table, or perhaps thrown it there, but now he's holding it again, like a club. She pours herself a glass of milk. It wasn't as if she'd found those Frenchmen tiresome, or taken it badly when they groped her. It's good to drink. It puts the world to rights. He pours more vodka into his glass. Siggi had looked at him. She finishes her milk. He tosses the magazine to her. Or at her. You, he says. You're just like your mother after all, a drunk with a new guy every month. Like Veiga, who fucked

260

Germans. Nazis. She's nuts. Your sister changes boyfriends more often than clothes. She's nuts, too. You're all nuts. Nuts! Nuts! Fucking nuts! Kobbi dear, she says. Kobbi dear, he mimics. Kobbi dear, she pleads. I'm Dickless Kobbi, he screams, he laughs. He kicks a chair. Kicks it again, and then something cracks inside him and wonderful energy rushes through him and he sees everything clearly. Everything. Everything is clear. Everything. He clenches his fist.

My brother in drink.

comfort

my fist
my brother in drink, disappointment, inadequacy
my comfort, my outlet
when everything fails, when
words betray, when
I don't want to hear
more,
when nothing is beautiful anymore
when life spits on me
my comfort, my
fist, my brother

Eastfjords

— PAST —

She thinks, This is nice

October, and the stars have vanished. There's scarcely been one clear sky the entire month, as if God felt she'd seen enough – though she did nothing bad. All she did was feel the warmth of his skin on the telescope eyepiece; that was it. And sensed his presence as they stood there together, as he talked about Jupiter's moons, explained gravity, how the Moon, for instance, pulls on the sea, and then she may have felt his gravity, how it pulled her blood to his. But she didn't do anything bad. Offered him her hand in parting; I thank the headmaster for his lesson, I doubt I'll ever look at the sky the same way again. He pulled the glove off his right hand and took hers, more firmly than she'd expected he would, more strongly, yet gently, and let his rest briefly in her palm. She still felt his gentle strength when she awoke the next morning. He had asked, without letting go of her hand, whether they should do this again . . . it's certainly more pleasant to gaze with others, as well as it being a joy for him to be allowed to teach her. Yes, thank you for the offer, since the headmaster is so . . . Please, call me Þorkell, he said.

Then the stars vanished.

What became of the blessed sky, Margrét sometimes says to Elín, it's usually the two of them at home during the day, Oddur and Þórður are at sea, or patching up the fishing gear, tending to things in the fishing shed, Hulda at the fish factory, Ólöf and Gunnar at school. Elín is so unhappy about not starting school, a whole year until it's her turn, that some mornings Margrét walks to the school with her, making sure that they're a good distance away from Gunnar, it mustn't look as if he needs to be accompanied. Sometimes Margrét and Elín even enter the foyer of this first concrete building in the village, but only for a moment or two, Margrét doesn't want to show herself too much. Come, silly, she says to Elín, pulling her out of the door. Once, however, her name is spoken, and he rests his hand on her shoulder, lightly. You're here, he says. No, not really, she says, it's my Elín, this little one here, who is so unhappy about not starting school that I walk here with her some mornings. The headmaster kneels down to Elín, speaks to her as if they've known each other a long time, and Elín looks as if she'll devour him with her eyes. The stars are hiding, he then says to Margrét – that was ten days ago.

They haven't gone into the foyer since then. Next time, Margrét always says, pulling unhappy Elín home with her.

Yes, she had said, they're so naughty, and she felt the force of gravity, the power of attraction. Later that day she saw the wife of Hjálmar the shopkeeper, so self-assured and beautiful, with her soft, gentle voice and regal bearing. Margrét reached for some raisins, pulled her hand back in a flash. How terribly ugly her hands are, she's never thought about it before; they resemble old fish. October passes through them, then comes November with snow, worse road conditions, the postman will be delayed, Margrét has to wait longer for *Skírnir*. The headmaster walks by with his telescope. Maybe she should go after him; our lives are so short and we mustn't die without knowing something, and she needs to talk to him about Þórður, too, needs to ask the headmaster to speak to the boy about his education, how much talent he has, he mustn't squander it. But her ugly hands hold tightly on to something, won't let her go. Þórður seems to be coming back, has started reading again, got the Italian poem from Tryggvi and the first volume of the newest novel by young Halldór Laxness, *Independent People*. It's a book that people argue about, that some literally hate its author for writing; and Þórður has again started telling Elín endless stories in the evenings. Lies there with her, she snuggles her face into the crook of his neck, some moments in life stay with us for ever, they're radiant stones that we take out when it grows dark. Early in the morning, if the sea looks promising, Margrét watches as father and son leave the house, Þórður a head taller, Oddur straight-backed, it's so good to have your son with you, it's like an affirmation that you've lived right, or at least decently. You must be careful not to wear him out, says Margrét to Oddur, knowing her husband's drive, and then he smiles, and his blue eyes shine. Oh, that smile . . . and the light in those blue eyes; had she forgotten how beautiful he is? How can she possibly be thinking about some headmaster when she has those blue eyes, that smile, this strong man – why can't she, isn't it innocent just to think, aren't you allowed to feel a little, enlarge your life a tiny bit? Can't she look to see how beautifully he walks, to see Jupiter's moons appear like unexpected specks of light in the telescope, is that a betrayal of Oddur, their life and memories? The reason she tells no-one about this, not even Áslaug, that she's gone up the slope in the middle of the night to look at the stars with the headmaster, is to protect his reputation.

Maybe also to have something just for herself.

She watches father and son walk away from the house in the morning's semi-darkness, Tryggvi comes out and greets them, she hears the echo of her brother's happy voice, he has said something funny to make them both laugh, Oddur and Þórður. She suddenly feels so happy inside that tears well up in her eyes. She makes some more coffee, half an hour until she has to wake Hulda to go to work at the fish factory. Pours herself a cup and sits down in Oddur's chair, which is still warm from him, and it feels as if she's sitting on Oddur's lap, as in the old days. Here he'd sat, smiling that smile of his. Night comes in, bringing stillness, and the sky is so thick with stars that it seems to be changing into a musical composition; which is probably why Margrét can't sleep. Oddur breathes heavily beside her, sunk in his dreams. She gets out of bed quietly, pours a glass of water, looks out, sees the headmaster pass by, so close to the house, she lets him disappear into the darkness, up the hill, forces herself to wait, counts to a hundred, then to a hundred again – and then is outside. She slips into her coat, puts on thick mittens to protect herself from the cold, to hide the ugliness of her hands. Hurries up the mountain, doesn't think about him walking beautifully, or about him walking at all, just about him having that telescope, and how his head is so filled with knowledge that he's willing to share with her, and isn't life a waste without seeking knowledge? Please, call me Þorkell, he says, probably for the tenth time. She stays with him for an hour, looks into the telescope, listens to him. Once he lets his hand rest on her lower back as he explains what she's looking at, bends over her, there's so much stillness, on earth and in the sky, that he instinctively speaks very softly, and must therefore bend over her, places his hand on her lower back, or his arm around her waist, actually. But just for a short time, as if accidentally. She thinks, This is nice.

And that's how life grows

She awakes fifteen years younger. Awakes as Oddur is getting out of bed, yawns, stretches at the bedside. She regards his sturdy-looking back. You're a beautiful man, she murmurs. Turning, he looks at her in surprise, sees her eyes, and she moans softly as he slips into her. A gentle breeze from the south, clouds sail the sky, the stars are gone, it's a dark morning. Margrét hums as she makes coffee, prepares lunches for her sailors, Þórður is reading *Independent People* by Halldór Laxness, sometimes reads out loud to his parents, and Oddur laughs three times. I like that lad, he says, maybe I should read his work sometime. Margrét watches them, she smiles. It was so good to feel Oddur inside her, feel his excitement, hear him moaning. She hugs them both as they leave, puts her arms around Þórður. You've grown so big, she says, and he smiles, kisses her hair, says, My darling mum.

Yet she had thought about the headmaster ... Þorkell ... when she and Oddur were together. Call me Þorkell, he had said in parting, and, somewhat flustered, she offered him her hand. He pulled off her mitten. She thought, Dammit, now he'll see how ugly my hand is, but he started kissing the back of it, smiled at her, kissed the back of her hand, not quickly, took his time, his lips warm on her skin. That's what she had thought, his warm lips, and had a deep orgasm with Oddur inside her. So deep that it almost hurt. Was that bad of her? She still loves Oddur, despite all the difficulties they've experienced, that they've had with each other, despite him being so unbending sometimes, insensitive, demanding, suffocating, despite his having . . . been with other women, perhaps. She still loves him. Those incredibly blue eyes. Can't help it. It was so beautiful to look at his back this morning ... but goodness gracious, how soft the headmaster's . . . Þorkell's . . . lips are. On the other hand, she'd once again forgotten to mention Þórður, to ask the headmaster to speak to him, because now was the perfect time, with him coming back, even whether the headmaster would be willing to tutor Þórður this winter, prepare him for

Reykjavík Secondary School. Except that she doesn't want to lose Þórður, it's so far to Reykjavík, she wouldn't see him for a whole winter, but Þórður's talents and desire for knowledge mustn't be allowed to slumber inside him and transform over time into unhappiness, bitterness. Few things are as bad as talents going to waste.

She forgot to mention Þórður . . . no, that's not quite right, she remembered it every so often, that now she should mention him, but felt so inferior that she couldn't bring herself to talk about her son, so selfish that she wanted to have this man all to herself for a bit longer. If there is such a thing as justice, she thinks, I'll be punished. Unless I make amends as soon as possible; but there will be no stars tonight. Breaths of wind from the south, the temperature rises from minus 5 to 8 degrees centigrade. She promises to walk to the school with Elín, they stroll over there, mother and daughter, well behind Gunnar, and go into the foyer, the headmaster sees them, he comes over and says to Elín, You know, we're looking for a woman to work here part-time, doing cleaning and various other chores, do you think I should speak to your mummy about it?

Elín skips, her heart pounds

Around noon, the fog rolls in. By its nature, Eastfjords fog is classified as *advection fog*, forming when warm air from the south streams over the cold sea here to the north. No stars tonight.

Perhaps it's for the best, thinks Margrét, she's tired, didn't get to sleep until around 2.00 a.m., her heart racing; it was because of life. Couldn't God have given her another starry night? Elín skipped round her mummy all the way home, asking over and over if she was going to start working at the school, the headmaster had said that Elín could write on the chalkboard when no-one was looking. That's just between us, he'd said, giving her a wink. The headmaster's offer is really nice, said Margrét, her hands behind her back, possibly to hide them, to keep him from seeing how ugly they were and then feeling ashamed of or regretting having kissed the back of her hand. Oh, why is it so difficult to call me Þorkell? he said, and laughed. Elín skipped all the way home and Margrét's heart thumped in her chest.

She had asked him to give her until the following morning, as if she really needed to think it over . . . Yet again she forgot to mention Þórður, which is perhaps understandable – the headmaster had taken her by surprise. Then the fog rolled in.

It's a long way to the Moon

It happened very quickly. They were sailing slowly back to land when a French fishing boat appeared out of nowhere and hit *Sleipnir* at full speed, smashed into it, amidships starboard. It's unclear what happened next, except that *Sleipnir* jerked to port, listed, the fog filled with shouts and curses in Icelandic and French, the sea poured into the fo'c'sle where most of the crew were, some asleep in their bunks, others smoking, playing cards, shooting the breeze. The crash threw all of them from their places, two were nearly knocked out, one man's head was bleeding, but it turned out not to be serious. Þórður had fled from the stale air of the fo'c'sle, having just finished the first volume of *Independent People*, wanted fresh air and peace to think, he and Tryggvi were going to sit down with some coffee when they came ashore and discuss the first two volumes. Tryggvi could hardly wait for Þórður to finish so that they could talk about the book and try to guess what came next. Bloody hell, it's good to be alive when they've started writing such big books again in Icelandic, not in Danish like that bastard Gunnar. The first world literature written in Icelandic in seven hundred years – in prose, that is.

They didn't immediately realise that Þórður was missing. Then someone spotted him, half-submerged a short distance from *Sleipnir*, about to disappear into the fog, rising and falling with the waves, as if they were lulling him to sleep.

They both jumped into the water at the same moment, the brothers-in-law Oddur and Tryggvi. Kicked off their boots, yanked off their woollen jumpers, Oddur a second ahead of Tryggvi, but Tryggvi the better swimmer and quicker to get to Þórður, he's competed in swimming competitions between Norðfjörður and Seyðisfjörður, no-one swims as fast as Tryggvi, it's nothing short of incredible how he cleaves the water, the sea, the waves. Once he was going to swim to the moon, which is approximately 380,000 kilometres away, that would have been a difficult swim, even for a champion like Tryggvi. How far is life from death, how many kilometres?

Þórður catches happiness

"Death is the prow of a boat sailing through life, changing it for a while into meaninglessness which is then transformed into bright eternity, but it happens at such a distance that we don't see it. We don't see that life is always bigger than death, because Jesus conquered death nearly two thousand years ago, which is why I can tell you this: Þórður may have left us who love him so much – this young, beautiful, kind and talented boy left us – but be comforted, because he left us to board one of the Lord's boats. Þórður is sailing on the sea of eternity, catching happiness."

Eternity, it's not a nice word

Margrét looked at Oddur's knuckles while the priest was speaking. She had her arms around Elín, was looking at his lacerated knuckles. He and Tryggvi had pulled Þórður back to *Sleipnir*, swam fast, frantically, but it was too late, far too late, because it was all too late and would be that way throughout eternity. Þórður had most likely been knocked out by the crash, been thrown against something and tumbled half-conscious or unconscious overboard. The French skipper had leapt over to *Sleipnir* when he saw Tryggvi and Oddur swim after Þórður, helped pull him aboard, and it was touching how he threw himself down, held Þórður's head and tried to breathe life into him, and wept when he saw how young the Icelandic sailor was. Oddur and Tryggvi knelt next to them and for several moments Oddur's blue eyes seemed to be transformed into open wounds. When the French skipper stopped trying to resuscitate Þórður, gave up, Oddur took Þórður's head in his hands, felt the wound from the blow beneath his thick hair, looked at the young face, they'd walked down the slope together that morning, having just said goodbye to Margrét, it had been such a beautiful morning, and it was nice to walk with Tryggvi and Þórður on either side of him. *Sleipnir* rose and fell on the sea, the men stood in a semicircle around the four of them, Oddur, Tryggvi, Þórður, the French skipper. Oddur shut his eyes for a second; it had been such a long time since he'd cradled his son's head in his hands. He thought about Elín, who often runs to meet them when they return from the sea, throws herself into

Þórður's arms. He stood up. As did the others, Tryggvi and the French captain, and then Oddur smelled drink on the French skipper, a heavy smell of cognac. He looked down at Þórður, then up at the skipper, who opened his arms, stepped towards Oddur, meaning to embrace him, show sympathy, human beings are often good and sympathy can make them beautiful. Oddur took half a step towards him and slammed his fist, rock-hard, into the skipper's face. The Frenchman fell back, dizzy, dumbfounded, but Oddur followed up with his left fist, and then the right again, then left, then right, and it took four men to make him stop. By then the Frenchman was covered in blood, with a broken nose, broken teeth, and his crew on its way over to *Sleipnir* like a crowd of profanities.

Margrét's lap is soaked with Elín's tears, the girl keeps her head buried there the entire time, unable to look at the casket, the box holding Þórður, doesn't want to. She cries and hates God. Headmaster Þorkell is in the centre of the church. Margrét knows she will never speak to him again.

Interlude

It's still night at the hospital, where Ari wanders alone down the half-lit corridors of eternity. I'll go to him soon – to the place where everything ends. Everyone dies in the end, night replaces day, everything vanishes, no power can prevent it – is that why we cast words like burning torches into the dark lands of death?

Someone is playing R.E.O. Speedwagon, "you should've seen by the look in my eyes, baby, there was something missing . . ."

Keflavík

— PRESENT —

Aw, shouldn't we listen to Megas instead?

The 1970s will be running the show for the next few hours, which is one good reason to turn up your radios, shouts the announcer on Gullbylgja. The huge bartender believes him, which is why we hear REO Speedwagon's every word, "and I'm gonna keep on loving you . . . I don't wanna sleep, I just wanna keep on loving you . . . I don't wanna sleep, I just wanna keep on loving you." Sleepless love. Ari and I know the sickly sweet yet melodic song. On his fifth glass, Svavar would often play it on his organ, drunk enough not to give a shit about me, Ari and Árni's lugubrious critiques, usually shutting his eyes during the refrain, just like the bartender, who bee-bops contentedly behind the bar, quite the opposite of the menacing troll I encountered when I came to the hotel twenty-four hours ago to meet Ari. I don't want to sleep, I just want to love and love you, but Bylgjan has occupied Hafnargata, and none other than Bó has come to Keflavík to sing one of his most popular songs, "Though Years and Centuries Pass", for the most loved-up couple in Keflavík. I look forward to singing for happiness and love, says Bó, and here in Keflavík, no less, in the cradle of Icelandic pop. The bartender refuses to play anything other than Gullbylgja, but Mayor Sigurjón listens to Bylgjan on his phone; he has an earbud in one ear, a man who pays attention, is in many places at once, a man of ideas. He talks about marketing Keflavík as "The Town of Love", says this to everyone, and wants to erect a huge statue of Rúnar Júlíusson between Njarðvík and Keflavík. He'd stand there, legs spread wide, holding his bass guitar, so huge that cars could drive between his legs. How symbolic would that be: to enter Keflavík, you'd have to drive between the legs of the sexiest man in the history of Iceland. Rúnni Júll, who, in the summer of 1966, was the highest-scoring player in the Icelandic Football League, was bass guitarist and singer in Iceland's most popular, best group, Hljómar, and married Iceland's newly crowned beauty queen – and spent his entire life with her. It truly was young love, though years and centuries passed! Sigurjón smiles, but Svavar locks up his tourist shop, slips out the back door and drives out of the town of love with a broken heart. He'd sent Snæfríður a text asking if she was enjoying herself, whether the chap she'd met for a meal seemed a decent man. Hi, I'm having fun, she'd answered, he's really great, and added a few smiley faces. Svavar puts some distance between himself and Keflavík; he's paralysed by sadness, though nervous, he'd had a few beers, was worried about being pulled over by the police and losing his licence. How could he explain that to his grandchildren? That he'd driven while drunk because his heart was broken?

Grandpa, heartbroken?! Useless writing a pop song about that; it wouldn't even make the Top 100. Has anyone in the whole world ever given a thought to heartbroken grandpas? Svavar turns towards the heath, away from the lights, he disappears into the darkness.

Aw, shouldn't we listen to Megas instead? says Jakob. They've finished eating, Anna had changed her clothes, is now wearing a short blue dress, a green cardigan. You look so young, he said, which brought a smile to her face and tears to her eyes. But really wants to listen to Bylgjan, doesn't want to miss Bó, his golden voice. We've got to hold on to love, darling; remember how lovely it was to be in love? As if the world had been created especially for you, which turned out to be nothing but an illusion, of course, yet it was a beautiful illusion; you actually existed for a little while, you lived!

The worst torments of Hell, says Jakob, after saying nothing for a long time, staring at the letter on the kitchen table, at Margrét's diaries on the coffee table, are suffered by those who didn't live enough. Only lived half-lives. Were neither good nor bad.

You're lively tonight, honey; Bó's never sung about that!

That's because it's from Dante. I'm not sure your Bó has ever read him. Tryggvi said that you haven't lived until you've read Dante. Do you know who he is? No, says Anna; should I? Would my life have been better if I had done? Jakob doesn't reply, totters over to the bookcase, pulls out a thick book, sits down with it. Hell, he says, is composed of nine circles, but I can't remember which circle they're in, the wretches who only lived half-lives. Is this your Dante? asks Anna, leaning over and stroking the back of Jakob's hand. He looks up, as if in surprise.

I: You visited your dad?

Ari looks at me. Dr Hook is on Gullbylgja, the song about Sylvia's mother. I see that the American couple knows it; he sings along and she leans over the table to kiss him. Her big breasts beneath her yellow cotton dress tip over their nearly empty bottle of white wine and a half-full glass; she doesn't notice, takes his hands, and they gaze into each other's eyes. The table is drenched with white wine.

Candidate for death

Do you want some coffee? asked Jakob, and Ari nodded instinctively, even though he didn't want any coffee, least of all Jakob's, which is always so weak that you can see the bottom of your cup

– you should be able to see to the bottom of your own life, not of your coffee cup. Jakob gets up from the sofa at his own pace, Megas managed to sing an entire verse in the meantime, but then the coffee maker purred, a good sound. Well now, said Jakob, so you're back from Copenhagen, how's life there, doesn't everyone ride bicycles? I suppose so, replied Ari.

Jakob: And they're in the European Union.

Yes.

Not us.

No.

Their currency isn't a laughing stock, the Danish krone.

No.

Nobody takes the Icelandic króna seriously, said Jakob. It's as useless as I am.

Anna: I've always preferred the dollar. It's always used as the standard. Using the Icelandic króna as the standard is like using clouds as a compass. In other words, we've no idea where we're headed.

Jakob: Those in charge get fat on the Icelandic króna. Profit is more important to them than people's lives. So what's new? Private interests have always taken precedence over people, here as elsewhere. Mum sometimes said that the problem with Icelanders is that they've always looked up to sharks, and consequently consider insolence a strength. That hasn't changed. Fantastic that I'll be dying soon; I won't ever have to witness this nonsense again. Capitalism has conquered the world, and happiness is printed in money machines. You've read Laxness?

Ari shrugged. Who hasn't read Laxness? he said. Not to mention the fact that I've been in the book business for decades. It's a bit like asking . . .

Why did you stop writing? asked Jakob, as if his temper suddenly flared, what was that all about, what were you afraid of? If only it were that simple, said Ari, who was about to get up to check on the coffee, but Anna beat him to it, stood up nimbly, as if nothing were weighing her down, as if her existence weighed nothing.

Jakob: Well, what do I know? Laxness was good because he dared to come forward and attack the world's bullies. He was never afraid to use his books to say what mattered, unlike those of you who stared at your feet while the banks and stockbroker arseholes nearly devoured the country, and you still stare at your feet and scratch your arses while the sharks shape society into any form they please. Laxness was man enough to fight back; he brought his weapons out for the big battles. The rest of you don't even step out of your adolescent bedrooms if you can help it, much less get out of bed.

Anna: You're so eloquent, darling. You should run for office.

Jakob: I'm a candidate for death, and I'm certain to be elected.

Anna: Do you mind if I shut the balcony door? All this fresh air has got you on such a roll that it'll kill you.

Goddammit, artists and young people are supposed to tear down walls so the air doesn't get stale, said Jakob, pounding on the living-room table with unexpected force. I didn't know, said Ari, that you wanted to tear down walls. I hate injustice, muttered Jakob, leaning back in the sofa, looking exhausted, as if he'd put all his energy into pounding the table, the declaration – and I hate politics, he added. Your uncle Tryggvi started working for the Yanks after he was injured at sea; he was never the same afterwards, resorted to working at the Base to get by and put his girls through school. But then his friends the leftists kicked him out. They staged their Keflavík march on the road that the Americans

283

laid for them, screamed themselves hoarse protesting against the military and everyone who worked for them. I hate politics, people aren't really any good, it's pure luxury not to have much time left, he said as he lit a cigarette, inhaled the smoke enthusiastically into his ruined lungs, perhaps imagining hastening his own death. I wish he were a little bit cuter, that Megas of yours, said Anna, and he could sing about love sometimes. I'm not sure he's happy.

Megas is the greatest artist we've ever had, and a great artist can't be happy in such a tiny nation, said Jakob, finishing his cigarette.

Ari stood up, said, Well then.

What? exclaimed Jakob, obviously surprised; you're leaving?

Yes, I have a few things to attend to. I'll be back tomorrow.

Why will you be back tomorrow?

Can't I visit you?

I guess I have no say in what you do, said Jakob angrily, I just don't understand why you have to leave while Megas is singing, especially about love, so everyone should be happy. The most beautiful song and poem that's ever been written in Iceland, and you're leaving, is that why you're publishing those ridiculous *Ten Tips* books?

Is that why; what do you mean by that? They sell pretty damned well, by the way.

Jakob: Sell well, is that the criterion now, to sell well? Coke sells well; does that make it important? You used to write once, you wrote books, what happened there?

Ari: Everything changes.

Jakob: And where's Þóra?

Ari: Where she belongs, I suppose.

Jakob: Why aren't you there?

Ari: As I said, everything changes.

Not Megas, said Jakob, raising his index finger and singing along: "The peaks around me circling drew; beyond them is nothing, for within them is you." Now that's a poem! You were going to leave without listening to those lines, and the ones that follow them!

Ari: I know the song.

Jakob: Know, like it's enough to know! Oh well, leave then; you're a total dud, anyway. He's not as much fun as us, huh, Anna?!

Oh, don't be like that, honey, there's more to life than fun.

More to life? There's nothing to me anymore! Death has gnawed it all away; all I've got left is my voice, and only to sing along with Megas, because it's no fun to sing alone.

Are you sure you want to risk it?

And that's how you parted? You didn't talk about anything you should have talked about?!

Ari: We still have time.

Not always, unfortunately, I say, and his expression darkens suddenly because those who die change into silence, they no longer know how to speak, perhaps not even to listen – everything we say to them vanishes into the void without a trace.

The crowd has grown at the hotel bar. All the tables are occupied, people stand at the bar. The two Norwegians, schoolmates of Mayor Sigurjón, have come to Keflavík to celebrate his sixtieth birthday, perhaps also in their roles as employees of an American company that Sigurjón is trying to lure to Keflavík, we don't know why they're here, they've moved to the American couple's table. They all laugh at something, then sing along to a song by Simply Red, "Holding Back the Years", if only we could hold back time, tie

285

that mad dog down. In the countryside, dogs that were hard to train were usually shot, then buried among the tussocks somewhere. Unfortunately, you can't execute time with a pistol and bury it among the tussocks somewhere; is that why we go in for singing old pop songs, because they make us feel younger, hold back the years? I'm going to visit Dad tomorrow, says Ari firmly, even enthusiastically, and will ask him about this memory of when the three of us stood by the window at Vífilsstaðir and she said, Now the universe is passing through us.

Are you sure you want to risk it? What if those words were never said? I'm prepared for that, he says; so much has happened, and some memories are such that they require no foundation in reality.

So much has happened, he repeats, and is about to add something, maybe explain what he means a bit better, but the Norwegians stand up, say goodbye to the American couple, walk over to where Sigurjón is sitting, in the place of honour at the biggest table in the bar, surrounded by smiles, has just spelled out his idea for changing Keflavík into The Town of Love. One of the Norwegians lightly taps the mayor on the shoulder, and he immediately stands up and goes with them. Stands straight-backed between them but somehow seems to shrink, if not shrivel up. One of the Norwegians puts his arm round the mayor's shoulder as if to say, It's O.K., unless he's saying something entirely different, and less pleasant. Ari and I watch as they walk off, and we notice Ásmundur and Sigga standing together at the end of the bar; my heart leaps – I haven't seen Sigga in almost thirty years, which is a long time in a person's life. She seems not to have aged. She was never considered to be pretty, what with her long neck, narrow face, small breasts, almost no hips – but her eyes were black and fiery, like burning lumps of coal. Almost thirty years. She has her hands in her pockets, looks up at Ásmundur, whom Ari had met just over a day ago under rather unusual circumstances, but whom I last saw one night at the very start of the '80s, when Ásmundur drove into someone's garden in upper Keflavík at 60 k.p.h.; Ari hammered in the passenger seat and "Polar Bear Blues" by Bubbi blasting from the stereo. Ari and I didn't get out of the car; we saw the lights go on, and then Gunnhildur and her husband came out of the house. She worked with us at the Skúli Million freezing plant, in her late twenties, mother of three, newly woken, so beautiful, and she took a step towards Ásmundur, who clambered, hammered on Budweiser beer, vodka and love, out of the car, shouted something, his declaration of love, he appeared not to see her husband. Twice they shut themselves in a freezer at Skúli Million while Ari and I stood guard. My God, how fucking much I love you, woman, shouted Ásmundur, he had to shout in order to drown out zealous Bubbi on the stereo. I want, he shouted, but was unable to finish, was unable to say what he wanted to say, because her husband sped into the garden and punched him, knocking him off his feet. Ásmundur was nineteen at the time, and so like his cousin Þórður that Margrét, who was elderly, confused and worn out, occasionally mixed them up and burst into tears on seeing her boy again. Ásmundur let her hug and kiss him, he dried her tears, embraced her, she weighed almost nothing now, and carried her to her bed. Sang old lullabies until she calmed down, until she stopped crying and fell asleep into a world where everyone is alive.

Someone is crying, but Elvis can open our hearts

We're going to Ásmundur's, says Sigga; it's impossible to hear yourself think in here. She grabs a bottle of Jack Daniels from the bar, and the four of us drive out of Keflavík. Sigga hands the whisky bottle to Ari, who's sitting next to her in the back seat. He accepts it with a smile. Ari and I haven't drunk bourbon whisky for thirty years, and every sip is a memory. Ásmundur steps on the gas, and when we're up on Miðnesheiði, asks, You've visited your dad, of course – how is he?

I wish I could give you a good answer, replies Ari, so quietly that Sigga squeezes his hand. He looks over at her, smiles faintly, but I look out towards Keflavík, where Jakob is sitting on the edge of his bed – it's dark in the small flat, and he gropes blindly for something, finds a pair of Anna's tights, quickly pulls them towards him and stuffs them in his mouth to stifle his crying. He trembles, he cries, but calms down a bit when Anna, half-asleep, sits up in bed, touches him, and says, Jakob dear.

It's so good when someone wants to say your name.

Jakob had recognised Anna immediately. He'd just arrived at the retirement home and was sitting in the dining room for the first time. The view from there had taken him by such surprise that he barely noticed the people around him. He was sitting alone at his table, deep in thought, when he was addressed by name, looked up, and there she stood with her food tray, smiling, apparently alert, possibly prepared to draw her sarcasm like a gun if necessary, if he pretended not to recognise her, pretended not to remember her. She addressed him companionably: Hello, Kobbi dear, may I sit with my old acquaintance? Yes, by all means, he said, and added, this is excellent beefsteak. She had sat down, smiled, not so you'd notice, but did smile, and said, As you know, I ended up studying English, perhaps too well. I know, he said, pouring some water into her glass; so that was settled. The only one she wanted to sit with. Some people wanted nothing to do with her – Anna the Yankee whore – and wouldn't even wish her good day, as if she didn't deserve a good day. Now she has sat up in bed, gently strokes Jakob's head, takes her tights, wet with saliva, out of his mouth, kisses him. The only person who has got Jakob to say the Serenity Prayer out loud, somewhere other than in rehab, which he has gone through twice, she three times: "God grant me the serenity to accept the things I cannot change; courage to change the things I can; and wisdom to know the difference."

Where should this wisdom come from, and what if God doesn't grant the necessary courage, maybe it's exhausted, sold out, you'll have to wait, we work in shifts here in Heaven and can't keep up with everything, Heaven has become too small for human suffering. Unless God simply doesn't want to give you courage or wisdom, give you anything at all, because you don't deserve it, aren't worth it, haven't earned it, your life is a failure, you've let everyone down, mainly yourself, lived like that for more than seventy years, what a waste.

Jakob cries. There, there, she whispers, hush now. She kisses his shoulders and then pulls him down to her, I'll help you, she mutters drowsily, it's never too late to change, not while you're alive, tomorrow is a new day and we'll have it together. Jakob calms down, she falls asleep, he listens to her breathing deepen and carefully, even affectionately, strokes her arm.

Nice boy you have, she'd said after Ari's visit, but someone needs to teach you how to talk to each other, you're both hurting, and you should probably have played something different than your dear Megas. I've always found my dear Elvis to be good at opening hearts. He shot his T.V., said Jakob. That was a sign of maturity, darling, he was always so sensitive, the sweetheart, and

289

saw what kind of a monster T.V. was becoming. Seriously, just look at the rubbish on it, it'll destroy your brain cells faster than alcohol! I'm just going to my room to change for dinner; I want to look nice for you and find a good Elvis C.D.

She went upstairs while Jakob tottered off to the storage room, got two boxes full of diaries and Margrét's letters, and had started going through the letters when Anna came downstairs in her nice dress. He looked up, said those lovely words, that she looked so young, she smiled, so happy, put Elvis on the C.D. player, then sat down beside him and was allowed to browse through the diaries while Jakob went through the letters, a substantial portion were letters to and from Tryggvi and Áslaug after they moved south to Vatnsleysuströnd. Many were quite thick, but one envelope was unopened, besides being addressed in different handwriting and sent from abroad: Margrét Guðmundsdóttir, Vík, Norðfirði, Iceland. Iceland, said Jakob in surprise – I wonder if it's from Canada? Yes, and from a secret admirer, said Anna excitedly, hopefully. It's old, Jakob muttered, staring at the postmark . . . and from Copenhagen. He turned the envelope over, from someone with the initials G. G. Oh, I hope it's a secret lover, said Anna, open the letter! Jakob stood up with difficulty, fetched a knife, sat down at the kitchen table, hesitated, sliced the envelope open, carefully smoothed out two densely written pages, looked hurriedly at the signature: Gunnar Gunnarsson. He started reading, soon looked up with an expression of surprise, if not astonishment, turned to look at one of the bookcases, at the collection of Gunnar's works that Margrét had given him and Ari's mother when it was published, and which certainly hadn't been cheap. Not Gunnar Gunnarsson the writer, asked Anna in surprise, when she saw what Jakob was looking at. So it would seem, he replied hesitantly. What does he say, why a letter from him to your mother, oh, how exciting this is, wasn't he a dreadful womaniser? Well, I don't know about that, no, not him, I don't think, muttered Jakob. She read a lot, your mother, didn't she? She was always reading, Dad sometimes said it was a disease, and she . . . really liked Gunnar. My collection is a gift from her.

Yet she didn't open a letter from him . . .

Jakob didn't reply, just stared at the letter without reading it. Maybe there was something between them, said Anna. My God, how interesting that would be! Interesting? Yes, that she had a secret life. Anna, smiling, shut her eyes, opened them again when Jakob said, almost harshly, angrily, No, she had no time whatsoever for that sort of thing. Dad took up too much space, he was the one who had the adventures. Maybe there's something here, said Anna, reaching for the diaries, but Jakob looked at the letter, read it.

A letter answered

Gunnar Gunnarsson's letter to Margrét, written in Copenhagen in the mid-'30s of the twentieth century, opened and read by her son more than seventy years later in Keflavík, is on two densely written pages, in ink. He thanks her for writing to him. Her letter had, unfortunately, lain "for a considerable time unread – one of many things undone – for which I apologise, and for the tardiness of my reply". But it gladdened my heart, writes Gunnar, when I saw that the letter was from the east; "I felt it bore the fragrance of heather and the mountains that I miss . . . yet I did not anticipate that the contents would stir my soul so profoundly. Your remarks about maternal love touched me deeply. Your love, pure and strong, for your son, who obviously has so much potential, touched me.

You must send him to school in Reykjavík. There is no need for him to strike out into the unknown, as I did. The times are different now, and I believe, despite Iceland's continually sad economic state, that there are considerably more, and better, possibilities there now than when I was his age. Send him to school, as soon as possible – the sooner the better – and I look forward to hearing how he gets on. His remarkable talents will not go unnoticed throughout his life . . . Maternal love – does a stronger, more beautiful force exist? Isn't it the force that powers life? I do not know if you have read my latest books, in which I describe a boy growing up in the east – a boy who could be me. He loses his mother at a young age, as I did. So I am able to bear witness to the fact that one can suffer no greater loss on earth, and the goal of all that I have done and experienced has perhaps been to make up for that loss. Which is doubtless a hopeless task. I could never speak of that loss to my father, which is probably my deepest sorrow apart from the loss of my mother. It was as if I had also lost my father . . . Was it perhaps the reason why I left at such a young age, to experience a new country, a new language? The human mind is a labyrinth. It is because of my losses, and because of how you wrote your letter, as well as the fact that you live in the east, not far from where I grew up, from my regret, that your letter moved me so deeply. Your son Þórður is blessed to have you as his mother."

Soon I'll finally be able to say the things that really matter

Jakob holds Anna's arm gently, presses his lips to the back of her hand, she murmurs tranquilly. He gets out of bed as quietly as he can so as not to wake her, one of her hands fumbles for him but then falls still, perhaps finding him in her dreams. He goes to the kitchen, turns on a light and re-reads Gunnar Gunnarsson's letter. Runs his fingers over the date in the upper corner, then reaches for a ballpoint pen and a Yahtzee score pad, tears off a sheet, writes on its reverse, in small letters, crooked and weak: "The sea makes us men, Dad used to say. He even wanted it put on his gravestone. I have never been able to forget those words. Perhaps it was a mistake to honour Mum's wish and never go to sea."

He tears another sheet off the pad, continues:

"Was I obeying her, or honouring her wish? Is it important to know the answer to this question? There is nothing as beautiful as the sea. I don't know what makes it so fair. Is it because it's so much bigger than humankind, yet possesses so much tranquillity?" – new sheet. "There's been little tranquillity in my life. It's my own fault. Worst of all is never to have known how to talk to those closest to me. To talk about things that mustn't be silenced. I managed to ruin so much by keeping quiet. I" – new sheet – ". . . no, I think I'll walk, or, well, totter down to the shore, have a look at the sea before I continue. Then I'm certain I'll finally be able to say the things that really matter."

That's how happiness knocks on your door

We've come to Sandgerði, make a left turn immediately and soon pass Svavar's two-storey wooden house. He lives there alone, has done since his marriage of nineteen years fell apart. It's just him and his organ, and his grandchildren when they fill the house with life. There are no children tonight. Just Svavar by the old organ, thinking about Snæfríður, how she's taking off her purple dress somewhere, and how someone better, more beautiful and smarter than him is watching her. Svavar fights to hold back the tears as

293

he plays songs about eternal love, whereas Ásmundur instinctively slows down when we see Snæfríður step out of her car outside the house. She gives us a quick look, then knocks on the door. Hard, three times. That's how happiness knocks on your door, remember that: three times.

Sigga laughs, Ásmundur grabs the whisky bottle as we approach his place, and Ari and I are astounded to see that it's old Kristján's little house – old Kristján with whom we worked at Drangey in the early '80s.

Turning, I exchange a glance with Ari in the back seat.

Sandgerði
— THE EARLY 1980S —

Kristján had asked the four of us, me, Ari, Árni and Svavar, to help him put his boat to sea. It was an April night, he'd lost most of his strength, wasn't able to launch it on his own.

It was a difficult night.

The four of us had just come from a dance at the community centre in Sandgerði, where Ari, Svavar and I tried to pluck up the courage to ask some of the girls to dance, while Árni seemed to prefer pondering how the lights flashing above the dance floor were wired up, how the band's sound system worked – he was lost in thoughts about direct and alternating current, so obviously spaced-out in the midst of all the drinking, the whirling dance, the hot kisses, that four sailors started messing with him. Their night hadn't gone as they had hoped it would. They were bored, started pushing him around, things escalated, they grabbed his arse, said they weren't really sure which sex he was, or on which side he should be fucked. Finally, they dragged Árni through the crowd and out into the night, without him putting up a struggle, as if he'd been switched off, or didn't care, which may be why no-one paid any attention. The sailors took him outside, while inside, Svavar had finally worked up the courage to ask a girl to dance and she had said yes, which was too good to be true. As it turned out they didn't get to dance very much, had hardly stepped onto the dance floor when a girlfriend of hers came over and asked Svavar about Árni, why he'd gone outside with those sailors. What sailors? asked Svavar in surprise.

The three of us went outside and found them behind the community centre, Árni lay face-down on the ground, motionless, they stood over him, had pulled off his trousers and underwear, his buttocks shone white, streaked with red as if he'd been whipped. Fucking losers, shouted Svavar, and we flew straight at them. Which was probably what they'd been hoping for. There was madness in their eyes, something dangerous, and we would most likely have ended up with broken noses, fewer teeth, fractured ribs, if Jonni the helmsman, later Jonni Thunderburger, hadn't appeared round the corner to take a piss, someone had wrecked the toilet inside, kicked it to pieces, and Jonni came round the corner, saw Árni bare-arsed on the ground, saw the rabid sailors, understood everything and flew into a cold rage. Leapt into action, yanked the biggest sailor towards him, so easily that he might as well have been handling a child rather than a bruiser strong as a bull, and broke his arm. In no more than five seconds. His companions were so shocked at his fury, his cold ruthlessness, that their madness vanished, they gave up the fight and led the screaming gorilla away. Disappeared into the night, where the Devil swallowed them in one bite.

You shouldn't go to dances, said Jonni to Árni, it just makes punks like them mad. What are you two doing, he added, looking at Ari and me, working here in the fish business? Every man has to find his own place in life – or he'll end up unhappy. My place is at sea, I don't know where your place is, except that it's definitely not here. It hurts to see a person in the wrong place in life; it's such a waste – makes me sad and angry. Jonni turned away to piss, then lit a cigarette, said, Life's a hell of a burden, inhaled, exhaled, added, Now get out of here. We immediately understood what he meant: out of this community centre, out of this village, out of this existence – find yourselves a different life.

We walked to Árni's place and got into the Saab, put a cassette in the tape player, turned it up loud: "Time takes a cigarette, puts it in your mouth." Drove off, but not far, headed for Hvalsnes church, to Hallgrímur and the little girls, towards the sadness, the grief, "oh no, love, you're not alone, gimme your hands, 'cause you're wonderful." We listened, looked out at the half-dark night, together yet poignantly alone, no matter how much Bowie tried to comfort us. Because it's hard not fitting in, feeling as if you don't belong anywhere. Saying nothing, we looked out at the half-bright spring night and saw old Kristján waddling down towards the beach. Where's he going in the middle of the night? I said. Árni parked the car on the soft verge, we got out, climbed over the fence, walked down the sloping hayfield to the old man, who'd started pulling at his boat with the powerlessness of old age, meaning that he'd barely managed to budge it, whereas he'd been able to carry it under one arm ten years ago, he told us. We saw that he'd put his volume of Einar Benediktsson's collected poems and an old tape player into the boat. Where are you going, Kristján my friend? Svavar asked. Kristján looked at us, straightened his back. He remained silent for quite some time, there was deep pain in his old eyes. I left a note on the kitchen table, he finally said hoarsely, a short letter that explains everything. This isn't an escape. Every person should have the chance to go with dignity. I don't want to die like a dog, old, crippled, in everyone's way. He seemed to want to say something else but fell silent, his lower lip trembled and his dark eyes had nearly turned black. Get in, said Ari. Kristján clambered stiffly into the boat, sat down on the thwart, bent, old, tired, but straightened up as we began pushing the boat down the beach and smiled when it was finally in the water, rocking slowly. He leaned over, lifted the tape player, pressed play, and Þorsteinn Ö. Stephensen began reading "The Open Sea": "For you am I homesick, wasteland of fear and glory."[12] Kristján looked at us, smiling, his eyes sparkled, he started the motor, sailed out to sea. Away. It's only now, more than thirty years later, that I realise why he was smiling, and so beautifully, as if feeling tremendously relieved, to the point of happiness – he smiled because he wasn't alone anymore. And because something of him would live on within us. His boat was found two days later, capsized, dozens of miles from shore.

She left so he could love me

The most beautiful place in Iceland, says Ásmundur after we've climbed out of the car, are standing in the dark outside the house

12 "The Open Sea" ("Útsær") is by the Icelandic Neo-Romantic poet Einar Benediktsson (1864–1940). Þorsteinn Ö. Stephensen (1904–1991) was an Icelandic actor who performed in more than six hundred radio plays.

and can hear the great din of the sea below, here we have peaceful-ness, grass and eternity, you don't need much more than that. I know that not many people agree with me, people here see little more than flatness, barrenness, yet it *is* beautiful, in every kind of weather. On the other hand, it's not the beauty of the grassy countryside, sky-blue mountains, and I'm not sure there are words in Icelandic for a place like this. For this . . . peculiar beauty that requires patience to sense. Who has such patience these days? I have you, says Sigga, that's the beauty of the world for me. Ásmun-dur smiles, which makes him look younger. The only decent man I've loved, Sigga would say that night.

He's made himself comfortable in the little house he bought and fixed up soon after his wife of fifteen years left him. She left, says Sigga, so that he could love me. Which is why I'm so fond of her. The living-room wall is covered with books, there must be a couple of thou-sand of them, which is surprising, we didn't know that he was a book-lover, but what do we know about Ásmundur, who dis-appeared from our lives after he drove into Gunnhildur's garden – she came out onto the steps, just out of bed, beautiful as the morning sun.

He makes coffee, brings out some hardfish and butter, Sigga fetches some beer, pours whisky into our glasses, this will most definitely be a good night, there's a fire in the fireplace and Paul McCartney is singing, "What if it rained, we didn't care . . . "

Sigga tucks her legs under her, snuggles up to Ásmundur on the sofa, smiles happily at having us there with her. But Ari dear, she asks after we've drunk, eaten hardfish, enjoyed being together, what's troubling you, why have you stopped writing . . . you know, I still have the poems you threw onto my balcony that night about . . . oh my God, thirty years ago – luckily, I haven't been sitting here drunk ever since!

I shut my eyes for a second.

And open them almost thirty years earlier.

Sandgerði
— THE LATE 1980S —

I prefer to drink straight from the bottle – it goes right to your core, says Sigga as she takes the vodka bottle from Þorlákur. It's evening, and there's a dance in Sandgerði to go to. It's the late '80s, and Ari and I have gone back to processing saltfish at Drangey in order to fund the printing of his first book of poetry. He's staying with his father, in a little three-bedroom flat that Jakob bought following his divorce; Ari gave no explanation as to why he'd quit university, said only that he needed money. As he was heading out to work on his third day back, he handed his father the slender black volume of poetry. He was wearing his work boots and his coat, had his thermos flask and lunch in one hand, when he said, Well, I just happened to publish this, handed Jakob the book, then reached for the doorknob. His father opened the book, read the first poem:

> I'm sorry –
> because of your great preoccupation
> with earning an income,
> finding the right clothes,
> the right look,
> your life will be cancelled
> today and the next few days

There's hardly anything on the fucking page! Is it supposed to be some smartypants message, to make such poor use of the page, or is that all you have to say?

I'm going to be late for work, replied Ari, and went out into the cold. Is that all you have to say: father and son said nothing more about the book.

There's a dance tonight at the community centre in Sandgerði, Upplyfting is playing, the village is quivering with anticipation, and Sigga is drinking from Þorlákur's vodka bottle. We managed to finish work before 9.00 p.m. by skipping dinner, but Máni had to give Linda a lift over the heath, to Keflavík. I can't let my poor darlings starve, she said apologetically, referring to her son Gummi and her husband, who is about 40 centimetres taller than she is. Perfect couple, said Þorlákur, after passing Sigga the bottle and her commenting that she'd rather drink straight from it, then cursing father and son both, they could bloody well have fixed their own dinner, they're grown men. Perfect couple, said Þorlákur. Linda is so short that she doesn't have to bend over to blow him. You've got two brain cells, Láki dear, said Sigga, one for thinking about sex, the other for fighting. I've got three, he corrected, the third's for holding you in my arms. She was gobsmacked, for once – and looked at Þorlákur as if seeing him for the first time.

Upplyfting is playing at the dance!

We wash down the stalls, the equipment, the floor, and Sigga dances over to Ari and me. You two are so terribly nice that I just love you, she says, hugging us, pressing her strong, thin body so tightly against us that we feel her small breasts. You're so soft, she says, her breath is warm, blended with vodka and tobacco. Come to the dance and I'll dance with you all night! I'm going to dance and dance, I have so much energy now that I'm afraid I'll get too drunk and wake up next to some nutter, some cute idiotic brute like the father of my child. Such a fucking loser but so cute that I

300

had his name tattooed under my left breast. You can read it by lift-ing my breast. Luckily, his name is so short that my breast covers it, small though it is – which he never grew tired of mentioning when he wanted to belittle me around other people, which was fairly often. As if you measure someone's importance by the size of their breasts . . . which men do, of course – please come to the dance, so I can kiss you, so I can dance with you. I've never danced with clouds in trousers!

Fucking losers – clouds in trousers. We'd told her about the Russian poet Mayakovsky, who was once sitting, tall and shaven-headed, in a train carriage when he was seized with a burning desire to talk to a girl sitting opposite him. They were alone in the carriage, Mayakovsky worried that his zeal and appearance would frighten the girl, so he said, Dear girl, you need not fear me, I am not a man but a cloud in trousers!

But Sigga also wanted to kiss us. So were we more to her than clouds in trousers? That's why she told us about her left breast, that we should lift it to see the name. Wasn't the message fairly clear?

Ari and I aren't going to the dance, however. Jakob is playing bridge up north in Akureyri, so we have the flat to ourselves; it's better to drink Jack Daniels and listen to Tom Waits than go to a dance. And write two poems about her breasts:

The left

I carefully lift it
as if it were fragile
and I see the name that you hate
my lips help you forget

The right

Shaped like a planet
or what moves me to tears
there are stars above me
– my desire is the darkness between them

Goddammit, I'm in love, says Ari.

Then night comes in through the window and we're outside Sigga's house. The lights are off in her room and Ari tosses pebbles at her window. Nothing happens. He crumples up the paper with the poems, throws it like a snowball at the window but is too drunk to throw properly and it lands on the balcony outside the room. He curses, bends down for a rock, throws it hard and hits the window – the rock goes through it. We freeze, lights go on in the room, and Þorlákur comes to the window, bare-chested. His sturdy body is on full display as we back deeper into the dark, just as Sigga appears at his side, her duvet around her, her shoulders bare and slender. Her left breast is shaped like that which moves you to tears.

Double glazing

Why oh why didn't you come to the dance? says Sigga, the December night lies against the windows of the house, so heavy that it takes double glazing to withstand the pressure.

That's where . . .

She found the poems a week later. Went out for a smoke while her little girl was sleeping. Sat down on the old wooden chair in the corner, it was cold, she shivered a bit and felt sad, perhaps because she'd begun to suspect that she'd fallen for the wrong man yet again. She also missed us, we'd quit our jobs at Drangey so abruptly, returned to Reykjavík where life is, opportunities, education. Sat hunched on the chair, felt as if she'd aged by decades and then saw the crumpled paper frozen into the snow. She freed it, smoothed it out distractedly and saw the poems. Knew instantly who had written them, thrown them onto the balcony – and who had broken the window with a rock.

I read the poems, she says, and started bawling. Sat sobbing on the balcony, smoked one cigarette after another, read the poems over and over, and I think I felt as if I was worth something for the first time since my stepfather raped me. I cried because I finally felt as if I possessed something beautiful, something that touched others in a beautiful way. Cried because I was sure that I would never experience happiness, that I would always make the wrong choices, not realise until it was too late that the charming confidence of the men I always seemed to fall for was little more than sterile complacency, their determination little more than awkward insolence – and, as if to prove her point, Þorlákur stopped by the house shortly thereafter, walked right in, cheerfully said hello to my mother, and then put his arms around me as if he owned me . . .

. . . *my strength comes from*

"Since my stepfather raped me":

That is why she was going to drown herself below the freezing plant in Keflavík at the start of the '80s, waded into the cold sea, didn't notice Ari's stepmother, who stood smoking by the wall.

Your stepmother – she's a good woman, says Sigga.

Still, Sigga had hit her, called her all sorts of foul names, as she dragged her back to shore. Then they cried together on the beach.

Yet the next day I acted as if she didn't exist. Didn't say a word to her until eighteen years later, after I'd finally gained the courage and strength to face up to my life, without the fear that I was a useless human being. It took me eighteen years to thank your stepmother for saving my life. I apologised for hitting her, calling her nasty names and completely ignoring her all those years. The blessed woman just put her arms round me and said, We all have our wounds, dear Sigga, and things can go badly for us if we don't heal them. I found it remarkable that she would say that, use those words, because I hadn't told anyone about the abuse I'd suffered. I'd been waiting for my mother to pass away. It was bad enough that my stepfather had poisoned my life and I couldn't bear the thought of him poisoning the final years of hers. Which is why I kept quiet, and waited. I felt she'd endured enough in this life.

Your stepmother told me to go home after dragging me out of the sea and us crying together. Go home now, you poor thing, she said, take a bath, I'll talk to Kalli – that was our foreman – and make up an excuse. No-one needs to know what happened here. It's nobody's business. Then we noticed one of the women standing with one of the freezing plant's lorry drivers, God only knows what they were doing there where no-one could see them, I know they were both married, and not to each other, but they'd likely been standing there for some time and seen your stepmother drag me kicking and screaming out of the sea. I went home, and shortly thereafter everyone seemed to know what had happened. That fucking crow and the lorry driver. How could you, asked my mother when I came home from work the next day, how could you do such a thing when your stepfather is suffering at death's door? You selfish bitch!

She said some other things, and much worse, but I said nothing. Just ran out of the door, slammed it behind me, went and got drunk, let some scumbag fuck me, forgive my language, teddy bear, she says, and kisses the back of Ásmundur's chunky hand. He started when I was seven. It went on for six years. Then it was as if he lost interest. He came at night when Mum wasn't at home, locked the door, turned out the lights. I hated him, but I felt paralysed as soon as he came into the room. Then he developed cancer and was bedridden at the hospital for a long time, until the end. I refused to visit him, which was the only time I stood up to him. When I knew that he couldn't get to me. Towards the end, though, Mum got me to go by pleading and threatening me. My stepfather had begged to see me. She waited in the corridor. He looked awful and spoke in such a low voice that I had to bend over to hear him. He grabbed my hand but was so weak that he only managed to whisper these two words: *Forgive me.* I put my lips to his ear, whispered, The Devil is devouring you from the inside. I snatched my hand away, left, and the next day your stepmother dragged me out of the sea. I wanted to kill myself because I was filthy, and to take my revenge on him. He would understand; that would be my answer to his plea for forgiveness, that he had murdered me when I was seven years old.

I tried to forget. Sometimes you have to forget in order to live. I drank, drank far too much, and every sip was darkness. The only light in my world was my little girl, and for many years I lived solely for her. I thought that would be enough, that in doing so, I would fulfil my destiny. One day I happened to attend a concert here in Keflavík, Kristinn Sigmundsson and Jónas Ingimundarson performed Schubert's "*Winterreise*". I'd never listened to classical music before, let alone gone to a concert, such things just didn't exist in my world. It was Sunday, I'd gone to the shop for a hamburger and cigarettes, hungover, sad, and then wandered down to the harbour, I didn't particularly want to live anymore, saw nicely dressed people streaming into the Duus Hus Cultural Centre – and before I knew it, found myself sitting in one of the concert halls. Of course, I immediately regretted it. The hall was full of posh people and I felt like a stupid fishwife, a foul stain on the atmosphere. I wanted to leave but didn't dare to stand up, was afraid of drawing attention to myself. Then the concert began and . . . I sobbed the entire time! Couldn't control myself. Tears ran down my cheeks. God in heaven, I couldn't understand how all those tears had fit inside this slender body of mine. The very next day, I registered for adult education classes at the comprehensive school here. I suddenly felt a desire to live, desired a life for myself. You've got to live for yourself to be able to give to others. That's where my strength comes from, from the desire to live. I also knew that I would have to recall everything. This applies to nations as well as individuals; those who don't know their past, or don't want to admit to it, will lose themselves in the future. Those who wish to go forward must sometimes first go back.

Somewhere in the vicinity
of the universe

It's much better to eat freshly baked cinnamon rolls than to die

Ari had wandered for a long time, many years perhaps, through the darkened corridors before he finally found her room. She was sitting up in bed, bathed in moonlight. She said, Oh my heart, and it was night. Armstrong had just jumped down onto the Moon's surface, jumped carefully, worried that the surface might crack.

Didn't Buzz jump too, asks Ari, weren't they together, he and Armstrong? Yes, Buzz jumped too, but later; long after that night, people will look at the Moon and talk about Armstrong, about how carefully he'd jumped, some will also mention his footprints, which were left behind on the Moon's surface, stamped in the dust, and will outlive him. But only a few people will mention Buzz, because Armstrong was first to step onto the Moon, Buzz was number 2, he was in the shadow. Maybe that's why he started drinking afterwards, became mired in unhappiness. It feels hard to be erased after having giving your all, accomplished just as much, been just as brave – erased from the whims of life, the fancies of fate.

How do you know this? Know what? About Buzz, that he's going to be forgotten, and that being forgotten will destroy him? Maybe because I'm bathed in moonlight, for me there's no longer any difference between a fraction of a second and eternity, but how brave you are to have come through all this darkness, weren't you afraid? Yes, but I wasn't alone, I had help. You're never truly alone, unless you really make the effort to be so, there's always help, somewhere. It's not always easy to believe in it, though.

What happens now, wasn't it enough for me to get here, to

conquer the darkness, can't we go home, because it will be morning soon, morning always comes, eventually, and Böðvar the baker has probably started baking cinnamon rolls, they're so good when they're still warm. Definitely better to eat a freshly baked cinnamon roll than to die.

Morning doesn't always come, some nights never end, and it's too late for a warm cinnamon roll. Soon it will be too late for everything. Nothing can stop death once it sets off; it steps down to earth and you're gone. Then you're forgotten.

Like Buzz?

Unless someone changes that; would you like some marble cake?

You're dying and you offer me marble cake!

I can't offer you life; besides, you've always loved marble cake, these are from Böðvar's bakery. Someone came to visit me. A stranger brought me flowers and two marble cakes, a woman. One represents her happiness, the other grief, guilt and a touch of fear. Which one would you like?

Who was this woman?

You'll get to know her; you'll be unfair to her, she'll be clumsy, not a good combination.

I don't understand, says Ari. I know, she says, you're only five years old. Five and a half. I know, she says, but don't you think the flowers are beautiful? Ari looks at them and spies a little notebook on the table, along with a new novel by Veiga: *The Shadow of the Earth*. "In memory of my beloved niece" reads the inscription at the beginning. Ari turns the book over, reads the text on the back cover:

> In this sharp, merciless novel, Iceland is controlled
> by foreign aluminium companies in cooperation with
> domestic stakeholders. Capital rules over everything;

politicians are either corrupt or weak. A young woman, Heiðrún, unexpectedly finds herself considered a threat to these forces. Her life, her very existence, hangs by a thread. Can she trust the man she loves? And who are the two mysterious Norwegians? Do they control everything, or nothing?

I was always a little afraid of her, says Ari, looking at the photo of Veiga on the cover. She was always picking on me, as if I'd done something bad to her. Sometimes Lilla would say to her, Don't behave like that with the boy. How different the sisters were, Lilla . . . she was like a radiator that would always warm you, that would dry your mittens, while Veiga . . .

Don't judge her too harshly, she wished you well, cared for you, but could be unfair because you reminded her of my betrayal, my surrender, which I didn't have a chance to correct. I visited her soon after I became pregnant with you and announced that I didn't need to write anymore. I would be writing you. You would be my creation. Good God, how angry she was! What betrayal did she mean, asks Ari, what . . . Shush, don't ask, we've got to continue, there's so little left of life, listen: "Everything was clear. Everything. He clenched his fists. My brother in drink."

Hvordan skal du arbeida hvis du har no arms?[13]
— REYKJAVÍK, THE 1960S —

Was it three blows, or four?

He remembers her slamming against the refrigerator.

Then everything became . . . hazy.

13 *"Hvordan skal du ..."* (Norwegian): "How can you work if you have [*no arms*]"?

Was somehow erased.

Jakob comes to, sitting, half-lying, on the sofa, the vodka bottle on its side on the floor, some of its contents have spilled. What a waste, he thinks, standing the bottle upright, regarding the little puddle. At first he doesn't remember anything, but gradually it all comes back. The day before, the joy, the evening, Naustið . . . he tenses. Sits up, it's dark, it's still night. He gets slowly to his feet, walks hesitantly into the bedroom, she's not there, goes into the kitchen, not there either. A kitchen chair is lying on its side. He looks at the refrigerator, sees a shallow dent. First he hit her with his palm, then with his fist. That wasn't enough. He also had to slam her against the fridge. He stares at it.

And rushes out.

Doesn't put on his coat, is just wearing a shirt, it's very cold, but he doesn't give a shit. It would be best for everyone, for her, his parents, the world, if he just died. He runs down Skaftahlíð and stops, breathless, by a small block of flats at the bottom where her father, my and Ari's grandfather, lives with a Norwegian woman. He stares at the intercom for a long time. His heart thuds violently. He rings the bell.

And several moments later is crying on his knees in their kitchen.

She is sitting at the table, arms around her knees, my and Ari's Norwegian step-grandmother is leaning against a cabinet, arms crossed, a stern look on her face, while Grandpa stands over Jakob. His knees buckled as he entered the kitchen and saw her at the table. He collapsed as if he'd been shot. Now he is crying, wretchedly, painfully. He reaches out, wails, Cut them off! Cut off my arms, he repeats loudly when they don't respond: Cut them off, I'm a monster!

Grandpa stares hard at Jakob. I'll kill the fucking bastard, he had said when Ari's mother had come to them, her nice dress torn, one eye swollen, her voice hollow when she told them what had happened, that Jakob had hit her and slammed her against the fridge, startling Grandpa; then came the rage. It gushed into his chest. He said, and meant it: I'll kill the fucking bastard. You *görer* no nonsense, said our Norwegian step-grandma, and he did nothing of the sort. Jakob's tears threw him off guard. Also the fact that he fell to his knees and begged them to cut off his arms. Grandpa looks at his daughter. She has pulled her knees up, hugs them to her chest, stares down at the tabletop. Grandpa sighs softly. Jakob holds out his arms again, says, Please do this for me; save me by cutting off my arms! Our Norwegian step-grandmother snorts, Stop this damned nonsense, *hvordan skal du arbeida hvis du har* no arms, she asks, putting desperation, grief, into such serene perspective that Grandpa shuts his eyes for a moment, uncertain whether he's doing so out of relief or sadness, but Jakob's arms fall to his sides, he gets up, sits down at the kitchen table, stares vaguely into the distance, while our step-grandmother makes coffee, rolls a cigarette. She offers one to Jakob and his fingers tremble so much that he nearly drops it on the floor. They smoke, wait for the coffee to brew. Ari's mother stares out of the window, to the east, where the light comes from. Something is paralysing her, perhaps it's life . . .

Pick red and think about sunshine

. . . because something, sometimes, seems to rebel against our dreams.

*

I didn't know he'd hit you, I hate him, I'm glad he's dying.

Oh, little one, that shouldn't have surprised you. There's no malice in Jakob, never has been, I think he couldn't handle life very well, or himself. He was convinced that he'd disappointed his father and had no place in his mother's dreams. I think he sometimes felt like an orphan. Which may be the reason why I was drawn to him: his vulnerability, and of course those blue eyes!

Didn't you love me more than him, Ari asks suddenly, asks obstinately, naively, desperately, in a human way, but she vanishes into the moonlight, then returns quickly and asks, Shall we play Ludo? God help me, how much I regret not being able to watch you grow, change, evolve – and . . . Oh, my little Pluto, it's such a swindle to have to die so young, you miss out on so much, nearly everything, and soon you'll start stuttering because death will become part of your language. What colour would you like for Ludo, take red, that's the best colour.

Why are you calling me Pluto? What's going to happen next?

I'll beat you at Ludo, disappear into the moonlight, you'll go on living, a planet in the darkness of the universe. Later on, it will turn out that you have no right to be called a planet; maybe a dwarf planet, at best. You won't have your own orbit, won't dare to go deeply enough into yourself, perhaps afraid of being unable to handle what you discover. You'll convince yourself that life is a horse that can be tamed, but then you'll kiss someone and fate will hurl a meteor in your direction, your horse will shy, turn wild, you'll go astray, become lost in the midst of your journey through life.

And then what, will I find the way?

You certainly do ask a lot of questions; do you think I know everything? Maybe I'll send you someone from the moon. The dead can do little to help the living, you must understand that, otherwise you'll never get anywhere.

What if you betray what mustn't be betrayed . . . Dad betrayed you, you know that now, what . . .

Yes, but what is betrayal? Maybe sometimes people have to betray in order to survive – we always rise after we fall. Otherwise, I suspect that the heart is too complicated for the reality that we've created. What a horrid mess. What can be done about it? And what is betrayal?

How am I supposed to answer that, I'm only five years old, it's night and I'm scared.

You don't have to reply, just live. Two of my four Ludo tokens have made it, I have two left, I'll die when the fourth reaches the finish. We have so little time left, I may have been happiest when I was nursing you. It's an experience that can hardly be described, when your child suckles your milk, I've never come as close to another life as I did then. I sometimes felt as if all of me was streaming into you. My third token is approaching the finish line: Think about sunshine.

She has never run so fast in her life
— NORÐFJÖRÐUR, PAST —

Because the sunshine fills the sky with its heat and light, melts the snow in the mountains, streams in through the kitchen window where Margrét is standing, staring out as Jakob suckles at her left breast. It's lovely to stand in the sunshine, to feel its warmth, feel the force of life, feel Jakob suckling her milk. He suckles, she gives, and the more she gives, the stronger they both become, and the bond between them. She looks out, there's Tryggvi and Áslaug's house – no, it's not their house anymore, of course; they're gone. Moved away three years ago, south to Vatnsleysuströnd, with their three girls. To her surprise, Áslaug never got over her homesickness, as relieved as she'd been to escape from there, nothing but flatness, lava rocks, the roaring sea, the incessant wind that seemed sometimes to want nothing more than to blow all life off the land. What a dream it had been to come here to the east, where the word *calm* has real meaning, and you knew you'd get nice summer days, warmth, sunshine. But then, unexpectedly, she began to dream about the open sea, serene and violent, a far horizon, freshness on the wind, silence in the lava. Yet she wasn't the one who spoke of moving; it was Tryggvi who did, suddenly he was gripped by *ennui*, as if the fjord had begun to close in on him. Maybe, he said to Margrét, explained, apologised, it's that you grow older and one day it dawns on you that you have only this one life for sure, and how should you spend it? You don't think about it in your younger years, when it's more than enough just to live, exist, drink life in. Then you wake up one day in the middle of your journey through life, as Dante writes, and feel in your bones how your possibilities lessen with each passing day – and how repetition takes up ever more space in your existence. You start longing for something else, a different horizon, not necessarily better, perhaps even worse in some sense, but for you, it's new. Something is added to your life, the wheel of repetition is slowed ever so slightly. Is that fleeing? I've asked myself the same questions. It's strange, sister, that you can't immediately recognise the difference between fleeing and the courage to change your life.

Jakob makes tranquil sounds, she closes her eyes, it isn't always easy to look at Tryggvi and Áslaug's house, remember their absence. But in return, she receives two, even three letters a month, they write to her separately, and consequently, it's as if Margrét acquires a tiny share in their new horizon. Tryggvi is now on a 40-ton fishing boat that sails from the village of Stapi, Áslaug is working in the fish factory there, they live just outside the village, in a nice house, the eldest girl is attending Reykjavík Secondary School, the first member from both sides of her family to go to secondary school. We did right, sister, and how lovely it would be if you moved here too, though I know that my brother-in-law couldn't be persuaded to do it, unless he could take the fjord with him, Nípa Point and preferably all of Snædalur Valley. How is he?

Margrét opens her eyes. How is he? It's as if something's happened between the brothers-in-law, as if something heavy has come between them, perhaps Oddur couldn't forgive his friend for moving away, he would be likely to feel that way, even view it as a betrayal, and become mired in that opinion, no-one can be as stubborn and unbending as Oddur, he can sometimes get so worked up about something that it approaches spite. "You can always," writes Áslaug, "come and visit us, even stay a few weeks. We have a spare room, we could go to Reykjavík, sit in cafés like foreign ladies, go to the cinema, the theatre, even get a bit drunk together!"

Yes, she writes back, yes, yes, yes!

She still hasn't gone. Has never gone farther than Seyðis-fjörður, the second fjord over, since she came from Canada, with a stop in Reykjavík. Twenty years ago. Reykjavík has changed . . . and she isn't the same person either. She still hasn't gone; there's so much holding us back. Oddur retreated into stubborn silence when she mentioned it, and then they had Jakob, who now suckles at her breast, drinks in her warm life as she stares out into the sunshine, sees the shore where Gunnar and his two friends are dragging something heavy behind them, most likely a raft that they've constructed. She reaches for the binoculars; yes, it's a raft. Gunnar turns to look as she is watching, as if apologetically. She's forbidden him so often to do things like that without an adult around, or at least close by. Gunnar promised – and it has always been a matter of pride to him to keep his promises. But it's hard to resist the sea, it's there before your eyes, from birth, filling your every moment. It's the sea that makes us men, Oddur has said more often than you can count, recites it like a creed; the sea decides whether you're a man or not. Gunnar could see no harm in helping his friends build the raft, he's much better with his hands than they are, he was only going to help them build and launch it, that could hardly be considered breaking his promise. But the sea sings such an alluring, enchanting song. That's why Gunnar looked up at the house, apologetically, as if to say, Sorry, Mum. Then they push off from the shore.

Margrét curses softly, gives Jakob a little nudge, wakes him, gets him to suckle better, calls to Ólöf and tells her to run down to the shore and forbid her brother from rowing out on the raft. Ólöf obeys reluctantly. She was sitting there mending her clothes, had planned to finish before a certain time, now her plan is ruined, all because of her brother who always gets his way, besides getting to play while she does all the hard work. She curses: if only the sea would swallow him! She goes out and Margrét can't help but smile at Ólöf's stubbornness and frustration, so obvious from her posture. Ólöf, however, starts running when she sees how well they're doing at pushing off, and by the time she stands panting on the beach, they're already a few metres out. After all, it's a brilliant day for starting a fishing company. Sun, and such profound calm that it's as if the winds have fallen asleep and sunk

318

into the sea. They row with their primitive oars and look up when Ólöf calls out, Is this how you keep a promise, you rascal? The others look at Gunnar, hesitantly, not quite as enthusiastic now, they're about fifteen metres from land and the sea is already deep. Gunnar shouts back, You don't understand, you don't know anything about such things, it's the sea that makes us men, see? And the land that makes you women!

Then he crouches down for his line, because now they're going to fish, start their fishing operation, become men – youth is behind them. Ólöf curses, grabs a rock, throws it at them, hoping to hit Gunnar, to silence his bragging, but misses. She hears them laugh and bends down for a bigger rock, throws it furiously in the direction of the laughter, the conceit, their freedom . . .

. . . the boys and the raft are no longer visible to Margrét, there are houses in the way, but she does see Ólöf bend over twice for rocks, throw one angrily the second time, put everything she has into the throw, then her entire body tenses. Margrét doesn't think twice: she rushes out of the door. Sticks Jakob under her arm like a sack and runs hard. Knows that something has happened, saw it in the way that Ólöf's body tensed. She rushes down the slope and sees that Ólöf has dashed into the sea, paddles out, barely able to swim, she sees the empty raft, two boys splashing in the water, hears their screams, the third one appears to be floating motionless, half-submerged.

Margrét has never run so fast in her life, she almost throws Jakob down on the beach in her rush, says, Don't move, as if he could understand, young as he is, the only thing he understands is her warmth and now she has tossed him aside, which is why he cries. She doesn't hear him, she doesn't listen, she yanks down her

319

skirt, wades into the water, starts swimming, past the exhausted Ólöf, who whispers, Mummy dear. Margrét forces herself to swim to the raft first and push it, unbearably slowly, towards the kicking boys, knows that they don't have much more strength to stay afloat, then swims to Gunnar, floating nearby. He starts to sink. As if he'd been waiting for her to come. So that she would get to see him drown. She sees his blonde head sink, disappear into the sea . . .

Life, our only resistance?

. . . I've always been afraid of the sea, she says, you know that your great-grandfather almost drowned in the harbour in Reykjavík; he was blind drunk, the old fool, then he caught pneumonia and died. Left your grandmother behind in the struggle.

Ari: Why don't you continue with the story of Margrét and Gunnar?

He's lying cuddled up to his mother, to sense her life force, has no idea whether he's five or fifty. I don't know, she says, maybe I just wanted you to know this, that I was afraid of the sea. Then I'm also going to be afraid of it; then we'll be the same. Yet the sea is incredibly beautiful, she says, I wish I could always be in its presence.

I want that too, says Ari, listening to her breathe.

Moonlight shines in through the window. It's up there, the Moon, with Armstrong's lonely footsteps on its surface. You want me to continue? she asks, after some time has passed, a few seconds, a few years, she has just breathed and the world doesn't need anything more. I don't know, he says, I want you to continue, but I'm also worried that you'll die when you've finished telling the story. You're right, I'll die when the story ends. Then stop, he says. I can't, dear heart, because then everything else would die, too. Death passes through everyone, it makes everything distant, erases everyone, our only resistance is to live and speak about it. Leave the life force behind in our words. It doesn't conquer death but perhaps prevents death from conquering life. Maybe, says Ari, reluctantly. Trust me, she says, stroking his fingers soothingly, then closes her eyes, and dives . . .

Don't say such things, she says
— NORÐFJÖRÐUR, PAST —

. . . after Gunnar. She has never dived into the sea. There's a heavy pounding down in the sea, and a hostile silence. She remembers this: the heavy pounding, the hostile silence. This she remembers. And herself swimming, frenzied, every cell in her body and life aimed at this one goal, to reach Gunnar before death does. She would wake so often to this dream in the coming years, decades. She, diving with all the power that life could grant her but not seeming to get anywhere. And Gunnar sinking.

But, says Ari in the moonlight at Vífilsstaðir, she reached him, right?

No, she didn't. She was too late.

Remembers this: Gunnar sinking, she's too late, much too late. She remembers nothing else.

Except that they're all on the pier, she, Gunnar, deathly pale, motionless, a few people and Þorkell the headmaster, who's kneeling, soaked to the bone, bare-chested, trying to breathe life into her boy.

I'm fine, says Gunnar, when someone mentions a doctor, that it would be better for a doctor to have a look at the boy. I'm just bloody freezing, he adds, shivering on the pier, despite wearing the headmaster's thick jumper. He'd been in his office on the upper floor of the school, sitting there writing an article, but had stood up to stretch and construct a sentence a bit better in his head, and then had seen someone running furiously down the slope. Recognised her instantly. And knew that something was terribly wrong. He didn't stop to think, ran outside, down to the pier and dove in – after tearing off his jacket and jumper and kicking off his shoes. He swam out, swam past Margrét, grabbed Gunnar, swam with him to the pier where eager hands helped the three of them out of the water. Several people had launched a boat and rowed out to Ólöf and the two boys, who were clinging to the raft. Þorkell blew life into Gunnar, who sat up shortly afterwards and vomited sea-water. He had a cut on his temple where the rock had hit him; it made him lose his balance, the raft went nearly vertical, dumping them all in the sea, unable to swim. He sat up, weak, shivering, threw up seawater and said, Dammit, man. Margrét laughed. She laughed, she kissed her boy, barely noticed when the headmaster put his jacket round her, his jumper on Gunnar, or when someone handed her Jakob. You poor thing, she says with a smile, as if she'd forgotten about him. She thanks the headmaster with a handshake. Her long, wet hair falls over his jacket. I thank the headmaster, she says in a muffled voice. He takes her hand, worn from hard work, with its long fingers. Piano fingers, he thinks, smiles faintly, and says, The pleasure is all mine. The first words that pass between them since that time on the mountain, in the night, beneath the stars, three years ago. The pleasure is all

mine, he says, I'm grateful to have had the chance to be of use. Then
he watches them walk home.

On the other hand, there are few, if any, better things than hot
cocoa when you're drenched to the skin, cold down to your bones
and nearly drowned. Margrét carefully folds the headmaster's
jumper, Ólöf chatters at Gunnar, who is wrapped in a blanket,
his forehead red from the rock. He shivers and is quiet for a long
time, finally looks at his mother and asks if she can forgive him
for breaking his promise. She kisses him, his hair, ears. You're
alive, she says, you're my boy. He smiles, happy. She turns to wipe
away her tears because Gunnar is alive, and because her longing
for Þórður suddenly becomes utterly unbearable . . . and perhaps
because she can't stop thinking about the time the headmaster
held her hand. She looks at her three children, Ólöf, Gunnar,
Elín, Hulda is out somewhere and Jakob is asleep. Elín had come
running in, having heard what had happened, came running
and leapt on Gunnar, nearly tipping the chair and Gunnar onto
the floor. Now they're sitting at the kitchen table, chatting away
happily, Margrét leans against the wall, running her hand, out of
old habit, over the pale wound left by the plate she once threw at
the wall with all her might, when something broke inside her,
threw the plate, as if to protest against life. Runs her hand over the
wound, watches her children, feels a warm sense of happiness.

I'll send the kids over with your jumper and jacket, she had
said when the headmaster wouldn't take back his garments,
despite shivering in the breeze, bare-chested, slim, delicate, yet
strong enough to save a life. As you wish, he said, I'll be at the
school, in my office, it's on the second floor, I have an extra jumper
there, I can dry my trousers. You're not going home to recover? I'll

recover best by working. Work, on a Sunday? Work, he said, that is perhaps too posh a word for what I am scribbling. It's the same for words as it is for fish, they're too witless to know the difference between Sunday and Monday. He smiled, almost shyly.

Gunnar's friends have arrived, those who were with him on the raft. The children laugh together. Gunnar is slower than usual, but he's happy. Her presence is no longer required. She grabs the head-master's jumper and jacket, asks Ólöf to look after Jakob, says that she's going to return the clothes, maybe walk up the mountain a bit. The children are having so much fun that they'll hardly notice whether she's there or up on the mountain. Or at the school, returning some clothes, a jumper and a jacket.

These garments are made from exceptionally fine fabric.

From Scotland, says the headmaster.

He had stood up when he heard someone coming, and thought, Whose footsteps might they be? Thought, Hopefully it's not someone coming to disturb me. He pretended not to notice his heart, that silly little creature, how it thudded. Forgive me for interrupting, she says. You're not interrupting. But the headmaster is working? I would hardly call it work, I thought I would start writing some articles about great scientists for *Eastfirthers*, we need grand thoughts from the wide, wide world in our everyday lives. You can work here, undisturbed? Oh, Margrét, call me Þorkell! There's no-one here to disturb me, not on a Sunday. I apologise again for disturbing you; I just wanted to return your clothes, and thank you again for what you did, though my thanks will never be sufficient. You may thank me by looking at me, he says unguardedly. Here are your clothes, she says, so considerate that she pretends not to have heard his nonsense; they're excep-

324

tionally fine. Scottish, he says; we could learn a lot from them, the Scots. Truth be told, we could learn a lot from the entire world. Sometimes we think so much about fish that it makes our minds more impoverished than they need to be – I'm not denigrating seamanship, he adds hurriedly. She hands him his clothes. He takes them.

Her errand is complete. No reason to waste time here, disturbing a learned man writing about grand thoughts, let alone when you've got such ugly hands.

Still, she just stands there, wasting both of their time. Or is it perhaps life that hesitates, as if it's standing, unsuspecting, at a crossroads, hesitating there, even gripped with fear? She turns, walks out, the moment has passed, she passed the test.

The article I'm writing, he says, is about a remarkable woman, Marie Curie, one of the most important scientists of our time, perhaps of all time. Indeed, says Margrét, hollowly, as if just being courteous, but she turns back to look at him. He nods, she passed away recently, he says, won the Nobel Prize twice, first in physics, then in chemistry. A great scientist, a great individual, and I want to enlarge our lives here in the east by writing about her. A woman, says Margrét. Yes, he says.

A mother, perhaps?

Two daughters. May I read you what I've written?

I don't want to disturb you any further.

He doesn't reply, goes to his desk, sits down, reaches for two densely written sheets, and Margrét follows him hesitantly. Afternoon light streams through the window and the headmaster reads what he has written about Marie Curie. His voice is soft and he reads enthusiastically. He finishes.

Margrét moves closer.

I'm a little more than halfway done, he says. Thank you, she says, for reading it to me; it was kind of you. He sits, she stands. Her flowing brown hair has begun to turn grey, but it's still thick. What did you mean, she asks suddenly. What, when? he asks. You said, "You may thank me by looking at me." Am I not allowed to say that? I don't understand, don't understand what you meant. I don't understand why you want to talk to me, and besides, I have very ugly hands. May I see them? No, she says, and holds them out. He takes them in his, caresses her fingers, turns them over, looks at her palms. It's as if all of life is in these hands, he says. Don't say such things. Forgive me. No, she says, and then takes his head in both of her hands, tilts it back, bites his lips, kisses him, bites his chin, kneels down to pull off his trousers, stands up, slips off her panties, looks at him. Parts her legs and sits on his lap. Still in her dress, she gropes with her right hand, finds his penis, strokes it gently as it hardens, swells, her eyes are half-closed, she strokes harder, squeezes a bit, he moans softly and she lowers herself onto him. Very slowly. Until he is all the way inside her. Just sits there. Looks into his eyes. Says his name. He says her name, and then she kisses him and begins to move. He takes a deep breath, she moans softly, moves slowly, then fast, they kiss, they cry. She whispers something, he . . .

Then what?

Why were they crying? asks Ari.

I hope because they were happy. But also because of sadness at . . . fitting together so well. Þorkell loved his wife, couldn't imagine life without her. And Margrét . . . they cried because they were doomed to betrayal every time they were together. Happiness that may not be revealed to the world holds great sorrow.

And then what? asks Ari.

"What will become of justice and beauty if ideals die?"
— SANDGERÐI, PRESENT —

No-one knew about it, says Ásmundur.

I sit by the window, look out and see the night stretching further than eyes can see. It streams into the house and fills me with what is, it fills me with times past, with life, and death, because Gunnar would die only eight years later, he froze to death between Seyðisfjörður and Norðfjörður, didn't have any particular business there, as Oddur put it. His first reaction to the news, and Margrét looked down at the kitchen table. When she looked up again, her love for Oddur was dead.

No-one knew about her and Þorkell's affair, which continued, it wasn't just that one intense, painful and beautiful moment on the top floor of the school, it continued until Þorkell died, sixteen years later. By then, Oddur was in the TB sanatorium in Eyjafjörður, out of action, the sea hero and enthusiast. He spent the final two decades of his life at that sanatorium and at Reykjalundur in Mosfellssveit, both so far from the sea that its smell couldn't reach them. Suffocating, and drains the life out of you, he often said, yet not enough to prevent him from having two children with two women, both considerably younger. Margrét didn't find out until after Oddur had passed away, and then purely by chance. "If only I'd known earlier," she wrote in her diary. "It would have eased my guilty conscience. Loving Þorkell would have been even better and more beautiful."

*

She started working at the school shortly after the incident with Gunnar. No-one knew about the affair, but when Þorkell became ill and lost his strength, the two of them would bathe him, his wife and Margrét. She got to touch his entire body, and then carry him to his bed in his final months, when Þorkell had withered to almost nothing. I'm dying, he whispered to her once, yet I have never lived as strongly. The pain was sufficiently bearable for him to sit up, read to her from the collection of articles that he wanted to finish. Margrét sat by the bed, wrote down what he said, and then Hrefna, his wife, came upstairs with coffee and cake for the three of them.

But no-one knew about their love, says Ásmundur. Grandma moved here to Keflavík and corresponded with Hrefna until the very end. Though Mum and I had to write her letters for her in her final days, and the two of them mentioned Þorkell in every letter: Please give him my greetings, sister, when next you go to the garden, Grandma would always end her letters. Shortly before her death she sent me with her diaries, quite a stack of them, covering more than four decades, down to the library with instructions that they remain sealed for thirty-five years. We found that strange. Her life seemed like an open book. No room for secrets, other than those held in thought. It crossed our minds that she'd written something harsh about Grandpa that she regretted. It wasn't always easy to live with Grandpa, of course; he was the skipper, the rest of us were deckhands, and she . . .

Thirty-five, says Ari, wasn't it thirty-five years since her death this September?

September 21. At nine in the morning Ásmundur and Sigga went down to the library to get them.

*

I don't know, says Ásmundur, whether your dad has read them, but it was decided long ago that he would have them first. I think he just put them into storage. Sigga, on the other hand, took no risks and spent two days photocopying every page.

And they turned out to be full of secrets, after all?

Yes, especially starting with that Sunday when Gunnar almost drowned. And some uncomfortably graphic descriptions of her and Þorkell's love.

No, says Sigga, not at all uncomfortable, but rather, unbearably beautiful, and Ari should publish them, of course. Publish them?! exclaims Ásmundur, shocked. Yes, teddy bear, publish them. They're too remarkable to be lost and forgotten. Of course it might be tough for some of you, your grandmother is incredibly blunt sometimes, not just about her and Þorkell's love life but also when she tells of her disappointment at how none of her children or grandchildren went in the directions she had imagined for them – and how none of them was Þórður. Everyone so busy with their own lives that no-one had the time for, or interest in, trying to change the world. Do you remember the entry from about a year before her death, when she wrote that no-one bothers to change anything but their hairstyle every now and then, and the direction in which the chairs face in their living rooms? "What will become of justice and beauty if ideals die?" A woman who writes like that has to appear in print. At some point, this family has got to dare to take a stand in life.

This is why I love you, says Ásmundur. You are what I should have been; you are the child that Grandma dreamed of. Sigga smiles, runs her fingers through Ásmundur's hair, and then looks at Ari: Margrét wrote quite a bit about your mother. Ari straightens up, asks, My mother? Yes, she . . .

329

. . . sometimes called me her daughter, sometimes her sister. I always meant to introduce them to each other, your grandmother and Veiga, but it's too late now. Soon everyone will be dead but you. Look – my Ludo token is on its way to the finish line.

Ari: So it's too late?

For me, yes, and for everyone else. Margrét, Veiga, Lilla, your grandfather and step-grandmother, Oddur, Tryggvi, Áslaug, Þórður, Gunnar, Elín . . . and Jakob. We can't go any further. We have to come to terms with what we did, regret what we didn't do. But the living can help the dead; raise us from the darkness of oblivion, let our beauty shine, clarify our betrayals and cowardice. Seek strength in what is good, learn from what is not. Only then will our bones rest peacefully for all eternity. Goodness, how awful you are at Ludo! It's your turn to roll the dice.

Every roll brings us closer to the end. I'll skip my turn, then I'll have you with me for eternity.

You have to roll the dice. You have to live. Why is that so difficult for you?

Did they discover the betrayal? asked my ex, Þóra, whom I still love. I can't stop doing so, she's in my blood. Did they discover the betrayal? she asked, after she'd arranged for my favourite cousin and role model, Ásmundur, to stick his index finger deep into my rectum – and he has long fingers. Betrayal? I love two women. That's what did me in.

It's not betrayal to love two women; it's a problem, an unfortunate happiness and pain. My betrayal was completely different.

What was it then? That I stopped writing? That seems to hurt all of you. Don't my own thoughts on the matter count? Even Dad spat something at me, why did I quit, as if that were a crime! He who didn't say a single word about my writing, even when it was published. What does it change if I write or I don't? As if literature makes any difference at all these days – you have no idea what the world has become. A few weeks ago, some fucking lunatics blew up a bus in southern Europe. Seven people were killed. Including a young woman and her child, not yet a year old. She'd just sent her husband a text, a quotation from a poem by Pessoa that she was reading on the bus. Few people have written better than Pessoa, but that's how useless his poems were when it came down to it. Anyway, fewer and fewer people read poetry now; it no longer makes a difference, it's just entertainment, a banquet ornament at best, and exam fodder in schools, just . . . Such is the world today – and you spin in your graves about writing! You cross the indefinable space between life and death . . . well, for what? To teach us how to live, to deal with our pain, to conquer injustice, cruelty? Absolutely not! You overcome the laws of nature because it frustrates you that I've stopped writing! Do you learn nothing there in eternity? Do you have no view? Don't you see that my books change nothing, no more than any other books? At best, I might be praised for my fine style, beautiful words, understanding of the human heart and soul, but that changes nothing, doesn't move the world; it's too heavy. Are you nourished, perhaps, by the praise accorded to me – which would mean that vanity is stronger than death?

What a bloody racket you make. Have you forgotten that it's night and we're in a hospital where most of the patients are dying? You'd started shouting. Even so, I'm happy with you, can see there's fire inside you still. It's too bad that you're so afraid.

Afraid of what?

You're right, Pluto, no-one should spend time writing unless he wants to give us new eyes, shed light on life's illusion, the betrayal, the cowardice, the injustice, yes, even defuse bombs. Beautiful words are worthless if they don't make us better people.

Has no-one told you
— SANDGERÐI, PRESENT —

... and why have you stopped writing? asks Sigga. I still have the poems you tossed onto my balcony that night. I was terribly proud of them, poems about my breasts; I didn't expect that! You can't imagine how important they were to me. Sometimes I read them to comfort me when I felt like my self-loathing would kill me. You wrote four books and then stopped, why? Don't you know that it's everyone's duty to make use of the power they've been given? Those with voices should sing. Those with the brains to calculate should wrestle with difficult mathematical problems. Those who have insight into the human condition should be psychologists or priests and comfort people. Has no-one told you that those who don't make use of their powers betray life, and themselves, and will die unhappy?

Sigga gives Ari a long look with those black eyes of hers. He opens his mouth to reply, but then the telephone rings.

Is cowardice the worst vice?

You swept everything off the breakfast table, stormed out, went north to Hólmavík because you were breaking down under the pressure of ...

Life, concludes Ari when his mother hesitates, or needs to rest.

... cowardice. I'm sorry to be so cruel, but I have little time

332

left, and almost no energy to treat you gently anymore. The things that have a lasting impact on a person are passed down from one generation to another. That's why families often wrestle with the same trolls, generation after generation, until, and if, someone manages to break the vicious cycle. Then the trolls turn to stone and it becomes easier to live. And die. For us, the troll is probably cowardice. Þórður bent to his father's will, I to your father's will and expectations, to my dad's and stepmother's, and thereby society's. Then we died. So young that we didn't get a chance to make up for it. Tryggvi never forgave himself for having stood by when he saw how Oddur tried to bend Þórður to his will, to his dreams, and something snapped inside Tryggvi when Oddur hit Þórður so hard that the boy was nearly knocked overboard. He never forgave himself for not stepping in, for not trying to comfort or help Þórður, or to talk to Oddur. Things were never the same between them after Þórður's death, which is why Tryggvi wanted to move away. He tried to make up for it by offering to take Jakob in down south. Oddur had called Jakob from the sanatorium in Eyjafjörður, to inform him that he'd got him a job on a good boat and that Jakob could start the following week. Two days later, your dad was, at Margrét's insistence, on his way south to Tryggvi, never to return to Norðfjörður; he'd got a job at the Base. Oddur took it badly.

But what did Dad want?

That's for you to find out . . . perhaps he sought strength beyond himself, in drink, in his friend Siggi . . . never felt whole, and happy, except when playing bridge. It was only then that he relied solely on his own strength. And now he's disappearing into the darkness . . .

Sandgerði, Keflavík

— PRESENT —

". . . I think that life is a bit fond of its weeds, as well"

A telephone rings a few times before Ari realises that it's his mobile. His fingers tremble as he pulls it from the pocket of his fleece, which he'd taken off and set aside when the living room had become too warm, because who would call in the middle of the night unless it was important, it couldn't wait, needed discussing right away . . . maybe it's Þóra? Maybe she woke up and longed to hear his voice, his breathing . . . Ari looks at the number, doesn't recognise it, answers hesitantly.

Is that you, honey, did I wake you? asks a woman's voice, a bit hoarse, worn. Ari recognises it immediately, but that word, *honey*, bothers him so much that he feigns ignorance and asks, Who's speaking, please? It's Anna, your father's friend . . . is that you, Ari? Yes. I found your number in your father's phone. I hope it's just me being hysterical, that I'm just a nervous old biddy, but I woke up about twenty minutes ago, it's night of course, and he's nowhere to be seen, my Kobbi. Your father, she adds when Ari says nothing. He can't have gone far, says Ari, staring into the flames in the fireplace, the man has trouble getting up from a sofa, let alone wandering off in the middle of the night . . . Hello, he says when she doesn't respond, hello, are you there? Yes, I'm sorry, I just found some bits of paper that he seems to have written on, they were under the letter, which is why I didn't see them. Slips of paper . . . what letter? Oh, from Gunnar, the writer, an extremely nice letter. Gunnar Gunnarsson? Yes, written with a fountain pen, exceptionally elegant and educated handwriting. A letter from Gunnar Gunnarsson to Dad? asks Ari in disbelief. He looks at us, Sigga sits up straighter, turns the music down. No, to your grandmother, Margrét, it was written in 1934, more than eighty years ago, and we found it last night, unopened. Imagine that, unopened after all these years! Why was Gunnar Gunnarsson writing to my grandmother . . . hello? he says when Anna says nothing. Oh, yes, sorry, I was just trying to read what your dad scribbled on these bits of paper, it's barely legible . . . Your grandmother appears to have written to Gunnar about her son Þórður, I understand that he died young and had been incredibly talented, and the writer is very sincere in his reply, your grandmother clearly touched him deeply . . . I think . . . he was going to go down to the shore, she interrupts herself. Who, Gunnar? No, darling, your dad, as far as I can make out. What does he say? That he's going to . . . totter down to the shore and . . . yes, look at the sea. It looks like it says: "Then I'm certain I'll finally be able to say the things that really matter." Did Dad write that?! Yes, who would have guessed it . . . I actually awoke to the sound of someone crying . . . he was crying . . . my Kobbi, but tried to stifle it, stuffed my tights into his mouth. Why can't you behave like proper human beings – no-one should have to cry alone, it's horribly painful. I'm going out to see if I can find him. Someone should teach you two how to talk to each other, and give you both a bit of a shake – I'll say no more.

Once we saw, says Ari, slowly, hesitantly, Dad and I, I mean, an old woman crying. It was many years ago. Decades. She was sitting against a wall of the retirement home above the Botanical Gardens, crying. Alone. No-one to comfort her and we just walked past. Pretended not to see her.

Ari stares at the coffee table. At the other end of the phone, only silence. We look at him, Nina Simone sings in a low voice, "I get along without you very well (except sometimes)," Ásmundur is ruffling Sigga's hair, and she wipes her eyes. My life, says Anna, after the long silence on the telephone, has never been good or beautiful. You may know that I was into Yanks. I dreamed of meeting someone who would take me away from Iceland. I didn't require much love, just trust, and to escape. I knew that I could be a good wife and mother. The world seemed so much bigger out there in America. With more room for happiness. I met your dad at the Base, it was night, and we were very young. I was there for the first time and he was incredibly cute, your dad, so sweet that I instantly felt attracted to him. Still, nothing happened between us, nor did we have time for anything, and . . . I didn't see your dad again until here in the retirement home . . . I was just seventeen, see, just a young thing; I'd run away from home after my mother died. She disappeared one night, her body was found at the shore two days later. That didn't really surprise anyone; she drank a tremendous amount, which back then was called being an alky; now there are fancier words for it . . . most likely fell dead-drunk into the sea, people said. I think she killed herself to get away from my dad. I ran away the day after the funeral, my dad . . . oh, he's dead now anyway, and they're probably still torturing him in Hell . . . but then I started going up to the Base, to try to get away from everything here, this small, oppressive world where men stepped on your toes while you were dancing, scratched their arses at the dinner table and never bothered to say anything nice to you . . . I'm sure you know that the word *away* possesses no magical powers . . . goodness, how you get me to talk, honey, you must have something truly special. I haven't just been jabbering, I've got dressed in the meantime, have my coat on, and my shoes. He's a beautiful man, your dad, even if he is the way he is. We're all the way we are. Now I'm outside in the cold and the night and I'm going to hurry to find your dad before he freezes. He's my flower of happiness. Maybe you find it stupid to hear an old alky and Yankee whore calling another alky her flower of happiness, but life is also a bit fond of its weeds, and therefore deigned to bring me happiness before it was too late.

So the world has come to this

Is he going down to the beach because his first memories are from there? Half-awake between some stones. His mother running away from him. Tossed him aside to go and save Gunnar.

Remembers and remembers – he wasn't even a year old, how could he remember?

Yet this is his first memory. Margrét tosses him aside. He remembers falling. Left him behind on the hard stones at the shore.

Remembers and remembers.

I picked you up off those stones like any old rubbish, Ásdís sometimes said to him. She worked for the shopkeeper, noticed a commotion, went outside, saw a group of people on the pier, saw Þorkell and Margrét in the sea with Gunnar, saw Ólöf hanging on to the raft along with the two boys – and then heard you on the stones, wailing, understanding nothing, naturally, without your mother, but you let me cuddle you as soon as I picked you up. Since then, I've always felt like a part of you is mine, said Ásdís, usually stroking Jakob's hair as she recalled the scene, which she did far too often. Smiled at him when he was sent down to the shop. He was always polite but couldn't stand her. Couldn't stand that it had been she who'd picked him up, not his mother. Couldn't stand the way she smiled at him. Sometimes she would sneak him

340

a few sweets when no-one was looking, wink at him, smile. Jakob would smile back but throw away the sweets as soon as he was outside the shop and in the clear, despite almost never getting sweets, except at Christmas. In fact, Jakob hated Ásdís. Who asked after him once he'd moved south. Ásdís was asking after you, says hi, was in more than one letter from Margrét. He hated her for thinking she had a claim on him. Because she'd picked him up from the rocks at the shore, forgotten by everyone. Forgotten, like Buzz. Þórður was Armstrong, Gunnar was Collins, who piloted the command module. The two of them had roles; he came later. What he did the two of them had already done, and better.

How terribly stupid I can be, thinks Jakob, stumbling between the sleeping houses, drawing nearer to Hafnargata, and the sea. It's remarkable how everything suddenly seems so clear. Maybe because he has to move so slowly, can't go any faster, has to stop and rest, has time to think . . . or can't avoid doing so. Maybe also because Gunnar Gunnarsson wrote that letter . . . and in it said what had been his greatest sorrow . . . If only he could thank Ásdís now for picking him up, and for being so kind to him over the years, and apologise for not having appreciated it. He would start with her . . . then Ari and . . . incredible how stupid he's been! There's self-pity in every drink, darling, Anna once said to him. It's so strange that life had possessed such benevolence and generosity to allow them to meet again, after all those years, all those difficulties, that heavy sea. He didn't deserve it. I'll make up for it, he says to himself, smiles, and has got to Hafnargata when it dawns on him that there's no reason for him to clamber down to the shore. Besides, it's difficult for him to reach the sea because of the boulders that have been piled up along the edge, Keflavík's old beach gone, filled with 3,000-year-old boulders from Helguvík, as if to underline the fact that the residents of Keflavík weren't allowed to fish anymore, they should just forget about the sea. I would break my neck on those bleeding rocks, mutters Jakob, his anger flaring suddenly, as always when he thinks about how the residents of Keflavík have been deprived of the sea, that such a thing could be possible, that the cold interests of a few filthy-rich individuals could effortlessly deprive a centuries-old fishing village of the sea. This is what the world has come to, thinks Jakob, now in the middle of Hafnargata, having abandoned his plan to go down to the shore. He just wants to go to Anna, hold her and let her hold him. If only he could turn back faster, if only he could run to her. It's good to be alive, he thinks, having completely forgotten about the cancer, that it's spreading like darkness inside him. Tomorrow, he thinks, Anna and I will go for a drive, drive around Keflavík and get real hamburgers at Jonni's, say a few spirited words about the fucking financial powers that want to destroy all of life with their insipid greed, and then . . . Jakob turns and looks. It's as if someone is saying his name. Very quietly, yet it seems to fill all existence, almost as if it's the universe itself that's whispering his name. Jakob turns and looks, and sees the light.

What a burden death is on life

The dead are selfish, says a Spanish poem, "they don't care if they make us cry . . . they refuse to walk, we're forced to carry them on our backs to the graveyard."

Ari has difficulty getting these lines out of his head. For a time, it's as if they replace both his thoughts and his emotions. Someone has covered Jakob with a blanket, wherever that came from, maybe from the bar across the road, a thick fleece blanket, as if to make sure that he doesn't get any colder. The door to the bar is ajar and music is carried out into the night. Patrons wander in and out, watching, some smoking, the smoke drifts up in the cold towards the bar's name, The First Kiss, after Hljómar's classic, youthful song. Anna puts her hand on Ari's shoulder. He looks at her and notices that she's trembling.

Her hoarse voice broke slightly as she told Ari what had happened, that two women had been smoking outside the bar when they saw a car coming flying down Hafnargata, carrying four laughing youngsters, blaring pounding music. Those kids need to learn how to fucking drive, one of them had said, and the other was about to agree when she noticed Jakob and screamed. He was in the middle of the road. Had crossed where the street-light is broken, the street dark as a consequence. The headlights illuminated him for a second before the car hit him. One of the youngsters, a sixteen-year-old girl in the passenger seat, said that the old man had been smiling, her words, the old man was smiling, and then added, like a much older person, I'll never forget that smile. Never forget. When Jakob was tossed like a sack by the blow from the car. The driver, little more than seventeen, had hit the brakes, tried to swerve past Jakob, but the front left fender threw him some three metres onto the pavement and against a building. The boy lost control of the car, which crashed through the window of the Síminn shop, and the shattering of the glass and blaring of the car alarm brought people running from the bar, and someone managed to catch up with the driver as he rushed crying down to the sea.

It'll be difficult for the poor thing to live with this, says Anna, you should talk to him, say something nice, it could help to reduce the damage. Yes, says Ari, looking down at his father on the pavement, beneath the fleece blanket, as if he'd decided to take a nap, take a breather from this difficult life. The dead are selfish, they just go to sleep and leave us to clean up after them, go through all the things they leave behind, decide what to do with the sofa, the cutlery, the socks, the food in the fridge. Their bills need to be sorted through, they have to be carried on our backs to the graveyard. Death is such a burden on life.

. . . while someone is alive

This song was one of his absolute favourites, says Anna.

She'd been planning to go straight up to her flat, handed Ari the key, smiled at us and bade us goodnight. You wouldn't like to come in? said Ari, surprised.

I don't want to be in the way.

If anyone, said Ari, has the right to go into Dad's flat, it's you.

She burst into tears, that strong woman. Sigga put her arms round her, led her crying inside, Ásmundur went and got some kitchen roll so she could blow her nose, dry her eyes, she laughed a little, said apologetically, I haven't cried in front of anyone since I was a child – except sometimes here, with my Kobbi, she managed to whisper, before starting to cry again. Ari sat in the chair opposite the sofa, clenched his fingers, that bloody poem still filling his head, and then his eyes met Sigga's, which said, Come and sit with us. He stood up, went and sat down next to them. They had Anna between them, Ari put his arm, hesitantly, almost shyly, around her shoulders. God help me, how many tears do I have, she whispered, and then leaned against him, cried on his shoulder, and he buried his face in her hair.

Ásmundur made coffee, and Anna asked if she could listen to "A Whiter Shade of Pale", since it had been such a favourite of Jakob's. She had handed Ari the letter from Gunnar to Margrét, along with the Yahtzee score sheets which Jakob had written on.

They drink coffee, Sigga and Ásmundur read Gunnar Gunnarsson's letter, and Ari reads Jakob's notes as the long, seductive notes of Procol Harum fill the flat: "certain I'll finally be able to say the things that really matter".

It makes everything more difficult if you don't know how to talk, says Anna, stroking the back of Ari's hand. You end up hurting everyone around you.

And now it's too late, says Ari softly, almost bitterly – a bitter self-accusation. Anna smiles weakly, strokes the back of his hand again, and says, Nonsense, it's never too late while you're still alive. While someone is alive.

Postlude

One

It is morning in the world. It's always morning somewhere, daylight is never exhausted, but some gets left behind in the darkness, disappears into it, with nothing to recall it when the new day dawns. Except for longing.

Day dawns in September at the hospital on a heath above Reykjavík, and in Keflavík in December, except that there the light is so sparse that it's closer to darkness. Yet day does dawn, we sense it, somewhere deep inside where the pain is, the desire for happiness. Morning comes, night retreats with its dreams, and a middle-aged nurse walks quietly into the room, stops when she sees the little boy in bed with the young woman. The boy breathes calmly, his arms wrapped around her arms as she lies close against him. She is no longer breathing. The nurse stands still as stone, as if paralysed, and the serene September light comes in through the window. She walks slowly to the bed, lays her palm gently on Ari's forehead, and he opens his eyes, sees the slowly falling snow fill the two hotel-room windows, and someone is singing softly in the next room. Some sort of lullaby in English, no, American, he recognises the voice, it's the American woman, singing for her husband. It's so good if you can wake up next to a person who means something to you, even means everything, as if life always wins, as if there's justice in the world. Is that why she's singing so beautifully? Ari gets up and goes to the window, gazes into the falling snow that connects worlds.

Two

Sigga had invited Ari to stay with her and Ásmundur in the cosy little house that once belonged to old Kristján, in a place for which the Icelandic language has no words. He had declined the invitation, said that he was going back to his hotel to try and get some sleep and then visit his stepmother. Take my car, then, said Sigga, the keys will be waiting for you at the reception desk.

Three

Ari and I drive out of Keflavík. Ari rang his stepmother soon after he woke up and told her the news, that Jakob was dead. She remained silent for a long time and he remained silent for a long time, but that was alright. It's just past ten in the morning and it's still dark. No month on earth is as deeply dark as December – sometimes it can be so gloomy that it's almost as if life should be banned. What messages, then, does the snow carry, that enormous quantity of whiteness sent to us by the sky?

Maybe the dead are talking to you, I say, trying to tell you something about darkness and light. Maybe, says Ari, turning up onto Miðnesheiði.

And you listen?

He looks over at me and smiles, traces of her lipstick on his cheek. Let me wipe this off, darling, Anna had said, trying to wipe off the lipstick, not entirely successfully, fortunately, because a kiss is a nice memory. I don't know, she had said, why I put on lipstick like some silly old biddy, hurried to do so when you rang and asked if you could stop by. As if I need to put on make-up now that the flower of my happiness is dead.

Her eyes were red, she'd slept a bit, hardly at all, just cried, sat with Jakob's favourite jumper in her arms, smelled it, held it, read Margrét's diaries, listened to Megas.

Even if his voice isn't really my cup of tea; I'm more into Elvis, and love, but I guess that's because I'm stupid.

She put on some lipstick as if it mattered how she looked. Ari hugged her. May I perhaps have a bit of you, she asked. As much as you like, he said, and she kissed him on the cheek.

Four

The car runs smoothly up onto the heath, it's snowing. Maybe the snowflakes are a message from the dead, but there were two texts on his mobile when he awoke after a short sleep; the first was from Svavar, the second from his daughters, Gréta and Hekla. They'd spent the evening together, cooked, looked at photos in the family album, cried, laughed, had a long chat with Sturla on Skype: "But Dad, check your e-mail, there's a song for you there. Come over right away, because life isn't as much fun when you aren't here."

The message from Svavar had been sent in the early morning: "Hey, you old ogre! I'm too happy to sleep! I just want to run up a mountain and shout something great about life from the top . . . because who do you think came to see me tonight? . . . You know, I just got a long e-mail from Árni. Remember how he disappeared the other year? Well, he's shown up again – but as a she! He's had himself turned into a woman! He's in the country and wants to meet up. Sent me a photo and everything. He, no, she (!) is bloody good-looking, too. Just as well that I'm head over heels in love and in seventh heaven, otherwise I might have developed a crush on my old friend . . . but the balls, man, to dare to change sex – isn't that true courage!?"

Five

"Grant me the strength to change what I can change."

So is there, after all, almost no limit to what you can change, is cowardice perhaps the biggest obstacle? This all began with a death, and soon I'll finally be able to tell you the things that really matter. Except that soon is sometimes too late for life, I say, as Ari parks at the side of the road, shuts off the engine, we're in the middle of the heath. Here's where I get out. I know, he says, which is why I'm not going to wait. I get out of the car, nothing more needs to be said.

Ari picks up his mobile as he's approaching Sandgerði, opens the e-mail from Gréta and Hekla. "You know this song, Dad, we listened to it a thousand times last night and were both bawling! P.S.: We sent the song to Mum, too . . ."

Ari clicks on the link and smiles as the phone plays "You Are Always on My Mind" by Elvis Presley.

He who knows how to open hearts.

Six

It's snowing over this low and nearly barren heath, but in some places moss grows on old rocks, even covers them, having started its job of changing the hard, lifeless rock into soil for colourful flowers. I see it all, how the rock becomes soil, how Ari parks the car outside his stepmother and Máni's house. I see it all as I merge slowly with the snowfall. Merge into it so perfectly that it's as if I never existed.
